To (Our) My brothers
Christ at Fuyama
Together we grew our love.

Marjorie & Clio Eldred
September 11, 2011

Seizing the Treasure

Nuggets of Vaughn-Kilpatrick Story

Marjorie Vaughn-Eldred

Copyright © 2011 by Marjorie Vaughn-Eldred

Golden Valley Gems
6403 241 Avenue East
Buckley, WA 98321

ISBN: 978-0-578-08210-3

All rights reserved. No part of this publication may be reproduced, stored in
a retrieval system or transmitted, in any form, or by any means, electronic,
mechanical, recorded, photocopied, or otherwise, without the prior written
permission of both the copyright owner and the above publisher of this book,
except by a reviewer who may quote brief passages in a review.

The scanning, uploading, and distribution of this book via the Internet or via any
other means without the permission of the publisher is illegal and punishable by
law. Please purchase only authorized electronic editions and do not participate
in or encourage electronic piracy of copyrightable materials. Your support of the
author's rights is appreciated.

Printed in the United States of America

To Mother and Dad
The ones who gave me life, poured out
their life's energies for me, and formed me
into the person that I am

Take time to remember, for the heart holds many treasures, golden moments that will always be a part of us.

From Feelings of the Heart calendar circa 1993

Author Unknown

Contents

ACKNOWLEDGEMENTS..15

PREFACE..19

PART ONE: MARION AND BLAND'S WORLD 21

  Prologue to Part One 23

  The Kilpatricks in Beaver County 24

  The Ghost of Two Buttes' Dream 29

  The Box Social Marion's Dream, 1928 42

  The Tuba Player 45

  The Literary 50

  The Dust Storm 53

  Marion's Decision and Diversion 56

  The Birthday Party 59

  Dr. Verity's Plan..64

  Box Social Surprise 69

  Parental Warnings 74

  Looking Forward 76

  Awakening...78

  Deep Thoughts 80

  Till Death Do Us Part 84

  Lone Star Bride Facts of Life on the Prairie 86

  Promise 91

  He's not Breathing! 93

  Unintentional Adventure 95

  Dusty Enemy 98

  Shall We Get a Puppy? 101

Unsettling Suggestion 103

I Know Who Holds the Future 106

Bland and Marion Vaughn's Travel 109

PART TWO: LIFE ON THE FARM IN OREGON 115

She Saved My Life 117

Dad's Legacy 121

Bread Alone 127

Grandpa's Girl? 129

Hungry Kids and Cinnamon Rolls 132

The Teacher Who Could Teach Pigs 134

Gooseberry Gobblers 136

No Bears out Tonight! 138

Round and Round 140

Perils of the Dairy Farm 141

Refuge in the Haystack 144

The Girl Who Wanted to Fly 145

Kids and Cows and Geese and Things 148

Imaginative? Or Mischievous? 153

The Boxing Glove Christmas 156

Another Fragrant Memory 158

Trombone and Trauma 160

The Milkmaid Trio Makes Its Debut 163

The Vaughn Girls 165

PART THREE: ADULT ADVENTURES 169

Choice of a Lifetime 171

Margie's Family Begins 182

A Crocodile Story 191

Dad and the Broiler Pan 194

The Santa Claus Gifts 195

The "I Don't Feel So Good" Sunday 196

Turkey Drumstick Disaster 197

Imperfect Angel 200

Balloons the Colors of Happy 203

Incriminating Attentions 206

A Letter, April 17, 1992 210

PART FOUR: GRANDCHILDREN **213**

Memories from Grandma's Bear Hug Journal 215

More Memories June 1992 218

Visit With the Texas Grandchildren: 1-8-92 222

January 4, 1993 224

July 4, 1993 226

PART FIVE" CLIO AND ME **229**

Why Is the Little Robin Lonely? How We First Met 231

Meet My Husband 234

An Invitation to Prison 246

Meatball Madness 249

PART SIX: AH LIFE! **253**

Gifts from my Garden 255

Holey Moley Desperation 260

Tornado in our Back Yard 264

It's Dr. Seuss's Birthday!! 267

There She Goes Miss Inquisitive 270

The First Square Dance 272

PART SEVEN: INTRODUCTION TO MY SIBLINGS **275**

The Little House That Grew Up 277

OOPS! I FORGOT THE DOG! 279

Musical Inclinations 281

On the Precipice 287

PART EIGHT: GOODBYES **291**

Where's Your Driver's License?!!! 293

Woops! 296

We Lost Our Mom 297

Last Gifts Mom Gave Us 299

Memorial Service Memories 301

Loving Absence 304

Epilogue: Seizing the Treasure 309

PART NINE: MORE ABOUT THE VAUGHNS

AND KILPATRICKS **311**

Prologue to Vaughn Ancestor's Stories 313

One: More about the Vaughn Ancestors

    Famous Friends Discontent 316

Greener and Greener Grass 319

Two: More about the Kilpatrick Ancestors Obituary,

    Samuel Allen Kilpatrick, June 10, 1952 329

Mother's Parents and Grandparents 332

About Two Buttes and the Kilpatricks 334

Poor Chicken 336

A Switch Story 337

Marion's Memories of her Siblings Stella Rachael Leona Kilpatrick 338

Marion's Memories of her older brother, John Franklin Kilpatrick .. 340

More on Uncle John Kilpatrick, per Ira Kilpatrick, October l, 2009 341

Marion's Memories of Tenney Elbertha Kilpatrick 343

Marion's Memories of Mayme Melvina Kilpatrick 344

Marion's Memories of William Allen Kilpatrick 346

Marion's Memories of Barney McCoy Kilpatrick 348

Memories of Bonnie Edwin Kilpatrick 350

Marion's Memories of her Twin Sister, Mildred Raye Kilpatrick 352

Marion's Memories of Neva Kilpatrick 355

About the Author, Marjorie Vaughn-Eldred 359

Acknowledgements

I owe the inspiration for this book to Erlene Phillips, my first cousin and the acknowledged genealogy expert in our Kilpatrick family. Her idea of combining family story with the names in our family tree spurred my desire to write our family's story. Thanks to Erlene and her sister, Luetta, for buying the first copies of this book way back in October.

From my Mother I learned many of the events in my parents' lives. Her patience in relating them to me as I took notes at my computer made much of the content of this book possible.

As my interest in the realities of life in the Dust Bowl grew I read numerous books:

Tim Egan's *The Worst Hard Time* expanded my knowledge of the causes of the dust storms and the suffering involved in living through those years in that location.

An *Owl on Every Post* by Sanora Babb acquainted me with the reality of disease-bringing-hunger in some areas of Baca County where residents did not have wells and found themselves dependent on the rains for their very lives.

I am grateful to Ira Kilpatrick, my cousin, who loaned me his copy of *Baca County* by the Baca County Historical Society (Thanks to the Baca County Historical Society, too) and allowed me to keep it for months. This book taught me many of the details related to the building of the Two Buttes Dam through writings by Virginia Campbell, a resident of Two Buttes whose husband had long collected historical data about the area. The book contained a wonderful index which enabled me to ferret out stories revealing who Dr. Verity was and his importance and popularity in the Two Buttes community. Ira also donated his valuable time by patiently answering my never-ending questions about life in Two Buttes. Sadly, he did not live to see this book in print. Thank you to his wife, Ann, who waited patiently during our long conversations for Ira to get off the phone.

I am indebted to Jeane Vaughn, my first cousin, who interviewed her dad—my father's youngest brother, Maynard Vaughn—and produced an audio tape of his story. From this tape I learned most of what I know about my Grandpa Vaughn and his life. Her brother, Ron added details about his relationship with Grandpa and information about the last years of Grandpa's life.

My Aunt Pearl left a detailed written record of Vaughn family history from which my sister, Mona, had 'grown' a family tree. Aunt Pearl's document also provided the information about my great grandparents that I have included in this book.

I am grateful to Mona and Jess Armas for their help and constant encouragement when my creative wells began to run dry. (Just to add a note of interest, Mona tells me that Eunice Vaughn, Uncle Maynard's late wife, kept faithful family records in a diary type book. Mona learned this when she talked on the phone with Eunice in her later years. I have not seen the diary.)

I want to thank the Harper County Historical Society for their wonderful editions of' *Sage and Sod*. From the Second Edition I gleaned information regarding the recreations enjoyed by the settlers on the plains and details of the struggles they endured while living in that harsh land.

The folks at RJ Communications deserve a lot of credit for taking my imperfect efforts and making them shine. Thank you to Jonathan Gullery who designed text and cover and Bob Powers who worked so hard answering my questions.

To Ed Bryant of Advanced Digital Solutions in Bellevue, Washington I owe my gratitude for all the times he rescued this project when I could do nothing to find it. Cyle and Kelly Eldred, Gary and Suzy Skelton, and Les Vaughn also spent precious time helping out in the computer department when I needed them.

ACKNOWLEDGEMENTS

My adult children have added so many encouragements and expressions of hope that were needed and supremely important to me. Special thanks to Barbara Albertson for her supportive notes and letters and spoken approval for what I was doing, to Doug Skelton for sharing bits and pieces he had found in his own search for family history and for his perusal of my manuscript and the positive reinforcement he gave just at the moment I needed to hear it.

Most of all I want to thank my wonderful husband, Clio, for all the hours he spent listening to me read the stories I had written and never failing to praise my efforts. I couldn't have stayed with this project without him.

If you are reading this book, I thank you, too. A book without a reader is unfinished. Have a wonderful time!

Preface

WE live with our families daily, sharing the ups and downs of life, hardly noticing the special love-gifts they share with us, smiling or bursting out in laughter at their humorous antics. We sit around our Thanksgiving tables with them and laugh at the various versions of their past notorious behaviors and adventurous acts. We cry with them when there is no one else to share the burdens. And then we forget all they do for us and take them for-granted.

The 2010 United States census counted one hundred fourteen million eight hundred thousand households. Few of these families have a habit of recording their family stories for their descendants or preserving the treasure that lives in the memory of each person. What loss!

My book, *Seizing the Treasure: Nuggets of Vaughn and Kilpatrick Story* overflows with family story, including a vignette of my GGG grandfather, Admiral Samuel Vaughan who reportedly sat at the Duke of Wellington's victory dinner after Napoleon's defeat at Waterloo. It records likely causes of my GG grandfather William's insurrection against the government of England and his consequent move to America to give his family a better life.

My great grandfather, Thomas Vaughn—spelling of the name was changed at naturalization—and my grandfather Charles were pioneers of the American West, ever drawn on by their desire for new land. My parents lived in the Dust Bowl of the thirties and during the great Depression. They left everything and traveled the long road to Oregon State, motivated by the desire to save their baby's life. There is much more.

This anthology of family history spans several generations and joins several genres: non-fiction, creative non-fiction, essay, and possibly even a bit of poetry. I hope you will enjoy every page.

If it can be said that "I am a part of all whom I have met," it may also be true that I have received much of who I am from those before me whom I have never met; that my ancestors have embroidered the first stitches of the tapestry of my life.

The stories in this book— written over a period of more than eight years —are an effort to preserve what I know and what I think I have learned about those who came before me. I included stories from my life. I hope the reading of this book will move you to write your own family stories, thus preserving the treasure now within your grasp before it is forever lost.

PART ONE

Marion and Bland's World

Prologue to Part One

MY parents met in Two Buttes, Colorado. For years that bit of information comprised almost everything I knew about their earlier lives, except, perhaps, for a bit of a story about dust storms or rattle snakes, or a mishap with a cow which my mother told. Then my cousin, Erlene, inspired me with her collection of family stories she had packaged along with a lot of genealogy.

I took my mother, Marion, to a Kilpatrick family reunion in Albuerquerque where we saw Erlene in the summer of 2003. When we returned, I found myself changed. Mom's stories now reached ears eager for every detail she could tell. I positioned her comfortably in an easy chair and seated myself at the computer, ready to record everything I heard. By the time we finished, her stories had inspired me to search for information about where my parents met and married and find facts about people they had known and loved, particularly Dr. Verity who played a major role in Mom's young life. The stories—which I shall label creative non-fiction—are the result. Dialogues included are mostly my creation, but represent—as accurately as I know how— the people my parents were.

An interest which came later centered on Beaver County, Oklahoma where Mom's family lived prior to their move to Two Buttes. Many of those years they lived in a "half-dug-out." My grandparents lived in Beaver County for nearly twenty-five years. My mother was born there and completed all her elementary school years in settler's homes — taught by eighteen-year-old graduates — and then when a teacher materialized—in the sod school building that was built in later years.

My anthology begins in Beaver County and sets the stage for the years in Two Buttes.

The Kilpatricks in Beaver County

Neva, Mildred, and Marion, Beaver County

Harvey Miller, Miss Sophie Miller and Joe Mitchell started a small store and post office in 1903 in Beaver County, Oklahoma and named it after Sophia who occupied the office of postmistress for the new community. Horse-drawn vehicles brought mail to the new settlers from

Gage, Oklahoma sixty miles to the east. Owners of this store and post office changed several times over the years; each time the owner changed he moved the store to his own land. Back and forth it went. In 1932 the post office and store closed.

In 1904, during the "Oklahoma Land Strips" distribution, Samuel Allen Kilpatrick staked a two-section claim—360 acres—one-half mile west of Sophia Post Office. He paid $1.00 per acre. Samuel built a half-dug-out for his wife, MaryLee, and seven children to live in. The plentiful grass of the plain provided a ready source for the sod he needed for the house.

He "proved up" the land by plowing the prairie land with a hand plow. A tired man came into the dug-out for lunch, took out his Bible, and sat on his stool by the door to read it. Particulars of how long the family lived in the dug-out remain an unknown, but eventually, he built a frame house near South Platte, practiced carpentry and continued to farm, growing cane and making sorghum for his own and other families.

Mrs. Kilpatrick swept the dirt floor with a wet broom often until it became hard and dust-free, wove rag rugs to cover it, and made curtains for the ground level windows. The family lived in the dugout long enough for Marion and Mildred to remember watching their mom feed the chickens through the kitchen window and hear her direct her and her sisters outside to act as the "vacuum cleaner" by beating rugs on the clothesline.

The family's close neighbors included Jim and Sophia Howard, the Joe Mickles, the Hunts, and Hershell and Flora Allen.

Miss Tanie Poland—an old maid school teacher and also a neighbor— couldn't understand why the Kilpatricks had such a large family. She voiced her concern one day after Neva, the tenth child, came into the world. "Mrs. Kilpatrick, how can you love them when you've got so many?"

Merica MaryLee had a ready answer. "Miss Tanie Poland, you're a school teacher, and you're a good one, but you don't know *anything* about raising kids. You don't know how to love them till you've got a few!"

Schooling for the children presented challenges for the settlers. Mothers or fathers taught their children in their homes or invited eighteen year-old graduates to help out. Finally, when a teacher materialized, the community built a sod schoolhouse and sent its kids walking to school. Some drove their children in buggies because of the large distance or extremely cold weather. School teachers could not continue teaching after they were married; this prohibition limited the tenures of many of the young teachers.

The Kilpatricks, Wesley Smiths, and Henry Mitchells met each Sunday to study the Bible and observe the Lord's Supper, at first taking turns in one another's homes, but eventually meeting in the sod school house. This group later became the South Platte Church of Christ. Settlers appreciated the presence of the only church in the area.

Camp meetings took place every summer at a place called Valley Park. Settlers named the location Valley Park because of a large grove of beautiful trees that grew in the little valley. The location afforded a great camping ground. People from all over the adjoining areas came to these meetings held under a large sheltering tree, and usually stayed several days. Families filled their "chuck boxes" with food to satisfy the hunger pangs that appeared regularly. Settlers—also hungry for companionship—valued these meetings for the opportunity to associate with neighbors as well as the spiritual content of the sermons presented.

The land opening generated much interest among families as well as young men and women past the required age of twenty-one. They filed on their own parcels or on a relinquishment—Some that filed never came to 'prove up' the claim; ownership went back to the government and another claimant was allowed to file on the parcel—The flood of questing people filled the land quickly between 1903 and 1907. People began to go further north into Colorado.

Filing a land claim may seem a highly masculine thing to do, but many women, old and young, wanted a part in the action. Though many more men filed than women, many families brought daughters; if a man needed a wife the numerous choices proved interesting. All the Kilpatrick young people married in Beaver County except Bonnie and the three youngest, Marion, Mildred, and Neva. Only the unfortunate guys traveled back the way they had come to find their partners. Beaver, the county seat twenty-five miles away sold the licenses needed for the marriages.

Kilpatrick Family 1918
Back Row, Left to Right: Bonnie, Bill, Barney, John. Middle Row: Mayme, Stella, Tennie
Front Row: Mildred, Samuel Allen, MaryLee, Marion. Center Front: Neva

This picture was taken in 1918, during World War I. Clyde Williams, Mayme's husband of only three months, had been called to serve our country. Mayme had moved back home to live while he served. The family lived in Beaver, Oklahoma. Marion, my mom, remembers that she spent a lot of time trying to keep Mayme from crying." Mom and Mildred were six years old at the time of the picture.

The oldest of the children—John, Stella, Tennie, and Mayme—were born in Tennessee. Barney, Bill, and Bonnie were born in Washita County, Oklahoma. Marion, Mildred, and Neva were born in Beaver County, Oklahoma.

When Mr. Kilpatrick went to the railroad for freight—hauling supplies presented an opportunity to earn cash—he brought back material to make clothing for the family. Muslin sold for five cents, a yard of gingham could be purchased for eight to ten cents. It took numerous yards to make a dress since styles stayed long, full, and ruffled—held out by abundant petticoats starched stiff and ironed with flat-irons heated on the stove. Ironing required a lot of time.

At first, the new land grew what people needed to eat, and gardens provided extra amounts for canning or drying for winter. Settlers learned to bury vegetables such as carrots and potatoes for storage and cover them with grass or hay until needed. They butchered beef and pork and wrapped and hung the meat high after the weather cooled. If the meat froze they just cut off a chunk and cooked it.

The Kilpatricks moved to Two Buttes, Colorado in 1928.

The Ghost of Two Buttes' Dream

OCTOBER 22, 1909 dawned bright and hot. Excitement trembled in the air on this Opening Day for the city of Two Buttes, Colorado. The plan the Townsite Committee devised to ensure a large crowd involved the arrival at the celebration of a "Horseless Carriage:" a two cylinder chain drive REO. Tales of these cars, manufactured from 1904 to 1908, fascinated the locals, but few had seen one. The attraction had done its work, drawing lookers for the car and buyers for the lots going on sale this day. Applications for homesteads had poured in since the State of Colorado had become involved in the dam project. Confidence ruled the day.

For twenty years people had talked about damming Two Buttes Creek. They thought the arid prairie needed a more constant source of water than the usual scant sixteen inches of rainfall. The reservoir of water that would result from the damming of the creek would furnish bountiful irrigation water for farms on its perimeter. The town would be called Two Buttes, for the twenty mile-distant twin buttes of the prairie. Born in an optimism that would later prove difficult to resurrect, this dream drove the founders on.

Fred L. Harris, recently moved to neighboring Lamar, Colorado, bought into the dream, became aggressively involved in building the dam, and persuaded his dear friend, Dr. William Porter Verity, to come to Two Buttes. Dr. Verity was fifty five years old. The year was 1909.

A bit of background on Doctor Verity seems important here. At the approximate age of twenty five, William P. Verity obtained his Medical Degree from Rush Medical College, Chicago, in 1879. He stayed on to work at Cook County Hospital, where he became a much respected surgeon, and eventually Chief of Surgery. Doctors and Interns worked without pay here at times, contributing to the city's indigent population, but the experience they gained in all types of diseases was reward enough.

Dr. Verity had directed his attentions toward fracture treatment, and had gained some reputation by devising a splint for especially-challenging compound fractures. The doctors called it "The Verity Suspension Splint," Some say he received national recognition for his work. Patients today can be grateful to Dr. Verity. Before his splint, doctors amputated compound fractures. The doctor was still at Cook County hospital in early 1909. An unwelcome interruption awaited him.

"Dr. Verity, would you please join us?" W.P. Verity, surprised, turned to Dr. Fenger with questioning eyes. "Sure. Let me finish this splint."

When Dr. Verity finished his work, he turned to see several specialists waiting outside a conference room; among them the doctor he had seen last week following his severe bout of fatigue. Puzzled, he entered the room and sat down, appreciating the brief opportunity for rest. He was over fifty now, and suspected that his fatigue was part of aging.

"Will, we are all concerned about you." Dr. Fenger turned to look at him. "You have worked so tirelessly for so many years, and given so much to your patients and this hospital . . . ."

"That's my job. You all work hard, too," Dr. Verity interrupted.

"Your exam showed an advanced case of tuberculosis, Will." The doctor sat speechless.

"You have to slow down. In fact, we believe medical practice is too demanding for you, and are suggesting a move to a much drier climate, maybe Arizona. We believe you should have five more years if you make this change. If not, less."

"Are you telling me I'm dying? I'm barely over fifty years old!"

"We're sorry, Will." Dr. Fenger closed the file he held. "You may go."

***

With a scene similar to this, W.P. Verity's life changed. Continued medical practice in this urban environment with hot summers and high humidity was no longer possible. Was it possible anywhere? Where would he go?

As he thought about possible changes of location, Arizona seemed like a good choice. What about Hattie? *She's so involved socially here in Chicago that she might not accept a move.*

His premonition grew and matured. Apparently Hattie didn't take kindly to the need for the move, and may have tried repeatedly to convince William to stay in Chicago and take his chances. But the doctor wanted to live, and he made the hard choice, at once leaving his home in Chicago, his medical practice, and possibly his wife.

The 'Akron Weekly Pioneer Press," December 20, 1912 tells of a maintenance agreement where Dr. Verity was ordered to pay $100.00 monthly, "until her husband returns to live with her." When the separation occurred— perhaps it was much earlier— we do not know. By the time of this agreement, Dr. Verity had been elected Mayor in Two Buttes, and would have been easily located.

I found no marriage record, divorce record, or additional information on Dr. Verity's life in Chicago. The above scenario is an assumption based on the maintenance agreement, a reference to his tuberculosis in Colorado Medicine, and information in Dr. Verity's obituary, apparently written by a friend in Two Buttes.

On his way to Arizona Dr. Verity stopped in Lamar, Colorado where his good Chicago friend, Fred L Harris, was now living. Fred—focused aggressively on building the dam on Two Buttes Creek in Baca County, Colorado—convinced Dr. Verity to stay in Two Buttes. This town had promise.

Fred Harris never quit pushing the dam project among the locals, or his friends, the business people of Chicago, and finally with the state, until funds were raised to proceed. Men interested in the dam banded together to form the Two Buttes Irrigation and Reservoir Company. The Board of Directors included A.N. Parrish and W.C. Gould, bankers from Lamar, and Mr. Harris, who contributed his persistent interest and his talents as a bond salesman, engineer and attorney. What would they have done without him? Would the dam exist today?

J.C. Lent and R.D. Holeman, drivers of the REO Automobile at the Townsite Opening, bought lots and opened businesses in Two Buttes— grocery and hardware stores to serve the homesteads that would surround the town. The Townsite Company built a hotel and restaurant structure that by 1912 also housed the Bank of Baca County. Behind the hotel they dug a well and built a watering trough for horses, the usual power behind transportation in those days. I read that Dr. Verity furnished the first water system in Two Buttes. Was it this well or a more sophisticated system at a later date? We do not know.

The Townsite Committee had completed surveying, maps for right of way and a contract for financing during 1907 and 1908. They awarded contracts for construction of the dam in October, 1909, shortly after the Townsite Opening Day, and construction of the dam's canals began. However, the contractor for the building of the dam structure procrastinated long enough that the Board of Directors cancelled his contract for non-performance, and the Two Buttes Irrigation and Reservoir Company took on construction management.

The construction camp included dining and cooking facilities, bunkhouses, a commissary, corrals and feeding stations for livestock. The irrigation company employed close to two hundred men. Arrangement for horses, mules, two graders, and forty six dump wagons completed the preparations.

Wages for a ten hour day ranged from two dollars to four dollars and fifty cents. The wage paid depended on what the man brought to the worksite— just himself, or himself plus a team or a wagon—and the work he performed; water boy, common laborer, team driver, carpenter, cook, or waiter.

During construction in the summer of 1910, the sun beat mercilessly on the dry prairie; the month of July brought temperatures of 100 to 106 degrees. Blowing dust complicated construction, causing frequent turnovers in the work force and multiplying unavoidable delays. One must wonder at the dogged determination and perseverance that caused those workers to endure through heat, dust and delay.

The drought ended in August with a rain of four and one half inches, three months before completion of the dam. The torrential rains damaged work in progress, but the disappointed people grieved most for the huge amount of water lost by the dam that was finished too late.

The project was completed on November 26, 1910. Forgetting the difficulties now past, the people rejoiced; they had realized their dream.

On September 25, 1911 the proud and hopeful people incorporated the town, and soon added sidewalks, a park, street lights, a moving picture house, and a newspaper office; amenities still scarce in other Baca County towns.

Dr. Verity had purchased farm land northeast of the town site, apparently intending to give up his medical career, but launched his second practice as a country doctor that year when he successfully treated J.C. Lent's difficult case of typhoid. His skills filled a need in the community. He became the most-loved doctor of Two Buttes.

His reputation grew rapidly. People remembered him. J.C. Lent walked around, healthy now, because of his intervention. Dr. Verity loved conversation—some say he was a lonely man—and lined his examining room with shelves for displaying interesting artifacts: a two-headed calf—its origin mysterious—a hand, blown apart by an exploding gun, amputated, and preserved as a lesson for overly adventurous young men; a large tarantula brought to him in a jam-soiled fruit jar by teen-agers, Ira Kilpatrick, and his friend; anything that might be interesting or instructive for his patients. Sometimes he displayed his live peacocks at the office, too. Ira remembers seeing them there.

People talked about the doctor: Some of his treatments seemed miraculous. He had a black salve that smelled pleasant and mysterious that he used for almost everything. He never refused calls, even if people couldn't pay. He didn't even *ask* whether people could pay. He believed that everyone would pay when they could. He never sent a bill. He would sell —or give— his black salve to his patients. He would come, in the midst of a snow storm, in the middle of the night, if you needed him.

Winds challenged men's presence on this prairie. Fires, many caused by lightening, threatened homes. Lightning struck men as they worked; their families found them where they fell. Blizzards covered roads and buried fences. Floods destroyed bridges and blocked roads. Dr. Verity braved all these conditions to treat his townspeople.

***

The pall of disappointment began to dampen the high spirits of the people as the rainfall failed to support adequate water levels in the reservoir. Though there were times the reservoir was full and providing irrigation water—heavy rains fell in 1914 and the reservoir was stocked with trout—droughts continued, severe enough to empty the reservoir and crust and crack the basin surface. So, in spite of the dam, they waited for rain. Without adequate rain, even dry land crops such as wheat and broomcorn could not grow through harvest. Some homesteaders did not have wells. Some suffered extreme hunger, even scurvy, from the lack of green vegetables, and ate what they could find, sometimes even mature Russian thistles, known as tumbleweeds.

When the dam-held reservoir was full, it irrigated farms, attracted waterfowl—ducks and wild geese—and provided fishing and recreation, furnishing an additional outing and enjoyment for the people of Baca County. When it dried, irrigated crops failed, necessitating more dry land crops, foreshadowing frustration in the end. The people of Two Buttes, having experienced the so-recently acquired and much-appreciated fishing and hunting, missed those activities and the presence of the birds. To their sorrow, the climate refused to bear the burden of their dream.

Two Buttes continued to grow through 1917, when a tornado roared through the town, damaging and destroying businesses and killing the man who printed the newspaper. Most business owners, sobered by the tragedy, moved on rather than rebuilding. New businesses did come, over the years nearly a hundred, but the owners usually found the climate— environmental and business—unacceptable, and left.

In 1918 during heavy snow and extreme cold weather, a new and especially virulent influenza virus attacked Two Buttes. Dr. Verity, dressed in his heavy bearskin coat, cap, and mittens, ministered his healing. So many people suffered that the town's only hotel filled with them. The casket-maker could not build enough caskets. Gravediggers were hard to find. Bodies waited in the freezing winter for friends or family to read scripture and say their good-byes. World-wide, this pandemic killed somewhere between thirty and one hundred million people—estimates vary widely—a large percentage of them young adults. Dr. Verity, in spite of the risks he took daily, the pain he felt when friends and neighbors died, the frigid weather, and his age, kept trudging through the days, doing what he needed to do. The town named him Dear Old Dr. Verity.

The new babies he brought into the world were the delight of his life. For years Dr. Verity was the lone physician in Two Buttes. They were his kids and he never forgot it.

Besides his medical practice and his farming, Dr. Verity served as Mayor for ten years, between 1912 and 1922. He brought the first electrical services to Two Buttes. He occupied the Coroner's post, beginning in 1914, and served his people in that office until 1940 when he became eighty seven years old.

Through the years, Dr. Verity found creative ways to enrich his people's lives. In 1921 W.W. Backus moved to town. The doctor learned of the man's musical talent and dedication gained over the years. Mr. Backus had educated himself, learning to play numerous musical instruments. He had worked in a circus, and he had played as a one-man-band for many years.

Dr. Verity invited Mr. Backus to organize and direct Two Buttes' municipal band. He looked around at his friends and neighbors, realized that many of them had no means of purchasing instruments for their children, and did it himself, enabling wide participation in the band.

Mr. Backus was a particular man, having a very business-like approach to directing. "Let's look again at that trombone run in Stars and Stripes. I don't like the way it's sounding. Tongue those notes! From the top! We're not going home until we do it right!" The students grew musically, and the city embraced its band, building a bandstand for summertime practices and performances in 1922. The park wherein it was located became a favorite gathering place.

Dr. Verity's Band

Dr. Verity dreamed big. That year he started a new tradition in Two Buttes, and called it Music Day. Each Labor Day he led the band in parade through the streets, himself the prancing drum major, stepping briskly to *Stars and Stripes Forever* or *King Cotton* marches, dressed in his white uniform and tall black bearskin hat, waving his baton. In time the residents of Two Buttes dubbed the band "Dr. Verity's Band." All afternoon the band played concerts in the park. Farmers brought their produce and set up stands. Residents of other Baca county towns learned to make Two Buttes' Music Day a priority, a time for visiting, reviewing Baca County history, music and dancing. At times several hundred people attended.

Springfield, Colorado, the County Seat about twenty five miles away, had a Music Day as early as 1908. Whether Dr. Verity participated there remains a mystery. Given the date of his arrival in Two Buttes (1908-9), it is possible that he did.

In 1927 Dr. Verity's Band went to a Colorado State competition where it played in massed band directed by John Phillip Sousa, the composer of the *Stars and Stripes Forever* and many other marches for bands. Mr. Sousa as judge, awarded Dr. Verity's band third place and rewarded them with a snare drum as prize. Ecstatic citizens of Two Buttes applauded.

Just a year or two later a young Marion Kilpatrick moved to town with her parents, twin sister, Mildred, and younger sister, Neva. Dr. Verity paid a visit.

"I'm Dr. Verity, the doctor in town. We have a great band here. I'd like to have your family involved."

Mr. Kilpatrick declined. "We've just moved. We haven't had a crop. We just don't have money to buy instruments for them."

"I'm prepared to help you. I'd really like Marion, Mildred, Neva, and Bonnie to be a part of the band. I'll buy instruments; whatever they choose." And so the Kilpatricks met Dr. Verity, became his fans, and a part of the band.

Two or three years later Dr. Verity summoned Marion. "I've heard you want to be a doctor," he said. "We need more doctors in Baca County. I want to help you get your education. I'll pay for your college and your books." An excited Marion rushed home to spread the good news only to be disappointed when her father refused the doctor's help. Young women were out of place in a doctor's world, he thought.

***

With the drought of the thirties, change came. Huge, brown-black dust storms rolled across the plowed prairies, powerful winds stealing the loose soil. Dust and freezing blizzards partnered with electricity from the storms, the dark of night in daytime, and non-breathable air to take their lives from them. Dust drifted against weeds and buildings, buried fences, machinery, and even cattle, sifted into homes and invaded people's last sanctuary. Helpless men, women and children cowered inside with the dust.

A day which started with bright sunshine turned suddenly into the hell of biting blowing dust. People developed hacking coughs, children died of dust pneumonia, foraging animals died from eating too much dirt, dust buried crops, and electrical storms blackened carefully nurtured gardens. The fields blew away, leaving only the packed sub-soils; with the fields went the people's dreams. The press described the area as "The Dust Bowl," and the title stuck.

After a decade of drought, thoroughly discouraged residents of Baca County entertained only feeble hopes for rain. To make bad matters worse, the dust storms accompanied plummeting wheat prices. Huge crops grown and marketed before the drought began had caused an over-supply. Wheat was the principal dry land crop, the crop on which they depended for cash. In order to break even, desperate farmers planted more wheat, unwittingly ensuring that their crop would be unmarketable next year, adding to the problem. Wheat rotted in the fields. Finally they could not grow even wheat. Depression ruled.

Some people left Baca County during these years, hoping for a brighter future; some did not. All through the thirties the dusty drought continued, rendering those who had chosen to stay desolate and almost hopeless; still, most refused to give up until all choice was gone.

***

Later in his life, Dr. Verity gave his library to the city, enabling the beginning of a library branch in Two Buttes. Volunteer labor kept the library open until the county provided funds to hire a librarian; temporarily as it turned out.

The habits of Dr. Verity's life were so giving, so compassionate, that by his eightieth birthday in 1933, the town reciprocated by giving him birthday parties. Three hundred people attended the first party, eight hundred, his eighty-fifth. The birthday parties continued as long as he lived.

He practiced medicine until age ninety three. W. Gerald Rainer, MD shared a story in Colorado Medicine about Dr. Verity in his last years. He heard it from Dr. Edwin C. Likes, a Lamar physician, who said he learned an enduring respect for Dr. Verity by the incident. It happened shortly before the doctor's death. The story told of a young child kicked in the head by a horse and said the blow fractured the skull. Infection, meningitis, and an abscess followed. Paralysis set in.

Dr. Verity, reportedly, called Dr. Likes and told him he had completed a series of diagrams and charts and knew where the abscess was located. "Will you do the surgery?" he asked. Dr. Likes agreed. As Dr. Verity gave him step by step directions, Dr. Likes drained the abscess, and the child made a marvelous recovery. Dr. Like located the abscess precisely where Dr. Verity predicted it would be.

After Dr. Verity's death in 1948, the community paid him tribute and redecorated his home and office on Main Street. His office became the city library. His home became a museum displaying mementos of his life, medical journals, and objects and treasures, some of which he had accepted in payment for his services.

At Dr. Verity's death he left a town full of friends. His legacy? A demonstration of what it means to "love your neighbor as yourself."

One of Dr. Verity's friends and admirers, when asked how people in Baca County had survived so many disasters, replied, "We had a Dr. Verity who… could be counted on to be there when the chips were down. What a privilege to have known him." (He was) "a legend in his own right." My mother, Marion Kilpatrick, was among those proud to have that privilege.

***

The dust storms caused a population decrease which plagues Baca County to this day. Two Buttes once had more than two hundred people. Today, the population consists of approximately forty adults and one child. The school in Two Buttes is gone, and a bus comes from Springfield for the child. People travel twenty five to fifty miles for a gallon of milk or a dozen eggs.

The Historical Society which created the book, *Baca County*, at the time I talked to the librarian had no phone. The library had no computer, no copy machine, and no phone. The volunteer librarian, Theresa Hendrix, answered the phone from her home and opened the doors once a week.

My phone visits with people in Two Buttes have been disheartening. Mary May Gourley says she has planned her last Two Buttes Reunion; most who would have come are no longer living.

November winds recently damaged the roof on Dr. Verity's home and office building which housed the library and museum., Theresa rescued the historical data, books and artifacts and moved them to the original bank building. Residents, reluctant to destroy a memento of the man who meant so much to all of them, cling to his home which brings cherished memories of brighter days.

About fifty of the hundreds of waterfowl that once visited the reservoir remain. The reservoir basin is mostly dry following a three year drought. The people are watching their town die, grieving their losses.

The once vibrant dream of Two Buttes' future has become The Ghost of Two Buttes' Past, haunting those few residents who remember better days. The present town resembles a modern day Camelot or Brigadoon, once vigorous, but now limping lamely into history.

Author Note

My cousins, Luetta and Erlene, and I visited Two Buttes this past summer. We walked through Dr. Verity's home and office. We visited the museum contents in the bank building. We saw and smelled Dr. Verity's black salve and were surprised at the pleasant aroma.

We met Theresa Hendrix and heard her story of recent happenings: a young boy found the town's records in the city dump. He and his father notified city officials and they retrieved them.

Theresa works tirelessly and daily to organize and preserve what she can. She plans to get grants to create new museum space and preserve Dr. Verity's home and office, and she is actually making progress. The population has grown by three or four people. A home has sold in Two Buttes recently. Hopefully, the ghost has fled and his hauntings have ceased.

The Box Social
Marion's Dream, 1928

"I'M definitely going to be a doctor," Marion said, looking at her twin sister who sat quietly sewing a quilt-top. "Doctors get to travel around, and see a lot of people, and they're smart. Just look at Dr. Verity. He knows how to help everyone. That black salve he makes heals almost anything. I wonder how he does it. I want to study so I can be like him."

Kilpatrick twins, Mildred and Marion

"Papa won't let you," Mildred looked up from her tiny stitches. "He thinks women need to stay in their homes and do women's work."

"Lots of women become doctors. I hear about them all the time at school. I just have to talk Papa into letting me!" Marion's intensity grew.

"Where would Papa get the money?" Mildred persisted. "You should learn to be content with your lot, and work harder learning to sew and keep house. It costs money to attend Medical School."

"I'll find a way. I have to. Let's don't talk about it any more." Marion turned away from the conversation, fearing the truths she had heard.

***

Marion, the first-born of the twins by several minutes, outgrew Mildred by an inch, stumbled more, and cared more. Stella, the oldest sister, said that when they were babies "If Mildred fell; Marion cried and tried to help her. If Marion fell, Mildred just kept going."

Mildred loved creative activities like sewing. Marion devoured books, wrote incessantly, and loved to cook. They were eighteen now. They had grown up in Beaver County, Oklahoma—'No Man's Land' in the Oklahoma Panhandle—where their Papa had made a three hundred sixty acre land claim in the early 1900's. Their lives began there.

Much of their time in Beaver County, they had lived in a "half-dug-out"— a house created by digging a hole into the ground and putting a roof over it. Ground-dwelling visitors were not usually excluded. Mama had worked hard making it a home, making rugs for the dirt floors from gunny sacks, white-washing the inside walls with lime, making curtains. They went to school in Beaver County, but not regularly, depending on whether there was a teacher, or whether the weather allowed. Because of this irregularity in schooling, Marion and Mildred had just entered their sophomore year.

About two years ago in 1928 when they were sixteen, they had moved to Two Buttes, Colorado, traveling the two hundred miles in a covered wagon, Marion sitting in the back leading their cow. The trip required eight long hot days, the riding relieved only by occasional walking and sightings of the prairie dog towns scattered across the plain.

"I'm tired, Mama. Can't we stop awhile?" Neva wanted to know.

"My sitter is sure getting tired," Marion turned and directed her words loudly toward the front of the wagon. But Papa pressed on to his goal.

They ended their trip in Two Buttes, Colorado, a small farm town with a doctor's office, a bank, a mercantile store, a grocer, and shops for car and farm machinery repair. Irrigated farms surrounded the town. Founders built the large dam, reservoir, and town around it between 1909 and 1911. The town exuded the energy and optimism of youth. People seemed to know and like one another.

The Kilpatricks lived now in a bigger, nicer, frame home with three rooms instead of the one room they had in their half-dug-out in Beaver County.

"Have you heard about the new family living down the road on John's property?" Mildred changed the subject. "They bought the south eighty acres of John's place. I heard their name is Vaughn. They have boys. One of them already teaches school."

"Yes, I've heard. Their daughter, Hazel is in our class. She's nice. I think we'll be friends. Let's ask Mama if we can invite the family over for Sunday dinner sometime soon. Some of them will probably come, and we could get to know them and show them they are welcome neighbors."

"Good idea, Marion. Let's do ask. We can help with the house and the cooking." Mildred lay her sewing aside and headed for Mama's bedroom.

Mama's health hadn't been good since the twins were born, perhaps a result of bearing ten children and working so hard. The girls habitually helped in the kitchen and outside with chores.

Mama thought their idea a good one and said she would check it out with Papa. Papa gave consent. Mama extended the invitation for a Sunday in late September. The family planned a trip to Two Buttes Dam Friday after school to pick wild plums; that new sweeter variety they found the last time they picked. They would make plum butter, always a welcome treat with any meal. The Vaughn boys would love home-made bread and plum butter!

The Tuba Player

LATE September finally came. Marion felt herself adjusting to the rhythms of school; reading, writing, studying, taking time out for band practice, and going home to read some more. When she went to band practice on Wednesday, she greeted her teacher, Mr. Backus, and went to her place in the cornet section. She was one of two trumpet players, and wanted to practice consistently to learn the music. She wanted to be ready when Mr. Backus asked them to play it.

Mr. Backus was particular; insistent that they play the music correctly. In fact, he wouldn't dismiss band practice until they succeeded. Marion, Mildred and Neva accepted the necessity of practice after two years in his band.

As Marion sorted through her music she glanced over at Mildred in the clarinet section and they smiled. As her eyes moved back to her music, she sensed other eyes on her, and turned her head just in time to see a tall good-looking young man she had never seen before. He held a tuba in his arms. He nodded his head and turned back to his music.

After class ended, Marion, placing her cornet in its case, contemplated the way he had looked at her. When she raised her eyes, she jumped, startled to see him standing in front of her.

"I'm Bland Vaughn," he said. "What's your name?"

"Marion Kilpatrick," she said, returning his smile. "I haven't seen you here before. Are you joining Dr. Verity's Band?"

"If you'll let me," he teased. "I teach school over in Wentworth. Mr. Backus said he needed a sousaphone player, so here I am. My folks live just outside of Two Buttes on the old Kilpatrick place."

"Permission granted." Marion smiled teasingly. "Your family is coming to our house for Sunday dinner. We're neighbors. Will I see you then?"

"Thanks for the invitation!" Bland said. "I think you *will*."

The tuba player walked away returning a teasing glance over his shoulder. Marion, suddenly light-hearted, skipped over to Mildred. "I met the schoolteacher. He's coming to dinner."

Two Buttes, Bland and Tuba

The Kilpatrick family's excitement over Sunday's plans grew as they made plum butter and pies, baked bread, churned butter, and helped dress the chickens. Marion's thoughts centered on Bland. *I wonder why he came over to talk to me in band class. He's really handsome. Doesn't he see how gangly I am?*

At last the chosen Sunday came. The girls dressed carefully and made sure Neva put on something pretty. The family traveled in their buggy to the long frame building that was the school, where the church met in the auditorium.

The congregation included a group of four families plus the Kilpatrick clan. The girls had four grown brothers whose families lived in Two Buttes; John, Barney, Bill and Bonnie. The Vaughn family came in, just a little late.

"Look at those good-looking guys!" Neva whispered loudly. Marion shushed her, and kept her eyes directed at the song book. After services were over, she looked around, questioning whether Bland was there. Gladly she saw him searching her out with his eyes. She hoped to spend time with him this afternoon.

Marion continued to greet her friends. Tom Bradshaw spoke to them, "Hi, Marion. Hi Mildred." He hugged Neva. Before walking away, he complimented Marion on her accomplishments in the band, and then, "Have you heard?" he asked, "Mrs. Carter has chosen *Windmills of Holland* for our school musical. I've heard you and Mildred sing great harmony. Be sure you try out for the lead. It'll be fun."

When Marion finished greeting her friends, the Vaughns had left the building. Marion felt disappointed but looked forward to the afternoon. The Kilpatrick family waited while Papa finished his duties so they could start for home. As they traveled, Marion revealed her dream to her father.

"Papa," she said. "I'm studying my science and math real hard. I want to be a doctor. I've watched, and I've seen lots of women doctors in *The Two Buttes Sentinel*. I could work in Springfield, at the medical center."

"Marion," he answered after thinking for awhile, "The Lord wanted women to serve their families at home, not go gallivanting all over the country. You'll make someone a good wife, someday."

She dropped the subject, not wanting to spoil the day. She could ask questions later.

Six of the Vaughn family came for dinner: Bland, his younger brothers, Merle and Maynard, his sister Hazel, and their parents, Mr. and Mrs. Charles Vaughn. Marion liked the family and enjoyed the banter among them and the questions and comments they directed to her family.

"How long have you folks lived in Two Buttes?" Mr. Vaughn asked Papa.

"We moved here from Beaver County, Oklahoma two years ago. We left our claim there and the South Platte Church of Christ to plant the church in Two Buttes and to give the girls a better school experience and more friends. We've been growing melon and squash seeds for the Rocky Ford seed Company. You're welcome to melons from our field any time you want, as long as you bring back the seeds. What about you? Where did you come from?"

"We just moved from Selman. Two of our oldest boys still have a garage there," Mr. Vaughn picked up his piece of fried chicken. "Chester didn't come tonight. Bland teaches school in Wentworth. He isn't home much any more."

"I think I'd like to be home more," Bland interjected, looking at Marion. "Would you consider walking over to the windbreak with me, Marion? There's good shade there, and we can talk." Marion felt the blush creep over her cheeks, but she nodded, flattered at his invitation.

They excused themselves from the table, got hat and bonnet from pegs by the door, and walked to the porch. "Mildred might like to go along," she suggested, not wanting to hurt Mildred's feelings.

"But I want to talk to *you*," Bland said. "Shall we?"

They walked in the heat along the dirt road, welcoming the scant shade given by their hats and the cool greenness of Papa's melon fields alongside.

Bland said, surprising her, "I'm interested to know. Who's the guy you were talking to this morning at church? Care to tell me?"

"Oh that was just a friend of mine, Tom Bradshaw. I've known him a long time. His dad preached for the South Platte Church of Christ in Beaver County. Tom is over here to finish his schooling as I am."

"I'd just as soon he'd go *back* to Beaver County," Bland declared strongly.

Marion, surprised by his bluntness, stopped walking. "Are you saying I shouldn't talk to my friends?" she asked.

"No. I'm interested in *seeing* you, and I don't like a lot of competition." Bland paused.

"Have you heard about the Literary Friday night?" he said, changing the subject. "I'd like to take you. I'll be back to Two Buttes by four o clock. I could pick you up at six. Will you go with me?"

Though Bland''s outburst bothered her, Marion answered politely. "Yes, I've heard about the Literary. In fact, I'm reciting a poem I just wrote. It's called *Why Not*? Would you like to hear it?"

"I really would. I'll look forward to seeing you Friday evening. Okay? And I'll see you in band practice Wednesday."

"Okay," answered Marion, tentatively. She pushed away the unsettled feelings knocking for admittance to her heart.

They walked back toward the house, the sun setting behind the locust and cedar trees of the windbreak. They found the party at the table breaking up; the pies served and eaten.

"Would you like some apple pie, or cherry, Bland?" Marion asked, setting plates for both of them on the table. "No time, now, Marion. Thanks anyway. See you Friday night."

The Literary

ALL the community gathered at the schoolhouse for the Literary on Friday night. The Powell family had practiced their singing, and was ready to perform. They sang an old hymn, *How Long Has It Been Since You Talked with the Lord?* Their voices blended closely as they harmonized in soprano, alto, tenor, and bass. Robert Temple recited *Hiawatha* by Henry Wadsworth Longfellow.

Marion's turn came next. The teacher, Mrs. Anita Staker, as the Master of Ceremonies, introduced her. "Our next performance is by a very promising student who has written her own poetry, Marion Kilpatrick. Welcome her, everyone." The crowd clapped enthusiastically, anticipating a treat.

When silence returned, Marion began: "The name of my poem is *Why Not?* Then she quoted words that had been born in her heart.

> *"Why get discouraged when things go wrong?*
> *Why not tackle each load with a song?*
> *Why think we're dying because we're hit?*
> *Why not keep on trying and hang to our grit?"*

> *"Why not give our comrade a slap on the back*
> *And point out to him the right of the track?*
> *Why not think of others instead of our rights*
> *And lead them on to pathways more bright?"*

> *"Why don't we encourage our fellow man?*
> *Why don't we help him when we can?*

THE LITERARY

*Why are we so selfish as to think of self
Whenever a friend is in need of our help?"*

*"Why not be examples of goodness and cheer?
Why not brush from someone's eyes, a tear?
Why not be sympathetic, kind-hearted and true
And encourage our friends to never be blue?"*

*"Oh!! I wish that I were the kind of friend
Who could help someone to a brighter end.
In my heart let others first always come
Until the setting of my life's sun!!"*

Marion Kilpatrick

School Teacher Bland

The applause thundered. People were on their feet, smiling and clapping for her. Marion smiled back at them and bowed her appreciation.

When she went to her seat by Bland, he looked at her admiringly. "You're even more beautiful than I thought. Your poem touched me."

"Thank you," Marion blushed again. "I like to write poetry. Sometimes I write essays, too."

As they traveled in Bland's car back to the house, he held her hand. "I love being with you. Shall we go on a picnic next weekend? We could go over to the Two Buttes Dam, or play tennis in town. Please say yes!"

"But Mr. Backus wants us to practice on Saturday! Won't you be there?"

"That's right. I almost forgot. We mustn't disappoint Mr. Backus. I'll be there." Bland tried again, "I hear Dr. Watt's wife is planning a Halloween party for the community. It's on the Friday night before Halloween, a masquerade party. Would you like to go?"

"Let me think about that," Marion brushed her hair back from her face. "I don't know what I'd do for a costume. We can't buy one. But maybe, just maybe, Mama could help me make something. She's not feeling very well these days, but I'll ask her and let you know in plenty of time. Thank you so much for taking me this evening. It was even more special with you there."

The Dust Storm

On a Saturday in mid-October, Marion, shaking rugs, thought an all too familiar haze hung over the day. She remembered other days like this and hoped the haze didn't mean what she feared. She had seen dust storms; the huge red-brown cloud rolling over the prairie toward them, enveloping them and bringing their lives almost to a halt. The dust obscured their vision, contaminated their air and water, sifted through the tiniest cracks into their home, and invaded even their imprisoned indoor existence. Usual activities ceased. Constant cleaning to reduce the threat of dust pneumonia replaced them. People died because of the dust. The storms halted transportation too.

Marion hoped this storm wouldn't come and prayed that, if it did, no one would get sick, or need a doctor.

Her thoughts jumped in another direction: She pondered what Papa had said about women being doctors. It concerned her because she loved her Papa and knew he loved the Lord. She wanted to please Papa *and* please the Lord. Would it really be wrong for her to become a doctor?

Marion had other worries. She couldn't forget the day Bland questioned her about talking to Tom, *almost as if he owned me. Maybe I shouldn't spend any more time with him. I've heard about women who marry possessive men, and all the troubles that come to them.* One thing she didn't want to do was make a mistake in marriage. That could ruin her whole life.

***

The date for the Halloween masquerade party approached. Marion, still ambivalent about whether she wanted to go, hadn't answered Bland's invitation or decided on a costume. *Maybe I should say "No" to his invitation.* She decided that on Wednesday, after band practice, she would tell him. *He can ask someone else if he wants.*

Suddenly, Marion realized the day was growing darker. She hurried out on the prairie far enough to see the horizon in the southwest, the direction from which the usual storm came. There the red-brown wall of dust roiled the dry earth and dominated the horizon.

A lot has to be done! Marion rushed into the house in near panic, "The dust is coming again; it's nearly here! We have to cover the windows right now! We should get the chickens in, and the cows. Right now! Everyone needs to help. Do we have enough food from the cellar? Mildred, would you check out the kitchen? Neva, please help me wet sheets and cover the windows. We need to pump extra water too. Hurry! Hurry! We must be ready!"

Mama heard the urgency in Marion's voice from her bed. "Do what Marion says," she ordered. "Do it now!"

Papa wasn't home yet. He had taken the horses and buggy to the Bradshaw's across town for an elders' meeting. It would be nearly impossible for him to get home after the storm hit.

Mama lay in her bed and prayed aloud for Samuel and for her family: "Dear Wonderful Lord in Heaven, You are Lord of all nature. You are stronger than the wind, and can see through the dust. Please keep us all safe in You, especially Samuel, out in the storm. In Jesus' Precious Name I pray. Amen."

The dust would make her breathing more difficult, compromised as her health was now. *The storm will be hard on Samuel.* He was almost seventy years old. "The Lord has cared for us over all these difficult years, and He will care for us now," she told Marion and Neva when they came close to her bed.

The storm struck about five pm. The house shook as the wind battered and pounded. The roar of the wind and the moans and creaks of the trembling house made conversation nearly impossible. The kerosene lamps' feeble lights challenged the dark, but dark remained, the flames only visible in the spots they occupied.

All the girls could do was walk around the rooms in the darkness, dusting. They checked the sheets to make sure they still covered the windows, worried about what they could eat for dinner, and dusted some more, hopelessly waiting for relief they knew might not come for days.

Marion anxiously remembered Papa, hoping he had not left the Bradshaw's home. *He always wants to be home when he can, sitting in the kitchen with Mama, reading his Bible to us. He'll come home.* She expectantly waited for him. He was probably struggling home now against this powerful wind and blinding, smothering dust. She prayed that God would give him supernatural strength and vision, and help him breathe, so he could get home safely.

The family waited hours, finally opening a jar of plum butter and cleaning surfaces again so they could slice a loaf of home-made bread for their dinner. They had almost finished when someone pounded on the door.

Reluctantly, expectantly, fearfully, they opened the door. There was Papa, red-brown dust in his hair, eyebrows, eyelashes, and covering his body. He nearly fell into the room, and they rushed to close the door. Hands fumbled awkwardly, helping him to remove his dusty clothing. Marion wiped his face and hair lovingly.

"Are you ok, Papa?" Mildred cried.

Neva hugged him, disregarding the dust still clinging to his body.

"Get me some clothes and I'll be better!" he answered Mildred. "Got anything around here to eat?"

Marion, weak with relief and eager to help her Papa, jumped up, dusted the table one more time, cut bread and spread it with plum butter. "Here, Papa Mine!" Marion offered, reverting to the familiar name she had used for Papa in her youth. "The plum butter is good. Eat it and you'll feel better."

Papa ate the food gratefully, and relaxed on his stool.

"How did you see to get home, Papa?" Marion asked a few moments later. Papa smiled. "I knew I couldn't do it, and the horses couldn't see either, but I knew God could see just fine. I didn't try to guide the horses. I asked God to do it, and He did. We had to stop a few times and rest because of the strong wind, but here we are! Let's say thank you to Him right now. Let's go to Mama, and we'll pray together."

Marion's Decision and Diversion

MONDAY morning the wind stopped. When the dust settled, it covered the fields with six inches of silt and drifted over tops of fences or any other obstacle in its path. Dust lay piled against the house, nearly to window height. The sun rose but with a sickly yellow color that brought no heat. Papa ventured outdoors to care for livestock and chickens with a bandana tied over his nose and mouth, for dust still hung heavy in the air.

School dismissed on the first day after the storm. Families busied themselves cleaning up their environments enough to live in them. They shoveled paths to the cellars, barns, and food supplies for the animals. They had to find the roads and clean them off. Dust obliterated every identifiable landmark making the scene surreal.

On Tuesday school started again. *Concentrating is so hard,* Marion thought, *with all the upset we've experienced.* And she dreaded band period on Wednesday when she would tell Bland she would not attend the masquerade party with him. *I hope he will understand.* Her anxious thoughts distracted her, and time passed slowly.

On Wednesday she entered the band room and greeted Mr. Backus who was always especially kind to her. *I'm glad he appreciates how hard I work on my music and my dependability when the band marches in a parade or does a concert. He treats me with respect. I like the way he treats me.*

Bland came in after rehearsal had started, stressed from his difficult drive. Practice centered on *Stars and Stripes Forever* by John Phillip Sousa; the rehearsal intense, each section—and sometimes individuals—being asked to play their parts. When it ended, Marion felt exhausted. She dreaded the talk with Bland, but he appeared before her, *Oh no! I can't avoid this now!.*

"Hi Bland. I'm glad you're okay after the storm. Were you over at Wentworth, or here with your parents?"

"I had to stay in Wentworth for a teacher's meeting on Saturday, and then it was too late to come home. What about you and your family? Are you all okay?"

"Papa was away from home when the storm struck, but he made it home okay. He said he asked God to guide him, and God did. We were so glad to see him! I hope your family is alright."

"Yes, they stayed safe at home."

"I'm glad," Marion said. "I want to talk to you. I've decided I won't go to the masquerade party. I'm telling you now so you can ask someone else if you wish."

"Why, Marion? Why are you refusing? There is no one else I'd like to ask. What did I do?" Bland asked.

"Nothing really. I was just bothered by the way you reacted when you saw me talking to my friend, Tom. Maybe we can go out again, sometime, but for right now I think we shouldn't be together too much. I'm only eighteen. It's much too soon to be getting serious. I hope you understand. I had fun with you."

"But I don't understand! See you around." Bland was gone, leaving Marion regretful, but relieved.

***

Marion concentrated her energies on her science and math, still feeding her dream of becoming a doctor. She saw Bland at band practice, but he no longer approached her. She felt deprived of his attentions, but she focused on other activities. She wrote a paper that protested women's' smoking, called it *"Flaming Fingers,"* and presented it at Literary. Bland was there watching but never approached.

Time for the spring musical came. Marion and Mildred tried out and got lead parts that featured songs with harmonies. Mrs. Carter held practices two or three times weekly. Attendance was mandatory.

They constantly traveled back and forth to school; added to their responsibilities at home, the musical kept them consistently busy. Mrs. Carter scheduled performances for the last weekend in March on Friday night and Saturday afternoon.

On the Friday of the first performance at five pm, the students of Two Buttes High School gathered for final preparations. They applied stage make up, checked the sets, touched up paint where needed, and practiced their lines and music.

Time passed quickly, and at seven pm the curtain rose to *Windmills of Holland*. The student actors poured their hearts into their performances. Marion and Mildred sang their duets flawlessly, and it ended.

A community, button-popping-proud of its young people, applauded enthusiastically and gave repeated curtain calls for the lead characters. In a dark corner, Bland applauded too, for the beautiful young Marion who had stolen his heart. He left quietly and quickly when the lights came on.

The Birthday Party

ON April 29, 1931 Marion and Mildred turned nineteen. Mama thought it was an important birthday and invited their neighbors, the Charles Vaughn family, to share it with them. They were to celebrate on the Friday night after the girls' birthday. Mildred and Marion were each allowed to invite two special friends.

The Twins and Neva did most of the preparatory work, since Mama lacked strength to help much. She did most of the planning, however: They would fix their usual company dinner: fried chicken, mashed potatoes and gravy, canned green beans and carrots, fresh rolls Marion made from scratch, and coffee with birthday cake for dessert. The girls would bake their cake, and Mama would decorate it. "I will plan the games," Mama said.

She's been very secretive, Marion thought, *not quite her usual self.*

Mama did have a secret. She had saved extra pennies, nickels and dimes for years, waiting for this birthday. She had pondered over catalogs, especially the pages showing the new "phonographs" which played "records." She knew the girls and their friends would certainly enjoy the surprise she planned. They would be able to listen to their favorite songs whenever they liked. Their radio which was a new addition to their home brought news daily, and introduced music such as *Three Little Words,* and *Bye Bye Blues.*

The girls had their favorites. As well as those favorites, Mama bought *Oh Susannah* and *Walkin' My Baby Back Home,* musical games which a group of young people could enjoy together. All the young people knew them from parties called "Jumping Around Parties," the substitute for dances that many parents provided. These games would be the main activity for the party. *It will be fun for everyone. If the weather is nice, we can do them outdoors. Otherwise we will push back the furniture.*

Marion and her sisters worked hard every evening after school getting ready for the party. On Thursday Marion baked. Mama decorated on Friday while they were at school. School dismissed at 3:30 pm, and they hurried home to fry the chicken; dinner was at 5:30 pm. The girls wanted to be ready for their company by five o'clock. They would need to be very efficient to pull it off.

When Marion, Mildred and Neva got home Friday afternoon, Mama hovered over the fry pan watching the chicken. Marion put potatoes on to cook at 4:45. At 5 they were almost done, so she moved them to the back of the stove to keep them warm. Mama's chicken waited, golden brown, and crisp, on the warming tray. The jars of beans and carrots were opened and ready to start cooking. The rolls were ready to put in the oven to warm. Papa came in from outdoors and headed for the bedroom to change. He found Mama there, recently arrived, trying to pull herself together.

Mildred's friends, Doris and Ross, were the first guests to arrive. Marion had invited her friend, Iver, and a girlfriend, Betty. They arrived next. At 5:30 the Vaughn family hadn't yet come, and Marion realized she was nervous about more than dinner. She put the beans and carrots on to cook and pulled the potatoes to the burner again. Just a few minutes, she told herself.

Will Bland come? He hasn't spoken to me for months now. Is he angry with me? Maybe he doesn't want to be friends anymore. Ending their friendship hadn't been her intent, and she felt sorry if he thought that's what she wanted.

The Vaughn family arrived but without Bland. Marion; disappointed, helped Mildred watch the food carefully, pulled off the potatoes and mashed them, and removed the bread from the warming oven. Wonderful, inviting aromas of fried chicken and freshly baked bread wafted through the house. Mama and Papa seated their guests. One chair remained empty. Papa led a prayer blessing the food, and the partying began.

Everyone seems to be having a good time, Marion thought; *everyone but me. It's silly to let his absence ruin my birthday.* She resolutely joked with Iver and shared her stories with Betty. Mildred centered her attentions on her friend, Ross and on Merle Vaughn, too. Neva and Maynard seemed to enjoy one another. Mama and Papa and the Vaughn parents conversed energetically.

When dinner was almost finished, someone knocked on the door. Marion jumped.

"Please answer the door, Marion," Papa said.

Marion rose quickly and hurried to the door. Bland stood there holding a large package.

"Anything left for me?" he asked.

"Yes, definitely! Please come in." Marion felt tongue-tied, not knowing how to break the long silence. She led Bland to the empty chair, noticeably beside hers, and said, "Please sit down, Bland. Pass the food around, everybody. This man's hungry."

Bland set his package down next to Marion's chair, and sneaked a knowing smile at Mama. "Sorry I'm late. I had an errand to do."

"We're so glad you're here, Bland. How have things been going at school?" Papa asked.

"We've just come back from district competition. My kids did really well. In fact, they took the first place ribbon in four of five subjects. I don't think they worked hard enough on their historical dates, so we took second in history, but I'm really proud of them."

"That's wonderful, Bland. You must have done a great job as a teacher to have them succeed like that!" Marion returned the platter holding the fried chicken to Bland.

"I use a lot of competition in the classroom. They love it, and it motivates them to work harder. It's a great teaching tool."

"Did you bring your guitar, Bland?" his mother asked.

"Yes, Mom. It's in the car if we need it. This is a great dinner, Mrs. Kilpatrick. The fried chicken is perfect."

"Marion and Mildred did the cooking. Don't give me the credit." Mama said.

"You did a birthday kind of job, Girls. It's wonderful eating!" Bland said, looking at Mildred, then at Marion for a long moment, a smile and a question in his eyes.

Marion smiled back at him. "We've missed you, Bland," she said, and lowered her gaze.

"I have a surprise for Marion and Mildred," Mama said. "Bland, why don't you give it to them?"

"My pleasure!" Bland picked up the package that arrived with him, and handed it to Mildred. "Here, why don't you open it? Don't let Marion see!" he teased.

"Mama, Mama, What is it?" Mildred squealed excitedly when she saw the package contents.

"It's a phonograph. See the turn-table? You put records on it, and it plays the music that's recorded on them." Mama reached under the table and handed another package to Neva. "Give it to Marion," she said.

Marion opened the package excitedly. "Oh! All our favorites! Thank you so much, Mama and Papa! Can we play them now?"

"As a matter of fact, that's what I'd planned for the rest of our evening. That's why I bought *Three Little Words and Oh, Susannah*. You kids know the games, don't you?"

"Oh yes!" Mildred jumped up from her chair. "How does this thing work?"

"I'll show you." Bland opened the lid. "Now, we just choose a record, and put it on the turn table. Start the turntable with this lever, pick up the needle arm, and set it down at the beginning of the record, like this. Which song will it be?"

"*Oh Susannah!*" Neva called. "Let's do *Oh Susannah!*"

"Choose your partners." Bland walked to Marion and held out his hand. Iver found Hazel, Maynard chose Neva, Merle, Betty. Mildred teamed up with Ross.

Bland's questioning eyes sought Marion's as they marched to the music. The air filled with laughter as the other couples followed them through the movements, sometimes losing their balance as they kicked, or missing a beat as they two-stepped at the end.

"Let's do it again!" Neva prompted. That was fun!"

The young people repeated the exercise over and over, alternating with *Walkin' My Baby Back Home.* When they tired and it was dark outside, they listened to the records Mama had bought and had contests memorizing the words.

Finally, about eleven pm, the Vaughn parents decided it was time to go home. "Thanks for the offer of the melons. We'll take you up on that." Mrs. Vaughn said, heading for the door.

Soon afterwards the others followed her lead, leaving only Bland waiting to talk to Marion.

Dr. Verity's Plan

"How did you like your birthday party?" Bland asked.

"I loved it, Bland. I'm so glad you came."

"I'm glad, too. But now, we need to talk. Can we sit on the porch?" He took Marion's hand and led her into the night. They sat in the porch swing.

Stars glittered in the expansive sky above, flirting with the full moon. Crickets chirped their melodic song from under the porch, and the far-off sound of coyotes' howling made Marion appreciate Bland's presence beside her.

Marion waited for Bland to start talking. *He has questions to ask.*

"I want to share some things with you. Is that okay?" he began.

"Definitely. Please do."

"I grew up on a farm near Selman, Oklahoma. When I turned eleven I started working hard like a man. I thought if my Dad saw how hard I worked, he would understand that the farm was important to me. Chester was a little older than I, and he worked too, but he really played at working, if you know what I mean. He didn't care much about the farm. When Dad ignored my hard work and rewarded Chester and I evenly, it really bothered me. I decided then that some day I would have my own farm. I've never been afraid of hard work. For now, I'm teaching school, but I really want to farm."

"I'm so sorry you were disappointed like that, Bland."

"I'm telling you this because you need to know it. What do you want to do with your life?"

"I've always wanted to be a doctor. It seems impossible, though. Papa says God wants women to stay in their homes and serve, but it seems like God is calling me to serve people by making them well. Medical school costs money, which Papa doesn't have. I haven't really talked it out with him. I guess I'm afraid he'll say 'No.' The other dream is to have a home and family of my own. I want a man who loves God, like Papa."

"You have big dreams, little lady." Bland smiled. I think I agree with your dad about the doctoring, but you can dream. Don't you think your dad is just a little too religious?"

"Papa's faith in God is firm." Marion stood suddenly. "He loves the Lord with all his heart. I want to be like him someday."

"I need to go now. Thank you for a nice evening. Happy birthday." Bland abruptly stood, and walked to his car.

"Thank you for coming, Bland. I was so glad to see you. Good Night." Marion followed him, watched him crank up the engine, and waved good-by. The night suddenly seemed less friendly, and Marion hurried inside.

***

Marion's junior year was drawing to a close. She enjoyed her friendships. Hazel checked in with her every day, and on Wednesdays she saw Bland. Sometimes he came over to greet her, but usually briefly. Marion wondered if he was upset about something she had said her birthday night when they were sharing dreams.

She thought about Bland almost constantly. *He seems uncomfortable, as if he has nothing to say,* she thought, *any time I talk about my faith, even though he is at church on Sundays. I must be imagining it,* she thought, and remembering her sister, Stella's poem,

Worry? What does worry do?
It never keeps a problem from over taking you.

It puts a frown upon your face,
A sharpness in your tone.
Unfit to live with others
And unfit to live alone, she dismissed the worry.

Stella Kilpatrick Maynard

SEIZING THE TREASURE

***

Mr. Backus approached Marion as she left band practice one day. "Marion, I need to talk to you. Do you have ten minutes?"

"Of course, Mr. Backus. I'm going home when I leave. What is it?"

"I've been talking to Dr. Verity about you. You've been working so hard. He's heard that you want to be a doctor. How are your plans coming along?"

"I'm a little discouraged. Papa isn't in favor of it, and wouldn't have the money if he approved. I don't see how it can happen."

"That's what I suspected. Dr. Verity has an idea for you. He wants to pay for your schooling so you can become the best doctor Baca County ever had. He'd like you to come to his office tomorrow after school. He'll be waiting for you. Will you go?"

Shocked, Marion blurted, "But he can't do that! It's just too much!"

"It's not too much if he wants to do it. And he wants to do it! See you tomorrow." Mr. Backus watched Marion walk away with a baffled look on her face.

The next day after school Marion walked the short distance from the school to the small frame house on Main Street where Dr. Verity lived and practiced A hot wind disarranged her hair, and she tried vainly to pat it back into place before she opened the door.

Dr. Verity waited at his desk. His unruly grey hair hung almost to his shoulders. Marion thought he had put on a little weight since she'd seen him last. *I hope he's well.*

The visit was brief. "Hi, Marion. Glad to see you. I have an idea I want to share. You don't know this, but I've been watching you. I'm impressed by your talents, your character, and your spirit. I've seen you at Literary and in the school musicals. I march with you in the band at every parade. I heard some time ago that you want to be a doctor," he said. "Is that correct?"

"Yes, Sir. I do want to be a doctor, but it can never happen. Mr. Backus told me what you want to do, and I appreciate it, down deep, but I could never accept that much money from anyone. I don't think Papa would let me, even if I could."

"Nonsense! You're nineteen, aren't you? Your parents will have nothing to do with it in a couple of years. I *want* to give it to you. We *need* doctors here in Baca County, and this is one way I can help get them. Think about it, Marion. I'd like to hear your decision within a couple of weeks. There comes my next patient; I need to go. Bye now."

Marion left Dr. Verity's office in a daze. *So it's really true, what Mr. Backus said. Dr. Verity does want to pay my college costs.* A future that she hadn't dared to imagine opened before her. *Tonight I must talk seriously to Papa; try to get his permission.*

She thought then about Bland's response when she told him she wanted to be a doctor. It didn't sound as if he approved either. *You have big dreams, little lady.* He hadn't encouraged her in that direction. *But Bland isn't around much these days, either, is he? I won't worry about him, at least. I already have plenty to worry about.*

Papa came in from his work that evening about six. He washed up, then sat on his stool in the kitchen and opened his Bible. Marion, waiting for him, pulled a chair and sat with him. She had asked Mildred to cook dinner tonight.

"Papa, we need to talk. Remember when I told you I want to be a doctor? It's still what I want, and I want your approval."

"Marion, I've told you what I think. Where did you get an idea like that any way? Women are much better off at home with their families."

"But Papa! Something wonderful has happened. Dr. Verity heard that I want to be a doctor, and he told me today that he wants to pay my way to medical school. Isn't that marvelous? It would make it possible for me to continue my education beyond high school. Please say I can do it. I'm nineteen now, almost adult. This is so important to me and I want to know you approve. It would mean so much if you'd say yes."

"We don't need charity, Marion. The Lord has given us what we need. You will be a 'keeper at home' as the Bible says women should be. Concentrate on the skills you will need when you have your own home. I believe this is what God wants for you."

Disappointment, needle sharp, pierced Marion's hope and deflated it. Papa would not relent, she knew. He'd already told her several times to concentrate on becoming the best home-maker she could.

She knew she *could* go against his wishes, but would it be worth what it cost their relationship; the pain it would bring them both? She tried to picture herself going to Dr. Verity and accepting his offer of money for college, disregarding Papa's wishes. She could not. *Papa has guided me with love and wisdom all my life.*

She pictured herself in Medical School, learning more about the human body and how to cure it, but always remembering that Papa did not approve. She envisioned herself a doctor, living over in Springfield, always embarrassed to come home and talk about her life. *My dream would cost too much,* she decided, and though the pain of it engulfed her, she gave it up.

Box Social Surprise

BUT life went on. Summer announced its coming. The school board always planned a box social just before school ended each year. The money earned helped to pay yearly school expenses, and the people of Two Buttes anticipated its arrival as friendly gossips looking forward to a new morsel of story. The occasion gave them plenty to chatter about for weeks.

Marion never felt adequate for the task of creating her box exterior. She relied on Mama's imagination, and Mama never failed her. Mildred was more creative, and made her own decorated box. Both boxes promised delicious contents.

Both would contain special treats like their own plum butter, and fried chicken. To complete their meal, they made their own potato salads, each different than the other. They baked pies; Marion a cherry, Mildred an apple, from fruits Mama had helped them can in season.

The Box Social took place on Saturday; the last Saturday before school was out. The bidding started at noon. No one knew how long it would last.

On Saturday morning the girls finished their cooking, packed their boxes, dressed in their prettiest, and traveled to the school. They carried each others' baskets—in an effort to disguise ownership—to the table dressed in a pink sheet and graced by a beautiful lace tablecloth. There the baskets waited, their sights and smells beckoning to men eager for bidding to start. The girls stood to the left of the table in a group. The men grouped to the right; busy trying to memorize the faces that deposited each basket.

Marion studied the group of men. She saw Iver, Maynard and Merle, but she couldn't spot Bland in the crowd. Disappointment clouded her vision;

she no longer cared who bought her basket, or who she would eat with. *I wish it was over.* She stood beside Mildred and Hazel blindly.

Mama had done her best on Marion's basket. She had covered it with crepe paper, made colorful flowers from contrasting paper, and used wild flowers from the fields to center each artificial flower. Bows and ribbons streamed from the handle. Marion knew it was beautiful, but to what benefit? Her attention strayed, and she watched the other girls nervously showing their excitement and anticipation by twirling their hair, tapping their feet, or giggling. She felt alone, excluded from the party atmosphere, an oddity, an oddity without a future. She grieved her lost dream and wondered what could possibly replace it.

Bidding had started, and several baskets had been sold; the happy couples searching and finding cool places against the building to settle, or searching for a tree within reasonable distance. Most home-owners had trees on the south and west of their houses, and on this day, for the box social, the yards became community property. The park offered lots of trees, too. Hot sunshine made shade a necessity.

Marion wondered if the bidding would ever end. The men delighted in bidding for the baskets they knew their friends wanted, thus stretching out the hours.

About two pm the auctioneer picked up Marion's basket. "Just look at the beautiful artistry in the design. I'll bet the meal inside is just as beautiful. Good eating in here. Do I hear five dollars? Yes, I have five! Six dollars? I have six!"

"Ten dollars!" Bland's voice startled Marion from her reverie. The unremarkable day turned special. Iver bid "Twelve," Bland bid "Fifteen," Iver bid "Seventeen," Bland bid "Twenty." The two men battled it out with their dollars; Bland finally buying the basket for forty dollars.

A welcome breeze stirred the air. Marion, suddenly hot and embarrassed, welcomed its coolness.

"Let's see the lady this box belongs to!" the auctioneer called.

Marion and Mildred Graduation

Marion stepped forward, the blush still fresh on her cheeks, to join Bland as he paid for her box. She'd been surprised at these men and their bids. They had bid for the privilege of eating with her. Wonderingly she stepped to Bland's side.

She and Bland walked down the street from the school, and found a nice shade tree in the Williams' yard. "Shall we stop here?" Bland asked.

"This'll be great. The shade should get even cooler as it gets later. Thank you, Bland. Thank you for paying so much for my box," she said.

"I would have paid whatever it took. I have a special reason for wanting to eat with you today. What are we having?"

"Fried chicken and the works, fresh rolls, plum butter, potato salad, greens, and cherry pie. Let's eat, shall we?" She held out her hand to Bland and bowed her head.

"Thank you for this food, and this good company, Amen. Please pass the chicken," he said, and then, slightly embarrassed, he added, "Two-thirty is mighty late for lunch, and I'm hungry."

As they ate, Bland shared what he had observed during the bidding. "Iver sure wanted your basket," he said, and went on to notice that Merle had bought Betty's. "He thinks about her a lot," he said. "He's always talking about her. Did you notice that Ross Indermill bought Mildred's dinner? Have they been spending time together?"

Marion was surprised at all he knew. "How do you guys know which basket belongs to which girl? We try so hard to keep it secret, but you always find out. I didn't think you were here. You totally surprised me."

"We have our own little grapevine, and I'll never tell." He smiled into her eyes. "As far as the surprise, I planned that too. I hung out behind the building until I saw your basket coming up for bids."

"You're the sneaky one, aren't you?" She smiled. "Are there any more surprises waiting?"

Suddenly Bland grew very serious and very quiet. "As a matter of fact, I do have something for you." He reached into his pocket and brought out a ring. "Marion, I have something to ask you. You don't have to answer me today, but I want you to know what I'm hoping. Marion, I love you. I want you to be my wife. Will you marry me? There is no one else in my life. You are the woman I want to share my life with."

A long-absent joy infused her empty heart. "Bland, I'm honored that you've chosen me. I admire you. I would appreciate a little time to think. I wasn't expecting this. I need to think. I'll let you know in two weeks. I hope to see you between now and then," she stammered on in a rush.

"We don't know each other very well. I couldn't get married until after I graduate. Are you willing to wait that long?"

"I'll give you as much time as you need, Marion. I love you." Bland put the ring back in his pocket, leaned over to Marion, and kissed her. "I'll be waiting."

Her future seemingly restored, Marion felt new and beautiful. She pictured herself as Bland's wife, the one the school teacher loved, the wife who would follow him wherever he led. She could make him happy, she felt sure of it. She could cook, sew a little, clean and decorate his home. She could even listen to him play that guitar, a pleasure she'd never yet enjoyed. She could talk to him, listen to his dreams, even help him to fulfill that farming dream he'd shared. She wasn't afraid of hard work, either.

Marion went home happy that night, giving thanks for Bland's love. She prayed for him, and for their marriage, giving their future to the God Who loved them more than life itself.

Parental Warnings

"DID you girls enjoy the box social?" Mama asked the next morning, "Mildred, who bought your dinner?"

"Ross Indermill! I was hoping against hope it would be him. He's such a nice guy, and so smart. He's already thinking of starting his own business, maybe stocking coffee machines. The machines are a new direction, and not many are out there, so competition shouldn't be too stiff for awhile. I could listen to him talk about his dreams all day!"

"You'll have to invite him to the house so Papa and I can visit with him. I'm so glad you had a good time. Marion, what about you?"

"I had a wonderful time once Bland started bidding for my box. At first I didn't think he was there, so I didn't care much till then. He and I went over to the Williams' yard and ate under their catalpa tree. Bland asked me to marry him! I'm so happy."

"Whoa! Slow down! Did you say what I thought I heard, that Bland asked you to marry him? I haven't seen him around much lately. This is a total surprise."

"He surprised me, too. He had a ring in his pocket, but I told him I needed some time to think. He's willing to wait until I've graduated."

"Do you think you know him well enough? You haven't really been together that much. Let's talk it all over with Papa when he comes home from the elder's meeting, or tomorrow, if it's too late tonight when he comes in."

"There's a whole year to get to know him. Don't worry, Mama."

***

"Marion, would you come outside with me for awhile?" Papa asked the next morning. "We need to talk."

Marion followed her Papa willingly. He went to the road, turned toward the windbreak, and they walked for several minutes before he spoke.

"Marion," Papa said, "Mama told me Bland asked you to marry him. Have you given him an answer?"

"No, Papa. Bland is willing to wait for my answer. I told him I'd let him know in two weeks."

"What will your answer be, Marion?"

"I'm still thinking, Papa, but I'm thinking a lot about how it will be when I am his wife. It's like I'm already living in my future."

"It sounds like your answer may be 'Yes.'"

"I think so, Papa. I really think I'm in love with him. I think about him constantly, even when we haven't been seeing one another much."

"Have you thought about how it will be when Bland is not pleased? It seems like he sure knows how to do the disappearing act. Have you noticed?"

"Well, yes. There have been periods when I thought I'd never see him again. I've wondered why he wasn't coming around any more."

"Had you considered that he might be punishing you for something you said?"

"No Papa. I hadn't considered that, not really. I did wonder, though."

"Marion, I'm afraid Bland might not treat you very well. At least think hard about your answer, and wait as long as you can to give it."

"But Papa! I told him I would give him the answer in two weeks!"

"Marion, you are choosing your whole life right now. Please don't rush into it."

"I don't have a life without Bland," Marion said. "Not any more."

They walked back toward the house. There was nothing more to say.

Looking Forward

BLAND showed up at her side anytime he was in Two Buttes... at band practice on Wednesdays, when she was home, after school, bringing in the wash from the clothes line or churning the morning's cream into butter. They became constant companions, enjoying walks on the prairie, picking wild flowers, picnicking on Saturdays, sitting together at church on Sundays.

In the fall, before school started, they took a picnic lunch to the Cedars in Western Baca County and spent the afternoon picking wild plums. They went to Literary and Iced Cream parties and Jumping Around Parties. They even went to a Medicine Show where a "doctor" pedaled his cure-all, and people actually bought it. There was always something to do, and they had marvelous fun doing it together.

Then school started. Bland, hired for a teaching job at Lone Star—a community near Two Buttes—still came to Two Buttes regularly on the weekends so they could be together.

Marion, at last interested in her trousseau, began to sew with more diligence than she had previously displayed. She made tea towels from flour sacks, embroidered them, and went on to pillow cases that she hemmed, embroidered, and gave to Mildred to crochet edging. She cut out and sewed new nightgowns from flannel, and Stella, when she heard of Marion's plans, volunteered to make her wedding dress.

Marion chose a soft lavender organdy for the creation. The dress Stella designed had a wide ruffle over the shoulders and around the open neckline, another wide ruffle flowing from side to side down the skirt, and a third ruffle at the calf-length hem. Marion rejoiced in its beauty, and anticipated the day she would wear it for Bland.

In the spring, Mrs. Carter selected *Daddy Long Legs* as the school musical, and Marion, Mildred and Neva had parts; Marion and Mildred, leading ladies once more, worked hard to perfect their singing.

Bland came to the performance, bragging to everyone that Marion was the girl he planned to marry. He came backstage to escort her out of the school, and took her to the drug store for a chocolate milk shake which they shared; each sipping through their own straw, heads close together, smiling into one another's eyes.

"I'm building us a small house near the school yard at Lone Star. It's not very big; more like a shed," he said. "I'm living in it now, and working on it after school each day. We can live there after we are married. On the southwest side of the house stands a large beautiful cottonwood tree. I wanted to take advantage of the shade during the hottest part of the day.

"I'm so glad, Bland. The shade will make things so much easier. Nicer, and cooler for me. Thank you for planning that. It'll seem hard adjusting to a small house again," said Marion, thinking out loud. "We've had three rooms in Two Buttes, not anything like what we had in Beaver County."

"I'm doing what I can, Marion. I thought you would appreciate it."

"But I do appreciate it. I didn't mean to be critical. It will be our home. That's all I need; a home and you." Marion's reassurances were greeted by silence. "Bland, please don't shut me out. I'm your friend. I love you."

"We should go home now, Marion. Sorry I'm so touchy. Sometimes I wonder what's the matter with me. Let's go. I'll take you home."

Awakening

"I'D like to ask Clyde Williams, my brother in law to marry us, Bland. Is that ok with you? Mama and Papa suggested we get married at our home." It was early July, and Bland was driving Marion up to show her the house at Lone Star. "I'm so excited to see our home."

Bland looked at Marion. "We haven't talked yet about a date for our wedding. Have you thought about it?"

"I've thought of nothing else. I've been considering August 21. It's a Sunday. I thought more people would be able to come on the weekend. We could get married in the afternoon. We'll fix desserts and ask everyone to come to our house. What do you think?"

"Any day will be fine with me. I'm glad you're ready to set the date. August is next month; I'll have the house finished enough that we can live in it. We'll just "camp" a little bit while I finish. Here we are."

Marion saw a small school building which appeared to be one room, and a small shed-like house located northeast of the school, a large cottonwood tree between the two buildings. The surroundings reminded her of those at home, rolling prairie as far as the eye could see, except here it was much emptier.

The only neighbor lived down a fence-line, about one half mile away. Suddenly Marion felt lonely; lonely for Papa and Mama, Mildred and Neva, Uncle John and Aunt Bertha across the field, Ira her cousin, Hazel, her friend, all the Kilpatrick cousins she knew so well. With her attention centered on Bland she hadn't thought much about all she was leaving; how much she was giving up.

"Shall we go in?" Bland interrupted her reverie, excited about what he had accomplished. He opened the car door and helped her out.

The walls were whitewashed and gave off light that dispelled the gloom of the closed room. Bland opened a boarded window in the kitchen, and light spilled in. "We can open the window when it's warm and the wind's not blowing. It may be a challenge to keep dust out, so I hope we don't have any more of those storms we've been having lately."

Marion noticed a wood stove for heat and cooking and a double bed in the opposite corner.

"We'll carry our water from the well at the school," he said. "It's not too far, and I'll help you with it. How do you like the table and chairs I've built?"

"Oh Bland, everything is better than I've expected. You've worked so hard, and your workmanship is lovely. We'll have everything we need here. Thank you."

"One thing we have to look out for is rattlesnakes." Bland continued to show her around outside. "This is less populated country, and they might be anywhere looking for food. Just watch where you step, and be careful where you put your hands."

The seriousness of the marriage commitment overwhelmed her. Now she realized the separations that were in her near future; the absence of her friends, the emptiness of the unknown prairie, and the uncertainty of unfamiliar neighbors. It was hard to picture her life here, even with Bland. *Oh Lord, Thou hast been my dwelling place in all generations. You will never leave me or forsake me,* she prayed. *Even here, on this lonely unfamiliar prairie, I have You.* She was comforted.

Deep Thoughts

SUNDAY, August 14 dawned beautiful and clear. *What a beautiful day it is,* Marion thought. *I hope our wedding day is like this.* She looked forward to seeing Bland at church and hoped they could have some time together so they could talk. She had been thinking about the kind of relationship she hoped they would grow into.

It had all started when she was reading with Neva. Mrs. Carter had loaned her a book called the Velveteen Rabbit by Margery Williams. The story was about toys becoming Real, but Marion thought *Real might happen to married couples, too, when they learn to understand one another and accept one another just the* way they are. In the story, the Skin Horse tells Velveteen Rabbit that when a child *really* loves him, he will be Real and that sometimes it hurts to be Real.

Yes, Marion thought. *We will have to decide to love one another even with all the faults we have; understand one another even when it's hard, and love no matter what happens.*

"It takes a long time," the Skin Horse told the rabbit. "It doesn't happen often to people who have sharp edges, or break easily, or have to be carefully kept."

That's what commitment means, Marion thought, *not allowing oneself to be easily hurt or broken, or to be too tender so others have to tip-toe around you. And it means not running away from each other when we have problems. I really want to talk with Bland about this.*

Bland sought Marion out and sat with her during services, holding her hand tenderly. *I'm beginning to feel safe with him, and appreciated.* The preacher talked about I Corinthians 13, the love chapter. She realized how much she could learn from that chapter, and resolved to study it to see if her love measured up to the standard it gave.

When services were over, she felt filled to the brim and eager to talk with Bland about all of it. "Would you like to take me home and stay for dinner with us?" she invited.

"Good idea. I'm glad you asked." Bland circled her waist with his arm. "This is our last weekend together before our wedding. We should spend it together and talk."

"That's what I was hoping we could do. Shall we walk over to the windbreak so we can be alone?" Marion looked into his eyes with a smile.

"That's a good idea too." Bland opened the car door and waited for Marion to get in, walked around the front, and slid into the driver's seat. "Alone with you is always nice."

"Thank you, Bland. I love being with you, too. I've been doing some reading," Marion said, "and would like to share what I've read with you. Is that all right? Something I've read really made me think about our marriage and what it will take to keep it growing."

"We love each other, Marion. What more should it take?"

"Bland, I know I have a lot of growing to do yet. I think everyone does, especially when they begin to grow a new relationship. Getting along can be hard. We will probably see things differently because of the differences in our growing up years." Marion paused, "Perhaps we should save the rest of this conversation for later. Right now, let's just look forward to dinner!"

An hour and one-half later they grabbed their hats and set out for the windbreak. Dinner had been enjoyable; conversation flowing easily between her parents and Bland. Neva, excited about the coming wedding, listened to every word.

"Now we can talk." Bland reached for her hand and brought her close. "What is it that you want to say to me, Marion?"

"It's just that I have a lot of faults, and I want to know that you'll love me even after you begin to see them; that you'll never criticize me because of them. I don't like my faults and I want to change them, but it's a slow process. Don't you feel like that too?"

"Not really, Marion. Nobody's perfect. I try to do the best I can, and I believe I'm a good person doing the right things. You're a good person, too. Just be happy with who you are. I love you right now. Why would that change?"

"May I tell you about the story I read?"

Bland nodded at Marion, smiling. "Go ahead," he said.

"The story's called the *Velveteen Rabbit*. The rabbit was a new toy, proud of his beautiful coat. He met the Skin Horse, all scruffy, torn, and broken in places. Rabbit couldn't understand why Skin Horse was so happy with all the torn places in his coat.

"It's because I'm Real, the Horse told him. "My boy loves me."

'Does it hurt?' Rabbit asked.

"Sometimes," said Skin Horse. "When you are Real you don't mind being hurt."

"Let me read a short bit to you." Marion took the small book out of her pocket and read,

'Does it happen all at once, like being wound up,' he asked, 'or bit by bit?'

"It doesn't happen all at once," said Skin Horse. "You become. It takes a long time. That's why it doesn't happen often to people who break easily, or have sharp edges, or who have to be carefully kept. Generally, by the time you are real, most of your hair has been loved off, and your eyes drop out and you get loose in the joints and very shabby. But these things don't matter at all, because once you are Real you can't be ugly, except to people who don't understand."

The Velveteen Rabbit, Margery Williams

"Cute story. But I don't see what it has to do with us." Bland stopped and searched her eyes.

"I think what I'm trying to say is, I want us to keep loving one another, even if we have hurt each other, and if our once shiny and new image is tarnished and torn, our faults hanging out in plain view. If we want that to happen, don't we have to make a firm decision to love even when we are hurting?"

"You think too much, Marion. Let's just take our life as it comes. I'll always love you."

Marion felt disappointed and dismissed. Bland had seemed to be listening to her but didn't understand the importance of what she had tried to say. He had treated her like a little girl who needed comfort. *At least I can make those important decisions,* she thought. *I will love Bland no matter what happens. I will love him now.*

Till Death Do Us Part

THE Wedding Day dawned clear and bright. Marion greeted the dawn with thanksgiving; for Bland, for the wonderful day, that today they would become man and wife. She remembered the loneliness that overcame her at Lone Star, and the answer that God had given her; the assurance that she was not alone, even there. She felt thankful for her family who had gathered around her to prepare for this day. The dress Stella had made fit so beautifully and complimented her coloring as she had hoped it would. Mildred had helped with the necessary sewing; beautiful crochet work trimmed several pair of pillowcases. Tasty cakes and pies waited in the kitchen for her friends and neighbors who would share the day with her.

The guests would start arriving soon; Clyde and Mayme would likely be first to arrive since they would want visiting time to be included in the day. She had visited with Clyde by telephone several weeks ago, sharing scripture she would like included in their ceremony.

"Don't worry about it," he said. "I'll probably use it all." Her brothers and sisters would sing the traditional wedding march, *Faithful and True*. Since the day was dry they would be married under the shade trees southwest of their home.

Before the guests arrived and confusion started, Marion wanted to pray.

Father in Heaven, I come before you today not knowing what kind of life is before me, but I know that You know. Bland is a complicated man, and I admit, I don't always know how to please him, but Father, I know how to please You. You are my strength when I am weak. Make me strong to do Your will, and give me the grace to please my husband. Help me to love and respect him through hurt and disappointment, through plenty and through want, through confidence and through fear, through joy and through anger or pain.

The Lord is my shepherd, I shall not want, He will provide for me, even in the presence of those who oppose me. He understands me, knows even the words I will speak; and understands Bland, too. I am leaving my father's house today to cleave to my husband as you have directed, to become one with this man. Please work through Your Spirit to make it happen as you have said, that our union will be for 'as long as we both shall live.

Marion looked up from her prayer to see Bland coming toward her, carrying a huge bouquet of red roses.

"For my beautiful bride," he said. "Are you ready to take our vows?"

Honeymoon camping

Lone Star Bride
Facts of Life on the Prairie

MARION had spent the day washing clothes and felt exhausted after several hours of hard work. She rested in a chair outside under the shade tree while she churned the butter. As she worked, she thought back over the previous months; their marriage on August twenty-first, 1932, the huge bouquet of red roses Bland had brought her just before the ceremony, their move to Lone Star, the hard months when she longed for her family and friends back in Two Buttes. The adjustments to, and total responsibility for the hard work involved in keeping house overwhelmed her.

The butter solidified; the long session of shaking the jar back and forth, back and forth, until the cream solids finally congealed was finished, and Marion was past tired, into fatigue. She rose, relieved, and started the walk across the prairie to the school yard where she would put the butter in the well house to cool.

As she stepped into the path, the dreaded sound of a Diamond-Back-Rattler warned her. She saw the snake coil to strike and panicked. Her butter jar hit the ground and shattered, making a sharp sound on the silent prairie. Screaming, she gripped—two-handed—the hoe she always carried and crashed it down toward the snake, hoping to remove its head. She missed and tried again. The snake writhed and slithered away looking for safety that it found in her shade tree. Marion ran for the house and slammed the door. She still cowered inside when Bland returned from school.

"I've never been so scared in my life," she told Bland shakily, "I've seen plenty of rattlesnakes, but usually after Papa had killed them. I never imagined I'd be the one swinging the hoe!"

"I'd hoped you'd never come across one," Bland said, "Are you okay? It didn't bite you did it?"

"No, it didn't bite me, but I'm still shaking, and I'll be killing snakes all night in my dreams. He's in my shade tree, the one where I work! What will I do without shade?"

Bland drew her to his side, hugging her, "The snake is probably already down from the tree." He smiled into her eyes. "I don't think you'll need to worry about it." But Marion *did* worry. The chores she was responsible for assumed mammoth proportions because they were done outside.

***

That night the storm came. Wind-blown dust swirled around and beat upon the twelve by eighteen foot house, trapping them inside and insidiously sifting through the almost invisible cracks to invade their only refuge from it. The air inside grew heavy, although the storm was scarcely two hours old. Marion had taken the measures she knew to be necessary, covering the cracks around the window and door with wet sheets, making sure they had food inside the house. Bland put the cow and chickens in the partially finished barn, and then they waited.

Bland paced nervously, restlessly, then sat down next to the kerosene lamp and tried to read. When he could not, he paced some more. Marion dusted every surface in the room over and over and went back to do it again.

The dust storm was familiar, but sharing it with Bland's nervous energy was not. Still, she could think of one benefit the dust storm offered. She could stay inside; she would not have to go outside with the snakes.

The storm ended by morning leaving an environment covered in silt, a house dusty, and clothes that had to be washed again. Bland carried water from the school-yard well until there was enough to fill the large washtub, and then he carried four more buckets of cold water. The washtub sat on the stove heating.

When it was hot, Marion dipped part of it into a bucket, carried it outside to another washtub, and added cold water. She got out the scrub board and the lye soap Mama had given her for a wedding gift, gathered the clothes—everything they had—and scrubbed each piece carefully, putting each article into the second tub for rinsing. After rubbing and rinsing, she wrung each piece by hand and put it into a third tub.

Bland had helped her set up her washing site under the tree, and while she worked Marion looked up fearfully, expecting the snake she had seen disappear there to drop down onto her. She prayed it wouldn't happen.

Before she had worked fifteen minutes, sweat ran from her hair, dripped into her eyes, and stuck her clothes to her body. She worked several hours before she could, at last, dump her water on the rose bush and hang the clothes on the line to dry. Exhausted, she escaped into the house and sat contemplating dinner and the work needed to prepare it.

Bland walked in from school. "Boy, I'm sure hungry," he said, Marion dissolved in tears.

"You're tired, aren't you," he said matter-of-factly. "Tomorrow is Friday. You won't have to work so hard tomorrow. Let's just boil eggs and eat them for dinner tonight."

***

Marion looked forward to Fridays. On that day she left the never-ending house work and went to school with Bland. His twelve students welcomed her and continued their morning activities. She delighted in watching Bland as he directed the work in the classroom.

The children were of all ages. Bland would first direct the youngest children in their tasks; penmanship, or learning their ABC's while the others worked on previously assigned tasks. Then he read them all a story and assigned varying activities according to age and ability. Each older student was responsible for a younger one and helped them while completing their own assignments; each student functioned as an assisting teacher, thus reinforcing their own learning.

Dad's class, Lone Star

Competition was an integral part of Bland's strategy. Following a classroom drill, children competed while learning math facts and history dates. They seemed to believe it was a game and learned new facts and new words every day.

Bland had a well-disciplined class. One Friday morning Marion observed him in action. The eighth grade son of a school board member, making sure that he had the teacher's attention, walked across the room on the desk-tops, secure in his belief that a teacher would never dare to discipline a school board member's son. Bland immediately turned the culprit over his knee. That was one boy's *last* challenge to the teacher's authority.

Time passed quickly in the classroom and Marion's admiration for Bland and his teaching abilities grew. She could see the students' knowledge increasing steadily.

Her favorite part of Friday happened after school. Bland always brought his guitar and played and sang. At first, Marion sat watching and listening, but the music drew her in and, increasingly, she found herself singing along.

"Marion, I think you should be a part of this," Bland invited, "Come up here beside me. We'll do a duet. You sing the harmony."

Bland started singing. "Let me call you sweetheart, I'm in love with you … …' As he sang the words, Bland turned his eyes toward Marion, directing the words to her. She looked at him, smiling, and sang back to him in a warm harmony, the watching kids believed what they saw, that Mr. Vaughn was smitten with his wife, and she with him. After the first Friday Marion sang with Bland, the class requested her regular presence for their weekly after-school fun.

Promise

IT was December 21, 1932, Bland's and Marion's four month anniversary. Marion was beginning her day reading in the Psalms: "Children are a heritage of the Lord. Happy is the man that has his quiver full of them."

I wonder if we'll have children. I hope so. She got up from her chair and walked to the kitchen where she cut slices of bread, got out some apple butter and spread it on bread, and put a fry pan on the burner. Bland was getting water from the school-yard well. They would have breakfast when he returned.

Suddenly the thought of food sickened her; the unusual turmoil in her stomach took her by surprise. She removed the fry pan from the burner and sat again. Feeling puzzled, she hoped she wasn't getting sick. And then, abruptly, she realized that it was past time for her period. *Last month's period was different, somehow, less, much less bleeding.* Now she knew why. *I'm pregnant with Bland's child.* Joy overwhelmed her.

"Thank you, Father. You are blessing us with your heritage. Guide us as we care for and teach this child. And bring him into this world safely." She rose and went back to her food preparations, first eating a very small morsel of bread to settle her stomach as she had seen her older sisters do many times.

When Bland came in she rushed to his side. "I've got something to tell you. I hope you're as happy as I am! We're going to have a baby!"

Bland looked surprised, and then he pulled her to him. "You couldn't give me a better gift," he said. "I hope we have a son. When will he be coming?"

"Oh Bland, I haven't even thought about that! Just *that* he's coming is enough for right now." Marion looked up into Bland's eyes. "I'll have to see a doctor soon. A doctor will know how far along I am."

"We'll make you an appointment in Springfield with Dr. Hamilton. Dr. Verity is just too far away. I've heard Dr. Hamilton is good. One of my student's mothers suggested I call him if we ever needed help."

***

The appointment with Dr. Hamilton went well. He confirmed the pregnancy and predicted an early June due date. They announced their good news to all the family, and Marion invited her mother to come and help her give birth.

At five months, Marion needed her first maternity clothes, and she felt the baby moving. In the ninth month Bland teased her about not being able to tie her own shoelaces.

Marion felt well through her pregnancy, but sometimes she wondered if her baby moved as much as he should. She prayed everyday for a safe delivery.

Early in June, Marion awakened from deep sleep, a familiar aching in her abdomen. She first thought her period had arrived again, then, realizing the nearness of her due date, she awakened Bland.

"Bland, I think the baby is coming soon. I'm cramping. Don't you think we should call Mama?"

"Why don't we wait and see if the cramping keeps happening? It could be something else, couldn't it?"

"I need Mama to help me. You'll need to go get her. We might not have much time."

Suddenly Bland jumped out of bed, pulling on his clothes. "You're right," he said. "We shouldn't waste any time. You call Mama and tell her I'm on the way."

Marion felt another deep aching cramp. "Hurry Bland. I don't know what to do without Mama."

"I'll be back as soon as I can. I love you, Marion. Don't worry."

And Bland was gone, driving into the night. She was alone.

He's not Breathing!

ARION was alone with her pain. She tried to relax between contractions, get a little more sleep, but found it impossible to do. Her anxiety grew with each pain, there was nothing to do but give it to God. He had said not to worry about anything, hadn't He? So she prayed, and finally she slept.

The returning car awakened her.

She heard her Mama's voice. "Bland, I never had such a ride in my life! I'm glad we made it. Get some water in the wash tub, quick. Put it on the stove to heat. Fill the second tub half-way. We may need it. Hurry!"

And then Marion, with increasing wakefulness, realized that her pain was much more intense.

Mama came close to her, watching. "Everything will be alright, Marion. Just concentrate on having this baby. If you feel like pushing, push."

Marion pushed. And she pushed again, and again. Her pain increased, and she pushed some more. Over and over she struggled to birth her precious baby. "O God, keep him safe," she prayed. "Help me!"

She was vaguely aware of Bland on the phone. "I need Dr. Hamilton," he said urgently. "Marion is in labor, and she's having a hard time. The doctor needs to come right away."

Time blurred. Marion tired with each additional effort until she was no longer aware of what was happening. Finally, after her last strength was gone, the baby came.

"Oh no!" Look at his skin. It's blue. And he's not breathing. It's a boy, and he's not breathing!" Mama rushed to the tubs of water with the baby. "We have to make him cry!"

She dipped the baby into the warm water, lifted him out, and dipped him into cooler water. Nothing. She tried again, into the warm water, then into the cool. Suddenly, the baby boy drew a deep breath and screamed. Marion broke into exhausted tears and cried out, "Oh thank you, God. Thank You!"

Mama wrapped the baby in a soft blanket and brought him to his mother. "What is his name?" She bent and put the baby into Marion's arms.

"Hello, my baby boy, Marion cried. You really scared me, but it's okay. You're safe now."

Bland was there at her side, bending over with his arms around both of them. "You were so brave, Marion. Thank you for my new son. Shall we call him Verlin? Maybe... let me think. Verlin Delano Vaughn. Then he's named after our new president, too. What do you think?"

But Marion didn't hear. She slept.

***

Dr. Hamilton arrived soon after Verlin's birth. Bland told him all that had happened.

"That was fast thinking," the doctor said to Mama. "You probably saved this baby's life. Everyone will be fine now."

"I don't know why I had Bland draw all that water," she said. "I think it was an answer to prayer."

The date was June 4, 1933.

Unintentional Adventure

ONE day in September when Marion had completed her chores except for watering Bessie, the cow, she put three-month-old Verlin into his buggy and pushed it out to the barn where the cow rested in the shade.

"You wait here," she said to Verlin. "Mama's going to get Bessie, and we'll take her over and give her a drink."

Marion left the buggy near the barn door and went inside. She fastened a rope to the cow's halter and then carefully and methodically wrapped the rope around her arm, freeing her hands so she could push the buggy along with her. She led the cow to the door and through it.

The cow, panic-stricken by the unfamiliar baby buggy sitting near her, bolted.

"Stop, Bessie! Stop!" Marion cried.

But Bessie did not stop. She ran out toward the prairie, dragging Marion, who fell, unable to run as fast as the cow. Marion cried, Verlin cried, and the cow kept running. Marion, dragged on her stomach behind the cow, wondered if this would be the day she died, and questioned, *who will take care of Verlin?* The rope came loose. She never knew why it did, but she was thankful.

Marion lay on the ground, hearing her baby cry, but helpless to respond. The shoulder of her left arm hurt dreadfully, and she had bruises from head to toe. She must get up. She must take care of her baby.

As she struggled to her feet, she heard Bland's voice. "What happened, Marion? Are you all right? Let me help you up."

"I can't talk about it now. Verlin's crying. Get him and take me to my bed."

Once she was in bed Marion sobbed violently. Fear, exhaustion, and pain poured out in torrents. She was angry at herself for tying the rope around her arm. Would she be able to care for her baby? She cried for almost an hour until spent, she slept.

***

A knock on the door awakened her the next morning. Marion struggled out of bed, hurting all over. She opened the door to a strange face, a small, toughened, older-looking woman wearing a house dress and apron.

"I'm Goldie Gentzler." I live just down the fence line from you. Sorry I haven't stopped in sooner to welcome you, but I'm here now. Bland said you needed me this morning. I'll fix up some breakfast for you and the baby."

"Thank you for coming, Mrs. Gentzler. I'm not quite up to the day. The cow dragged me across the prairie yesterday afternoon." Talking about it caused Marion to cry. "I've been in bed since, wondering how I could take care of Verlin."

"Don't cry, Honey. I'm here to help." Mrs. Gentzler put a gentle arm around Marion's shoulders.

"He's been stirring for about thirty minutes now. I'm sure he's hungry." Marion moved toward her bed. "I'll get back in bed if you don't mind, and you can bring him to me. He can nurse, then he'll go back to sleep." She sat carefully on the bed, gingerly moved to a lying position, and reached up for the baby. "Ouch!" she exclaimed. "That cow hurt my left arm."

"Let me change him first, Honey, then he's all yours!" Mrs. Gentzler sat on the opposite side of the bed, put Verlin down in front of her, and changed the diaper expertly. "Here he is. Chowtime!" She smiled down at Marion and lowered the baby onto her arm and shoulder. Verlin nuzzled into his familiar place and nursed contentedly.

"Now, what would you like for breakfast, dear?"

"Just some fruit and toast. You'll need to get the fruit from the cellar. I used the last from the house yesterday."

"How about a boiled egg to go with that? Your body is repairing itself now. The protein would help." Mrs. Gentzler moved efficiently around the small kitchen area, buttering bread, putting water on to boil. Then she headed outdoors to the cellar to retrieve the jars of fruit. She came back with peaches and prunes Marion had canned during the summer.

When the baby was fed and Marion had finished her breakfast, she felt exhausted. Mrs. Gentzler took her leave promising to be back in about four hours.

Dusty Enemy

ATURDAY, November eleventh,1933 dawned brightly, the sun sending its brilliant burning rays to earth and settling them dully on the dusty prairie. The breezes, for a change, were sparse, leaving fresher air to breathe, but robbing the morning of its coolness.

Marion planned to bake; their bread supply was low. She gave five-month-old Verlin his cereal, sneaking bites past his grabbing hands into his mouth, and she crushed some canned peaches for him. He played happily with the food, feeling it with his fingers, putting it in his hair. Marion smiled and washed his face and hands, kissing him. "Such a sweet boy, she said.

She looked out the window, and seeing the accumulated dust on the prairie, yearned for the waving grass and blooming flowers she could remember, but which were long gone, vanished with the wind, drought, and dust that had been their lot for these last years.

She stepped out the door to look at her rose bush, still growing, but only because of her constant washing and watering each time she emptied bath water or morning dish water. The bush was bravely sending out new shoots, even though it was November. Needing to be outdoors, she walked around the house past her tree. The horizon in the north looked strange, gray-black and cloudy.

Oh no! Not again. Not another one of those Black Northers! Running now, she entered the house and closed the window, hoping Bland would bring a bucket of water when he came home; he needed to come right now. He was working on his lessons; hopefully he would see what was coming. She needed to close things up.

While she waited for Bland she ran to the cellar and brought extra fruit and vegetables to the kitchen. You could never tell how long these storms would last.

Bessie was still in the barn; she would need extra water, too. The chickens should be okay outside, she thought, as she gathered sheets and towels and wet them. She would cover the windows with them, and the door, too, once Bland was home.

Verlin would need to be off the floor in his crib. *Babies and dust storms just don't mix,* she thought.

Bland hurried home with two buckets of water just before the storm hit. Together they hung wet sheets over the window and door.

The wind blasted the house like an explosion, and they felt the temperatures inside the house cool and near-darkness descend. Verlin cried, startled by the unexpected sound and sudden darkness. Marion went to him, planning to wash and lift him from his chair. When she touched the baby she felt an electric shock, and Verlin screamed frantically. She got a small blanket and tried again, this time successfully. She rocked the baby over and over, until he finally slept. She put him in his crib where he slept for several hours.

The house gathered dust rapidly. The wind and dust still pounded, sifting steadily inward. Marion and Bland sat with wet washcloths over their mouths and noses and tried to keep the sleeping baby protected, too, but his movements repeatedly ripped the cloth from his face. Marion, exhausted from her efforts to keep the dust cleaned from surfaces, went back and forth to Verlin's crib, vainly trying to shield her precious baby from the dangerous dusty enemy.

Bland paced distractedly, discontentedly, occasionally pausing to check Verlin's breathing. Together they worried about their child. They had heard of people dying as a result of these storms. He was still so young, and he'd had trouble breathing the day he was born!

The wind and dust continued to trespass into their world leaving them touchy and tense, gloomy and grouchy, peevish and petulant, for two days and one night. When quiet and light returned they felt startled and suspicious, fearful the storm wasn't really gone.

Verlin still slept, as if retreating from a reality too fearsome for his baby mind to tolerate. When he woke he was fretful and quiet by turns; his usual sunny disposition was seemingly gone. Holding him in her arms, Marion thought his breathing sounded ragged. *He needs fresh air,* she thought. *Maybe tomorrow the air will be clearer. Dear Lord, let it be clearer. Keep our baby safe.*

Bland stayed home from school on Monday, trying to restore their way of life. He came into the house, saying, "The chickens are nowhere to be found."

"I thought they'd go into the barn," Marion protested. "I wonder where they are."

"I've heard of chickens blowing away in the high winds and dust, and never being seen again."

Oh! No! We need the chickens!" Marion exclaimed, running for the door. "We've got to find them!"

"I've looked everywhere," Bland said. "I should have told you what I'd heard. This was an especially bad storm with extra strong winds. I think they're gone for good."

"But what will we eat? Where will we get eggs?" Marion burst into frustrated tears. "Why does everything have to be so hard?"

"We'll get by," Bland said. "I'll have to start hunting rabbits. Couldn't we eat cottage cheese instead of eggs?"

The air gradually cleared, but the baby's breathing took longer to improve. For two weeks he fussed and fumed, expressing his discomfort. Thankfully, the weather stayed calm.

Busy weeks multiplied, and before Marion could believe it, Thanksgiving and Christmas were nearly upon them.

Shall We Get a Puppy?

THAT Christmas, the first for their little family of three, was a joyous time. They found tumbleweed out on the prairie and brought it in. Marion had watched her mother decorate tumbleweeds many times, and knew how to flock the tumbleweed with a thick soap suds and lime mixture. The rest was fun. They made green paper chains and popped corn to make small balls, and hung them on the branches.

"Verlin needs a dog," Bland said. "Every boy should have one

"Do you think we could get an older puppy, one that has been trained?" Marion suggested. "A dog is a great idea."

"A puppy would be better for Verlin," Bland said. "They can grow up together and become the best of friends. The Gentzlers have a new litter now, real cute ones. One is brown, black and white. The tips of his ears are white. I'd like to get him."

"Let's wait and get him at Christmas time—for a Christmas present, you know— He probably needs to stay with his mother for awhile, don't you think?" Marion smiled into Bland's eyes. Christmas would be so much fun with a new puppy."

"Christmas is about five weeks away." Bland took her hand in his. "That's about when the neighbors said we could have him What shall we call him?"

"Sounds like a 'Tippy' to me." Marion pulled Bland to her and snuggled into his warmth, anticipating Verlin's joy.

They spent Christmas vacation watching their child crawl over to the tree and touch it with his hand. Savoring the wonder in his eyes, they moved him away and watched him return to the intriguing feel of it.

They read his new books to him. Bland had located the "Little Giant

Book Series" by Whitman Publishing Company, and ordered it for Verlin. The stories were *Toddles, Bob and Mr. Bunny, Bubbles, Little Brown Teddy, and Topsy and Toby.* Verlin clapped his hands and jabbered every time they read *Little Brown Teddy.*

Tippy arrived on Christmas morning. Much laughter and a few tears came with him. By the end of Christmas vacation Verlin and Tippy were playing together happily, learning love for one another.

***

Christmas and the New Year had come and gone. There had been no more severe dust storms since the November 11th one had ended. Verlin had recovered his easy breathing pattern and his happy spirits.

Bland was back in school, preparing his class for the competitions that always come in the spring. Marion was using her time during the winter months to sew some new dresses from fabric Mama and Papa had given her for Christmas.

Verlin and Tippy were becoming friends as Bland had predicted; Verlin laughing while Tippy tickled his toes or licked his fingers. Tippy followed when Verlin needed changing or ate his meals, becoming an expert janitor around the high chair, enjoying the food Verlin had dropped or thrown. Marion loved his puppy ways and the way he made Verlin laugh.

The dark spot in their world was the dust that covered their yard, the fields, and the road to civilization.

Unsettling Suggestion

Lone Star House and New Vaughn Family

MARION looked out the small kitchen window at the dust that covered the prairie, It lay in drifts against the school, the house, the tree, and the fence line that led down to the Gentzlers.' It clogged the roads, making it necessary to follow the tracks of whatever brave traveler had made them, car, or footprint.

I'm so very weary of it. The prairie used to be so beautiful. Every trace of beauty had disappeared. Marion picked up dirty dishes from the table and put them in the dishpan.

Very few people braved travel these days. They made do with what they had. Some people—mostly farmers who had no cash and no well—were eating tumbleweed; growing a garden having been impossible without the water. Though tough and tasteless, the mature Russian Thistles filled one's stomach.

Marion still had canned fruit and vegetables from the garden she had nourished by carrying used wash water. They ate mostly fruit, vegetables, and, as long as they had flour, Marion could make bread.

I should be more thankful, she scolded herself. Rabbits had proven hard to find, colored as they were like the dust. *We have food. But days are so long and dreary.*

On April fourteenth the dust came again. Huge storms carried tons of dirt east to Chicago, New York, and the Atlantic Ocean. News Media dubbed the day "Black Sunday" because there were so many dust storms.

In Lone Star, Marion and Bland watched their ten-month-old son struggle, his breathing becoming more and more labored.

"Marion, I think we have to consider leaving Colorado," Bland said one day in late April. "I don't think Verlin can survive these dusty conditions much longer."

"Leave Colorado? Where would we go?" Marion protested.

"I've been thinking about Idaho, or maybe Oregon State. There is land there that maybe we could get onto. Maybe we could buy our farm if there's a government program to help us."

"But all my family lives in Colorado and Oklahoma. I really don't want to leave them." Marion's eyes filled with tears. "Do you really think we have to leave?"

"We need to talk to Dr. Hamilton about Verlin's risk, but if it were up to me, I'd leave. It just seems advisable." Bland looked at Marion solemnly. "It might make the difference between Verlin's life and death."

Then let's talk to Dr. Hamilton, and soon." Marion dried her tears. "I couldn't bear to lose our little boy."

They made their appointment with the doctor for May twenty-seventh.

While they waited their lives were in a kind of limbo; their plans remained vague and indefinite. May twenty-seventh would be decision day, the day they would choose their future.

Bland planned constantly for the trip they might need to make. His car was not old, but old enough that a long trip might bring on mechanical trouble. To forestall any possibility of that, he went to a dealer and traded for a new one. They would need to take necessary items along if they went. He purchased a tent, sleeping bags, a camping stove, food that could be easily prepared, and a trailer to pack it all in. It would be hard to leave their things, but they could take only what could be packed in the trailer.

Marion observed Bland's actions and knew. Bland was really worried. She looked at their meager possessions and struggled to decide what she could do without if she had to. *The table and chairs Bland had made? The bed? The small table that Papa had made for her? It had to go along, no matter what, and the rug Mama had made for their floor. I need these momentos of my family.*

Verlin's Kiddy Car was a necessity, and Tippy. Verlin's books would help during the long hours in the car. *Cooking. What can I take to make it easier? How can I take all my washing equipment?* The questions and the worry circled round and round the same weary path. Finally, she gave the decisions to the Lord and asked that He make them for her.

I Know Who Holds
the Future

"OH Bland! This can't be happening again. Verlin got so sick last time. His breathing is getting worse and worse already. What can we do?" It was May eleventh, 1934. Another huge dust storm challenged their right to live on the prairie. Strong icy winds carried their burden of displaced dust, dropped it on top of their lives, and deposited it in and on their home.

With it came fear for Verlin that crowded around their hearts, monopolized their thoughts and settled their resolve. As soon as school was out and Verlin had recovered from this storm they would leave for Oregon.

Verlin struggled against the dust, his breathing became more rapid and ragged, worse than ever before "Will you go and get Mrs. Gentzler, Bland? Maybe she can think of something to do. I've tried everything I know and nothing is working."

The dust was blowing, visibility almost zero, when Bland left the house. The road was invisible, and knowing he could get lost, he searched for the fence line. About a foot of the six-foot posts were still dimly visible, and he was able to follow them for the half mile to the neighbor's house. Every step he labored against the deep dust.

Mrs. Gentzler put on her coat, glasses, a hat and boots, and followed Bland back to the house. When she heard Verlin's breathing, she advised. "If you want to save your baby you must get him to a doctor." Marion felt the panic rise within her. "Bland, call Dr. Hamilton! We've got to take Verlin to him!"

Marion wet a washcloth again and vainly tried to keep Verlin's mouth and nose covered against the dust while they rushed him to the car. Marion hoped that visibility would improve. The trip to Springfield was about twenty-five miles, an almost interminable distance in this dust. *God help us, God help us, God help us,* Marion prayed. The wind decreased in speed and with it the visibility improved. They could see a car-length ahead. It was enough.

Marion, Bland and Verlin on running board

The day was almost gone when they reached Springfield. Dr. Hamilton waited for them in an interior rented motel room, windows sealed tightly against the dust, doors closed and taped. He had brought a portable incubator along with a supply of oxygen.

For several days Marion, Bland, and Dr. Hamilton watched over little Verlin in the incubator, each making sure he was breathing the rich oxygen, nudging him if he stopped breathing. On the fourth day Verlin's skin turned from sallow to pink, his energy began to return, and Dr. Hamilton permitted Marion to lift him from the incubator.

"Thank you, God. Thank you, God, for our baby," Marion prayed.

Dr. Hamilton strongly advised them to take Verlin and move to a climate with cleaner air. "He likely wouldn't live through another dust storm," he said, thus making their decision firm. The day after school ended they would leave Colorado to begin their lives in Oregon. Goodbyes would need to be said, some perhaps for the last time. Decisions needed to be made. By God's grace they would save their son. By God's grace they would live each day.

They would start their lives again in a strange land with people that only God knew. They would trust Him for the direction and the help they needed. This was no time for tears. They would take one step at a time. They would move on to Oregon.

The End

Bland and Marion Vaughn's Travel

As told by Ninety One year old Marion, November 2003 Quotations indicate actual words spoken by Marion. (Parenthesis added by author for clarity. Other areas are paraphrased by author.)

"WE were married in 1932, August 21. Verlin was born June 4, 1933 at Lone Star, Colorado, about twenty miles from Two Buttes. I had a hard time delivering Verlin. He weighed 10 pounds and was 23 inches long."

"Verlin was a 'blue baby. Mama had tepid water ready for the birth and saved Verlin by first dipping him into cold water and then into the tepid to help him start breathing. Bland had gone to Two Buttes to get Mama to be with me. He drove his car, and was in such a hurry that Mama said she'd never had such a ride in her life. "We called Dr. Hamilton." (He came to the house.) "He said that without Mama's quick thinking we might not have saved Verlin."

There were lots of dust storms in the early thirties. Prolonged drought had "turned the fields to dust," making crops impossible. Mom and Dad were living at Lone Star; Dad was teaching school. Verlin got very ill. They needed help. Dad went outside and — because he couldn't see through the dust storm—followed the fence line to get to the neighbor's for help. "You'd better get this baby to a doctor if you want to save his life," the neighbor told her. "I'm afraid mustard plasters won't do him any good now."

"We got in the car and rushed to Springfield where Dr. Hamilton's office was. Dr. Hamilton had hung wet sheets over the windows in a motel room to catch the dust. The dust collected on the back of the wet sheets till it became mud."

Dad cancelled school for several days, and Mom and Dad took turns sitting by Verlin making sure he was breathing.

"The dust was covering fence lines; the winds were just blowing the fields away." Sage and Sod, Second Edition notes that "during the years between1934-1938 some areas in Texas and Oklahoma lost as much as a foot of topsoil in these storms. There were 263 such storms during these years."

After my parents took Verlin home they continued to use sheets on the windows and over Verlin's crib, an effort many people made to ensure children were breathing clean air.

Many children and adults died of *dust pneumonia,* and this became the motivation for Mom and Dad to leave Colorado and head for Oregon. After the school year was finished they departed, "traveling in a new car" which pulled a trailer behind it, and leaving everything that would not fit into the car or the trailer.

"We brought our dog along to Oregon. His name was Tippy. He was the one Verlin later fed the fresh bread to. He rode in the back seat. Verlin was two years old."

Memories: "We set up our tent close to a creek, and during the night it rained. The creek flooded during the night. We had to move our tent." Flash floods were common in the Midwest. They were blessed not to have lost their lives. Many people did.

"At Jackson Hole, Wyoming"—located at the end of a big valley with mountain ranges on west, south, and east—we came to a creek which we would have to ford in the car. Bland made me get out of the car with Verlin until he had driven the car across and was sure it could be done safely. Then he came back for us."

"After we got to Idaho we spent our time helping in the harvest. One family we worked for was the Stams at Buhl, Idaho. After we had finished the hay harvest at the Stams we were preparing to leave the next morning. Bland was in the car. He had gone to town and was just returning. We were having a storm. I was out by the tent getting things ready to leave. Suddenly I heard a rustling sound like a low rumble. The next thing I knew leaves and branches were falling off the tree and I saw Tippy, our dog, who had been lying by the tree, having convulsions where he lay."

"Mr. Stam opened the door to the house and yelled, 'Are you okay, Marion?'"

"I said, 'I'm okay, but I think my dog's dead.'"

"Mr. Stam yelled, '"You get in this house right now!!'"

"Bland was still sitting in the car, so frightened by what he had seen, and how close the lightning had been to me that he couldn't even get out of the car, he was so weak." Tippy lived through his experience, thankfully.

"When we arrived in Buhl, Idaho, Verlin had a "kiddy car" he liked to ride on. We stopped at Bland's Aunt Augusta's. We spent the first night in the house, but they had so many bed-bugs that they just ate up Verlin and left big welts all over him."(I read that bed-bugs often came in with new lumber, but don't know whether it is accurate.)

"The next day we set up our tent again, and moved out there. The tent was only big enough to hold our bed; not much more. We lived in that tent until we were finally in our own house." (In Oregon)

"We stayed there with them for some time, Bland working in the fields for his Uncle Al Shriver, and I worked in the house helping Aunt Augusta with meals to feed harvest crews."

"We continued to follow the harvest all through the fall, eventually ending up in Harper, Oregon working for Earl and Vaye Flock."

By the time Mom and Dad reached Harper where the Flocks lived they were nearly destitute. Mom never mentioned it. Vaye Flock told her granddaughter, Marlene, that the first time she met Mom was at church. "She was wearing a ragged dress and her baby was hungry. They were living in a tent. We took them home with us and helped them out." Dad had been working for the Civilian Conservation Corps.

Marion continues her story. "It seems to me now that Bland got a job teaching sometime around this, and built a little shack for us to live in on the county school ground between Harper and Vale."(We have a picture of Dad with this class. I counted at least forty students.)

"Eventually we bought our farm in Vale through the FHA which was making down payments for people who were willing to take the land out of sage-brush and greasewood"—My brother, Les just told me that Dad said that he used his pigs to dig the sage brush and grease wood out of the land. I'd never heard that before—"Since it was the Depression, the government was trying to help people get started again."

***

Dad continued to teach at the school between Harper and Vale for several years after he bought the farm. He rode to school on a horse and crossed Bully Creek daily, sometimes while it flooded.

The shell of a small house stood on the farm Dad and Mom bought. Mom says Dad tacked heavy building paper over the inside walls to make it more air-tight. She tells of the winters when it froze, and the only way she and Verlin could keep warm was to get in bed.

"I was carrying Margie then (1937). Verlin would feel her kick and asked lots of questions. '"Mommy, how did the baby get in there?'"

They did have a wood-burning stove in which they burned sagebrush. Daddy would gather it daily, but it burned so fast that most of the day there was no warmth in the house. Mom tells of going up the hill and gathering sagebrush, then carrying it down the hill to the house.

When we children were older, Mom would heat bricks before bedtime to keep our feet warm, just as she had seen her mother do. Daddy would leave the farm early each morning to go over to the school house and teach, so Mom had her hands full trying to take care of two small children and keep the house warm enough to survive. Laundry was done with a wash board and a tub "until Grandpa Vaughn finally insisted that we get a washing machine" (a Maytag). Even with the washing machine, the clothes had to be put through a wringer by hand. (It was)"very hard work, but better than a washboard, at that."

Originally, Mom obtained water from the irrigation ditches to do the wash and heated it on the stove. "Finally we hired a well-digger to put in a well for us. After that we could just pump water when we needed it."

"We started our dairy herd with a jersey bull and several cows. We built our herd with their offspring." Dad grew crops such as corn, alfalfa, and wheat that helped feed the herd.

PART TWO

Life on the Farm in Oregon

She Saved My Life

Up the hill and about a mile from Dad and Mom's new farm sat another new farm. The George Bakers—George and Violet and their three sons, Jim, Jerry, and Ricky—inhabited these acres, and the Vaughn and the Bakers became friends and constant support for each other. Much of this support took the form of helping with harvest.

The two women became much more to each other. Violet told me many years later, "She saved my life. I thought we had moved to a wilderness!"

A wilderness it was, filled with sagebrush and greasewood. The country was wild, and had insufficient rainfall to grow crops, so irrigation became a daily necessity, the responsibility for which fell to my Dad. One of my memories of Dad is of a tired, hot, man, dressed in overalls and irrigation boots, and carrying that irrigation shovel over his shoulder. He toiled through each field on the forty acres, opening one furrow, and plugging the water flow in another, fighting an endless war against the gophers, rodents that because of their burrowing habits were the cause of a huge loss of water. Eventually, the farm was bordered by large irrigation canals from which Dad created connections to his fields.

Besides the irrigation, such a crucial part of growing a crop, there was always the field preparation, planting, and harvesting. These chores took almost one hundred per cent of Dad's time, leaving most of the chores such as feeding the animals to be completed when it was too dark to irrigate.

Mother became a constant inhabitant of the milk barn, and Dad's companion during many of the other farm chores, in addition to her job as the mother of young children. It was a difficult and demanding life they led there on that farm.

I remember much of the tension that was a constant in my Dad's life, and as a result, in Mother's, and in ours.

***

When Marion and Bland moved to the farm they had purchased, they found a frame home without insulation of any kind. Mom told of Dad putting heavy building paper on the walls to cut down the movement in of the cold air outside. She also told of cutting sagebrush and greasewood for heat. She said Dad would pile it to the ceiling before he left for school, but that it burned so rapidly that she would either have to take Verlin out into the cold while she gathered a new supply, or go to bed, the only way to keep them both warm.

Into this cold, stark, difficult environment, I came, four years after Verlin's birth. Two and one-half years later, Mona blessed the family giving Marjorie a sister, and about four years later, the second son, Leslie came along. Al came along in 1946, and ended the growth of our family

About five years after Mona's birth, the Bakers bought their farm about ½ mile from ours, and up a fairly steep hill. George finalized arrangements for the farm in Violet's absence because of an accident that had put their middle son, Jerry in the hospital.

Having no opportunity to go with George to view the farm because of her need to be with Jerry, Violet told him, "I guess if you want to buy a farm, you'll have to buy it." Later when she at last viewed the farm, she took one look at George and said, "Were you *drunk* when you bought it?" ("I knew George didn't drink, but could not believe he could have been thinking clearly," she told me later.) "I didn't know God made country like this!"

Having never lived on a farm previously, Violet felt totally at a loss. She did not know how to live on a farm. She did not know how to cook with the equipment she had. She did not know how to cope with her difficult surroundings. She did not know how to feed a harvest crew when they came to help with the harvest. Of Mom, Violet said, "She saved my life."

Mom, who had been a farm girl all her life, and always eager to help, was glad to meet the needs Violet had. And Violet was able to make Mom's life easier as well. "The first time I ever saw you kids, you, and Verlin, and Mona had walked up the hill and into my driveway carrying buckets. Violet remembers that she thought, *There are some girls. I wish I had a girl!* We had come to get water. Violet said, "We had the only soft water well on the bench (hill), and we gave away a lot of water." Violet and George parented three boys.

From this beginning a lifelong friendship grew. The two women would walk back and forth to visit occasionally, and, since Violet had never driven a car, Mom provided rides to town when it was time to buy groceries. Mom also invited her to visit the church of Christ meeting with her, and Violet did go, if only a few times. "You don't have music in the church, do you?" she said in response to our a cappella hymns.

One thing Violet and Mom shared numerous times: They gave each other permanents, usually uneventfully. However, Violet reports that there was a slip-up one day. "You kids came home from school, and you were hungry." —too bad for the permanent recipient, who happened to be Violet.

"I wondered, afterwards, why my hair was so dry and frizzy. I couldn't do anything with it. When I look back at the pictures taken at that time, I always had my scarf on."

Mom didn't confess until months later what had happened. She had found the unused neutralizer on the table behind the mayonnaise! That, however, was not the last of the permanents. Violet had a forgiving spirit. She proved her forgiveness one Christmas, when she made clothing for the dolls Mom had purchased for Mona and I. She also convinced George to build wardrobe boxes for those clothes. Was she pretending, just for a moment, that we were *her* girls?

Though times, circumstances, and surroundings were daunting, each woman found the other a bringer of relief, a source of humor, and always a listening ear.

The dairy farm was a demanding master. As we children grew, we took on our responsibility to help out with the milking chore. Since we shared the job with Mother, the time in the milk barn became the catalyst for growing relationships between mother and children. There was much opportunity for conversation, and as our children's voices developed, precious time was put to good use as we harmonized together. Such wonderful memories!

In our teen-age years television came to our house, and a favorite—and regularly watched—Saturday night program was *Your Hit Parade*. Thus, we learned many songs to try out together: *I Understand, Joey, Sentimental Journey, You Belong to Me.* We also sang an endless number of hymns we had learned at our weekly church meetings.

This singing activity culminated in a trip to the county fair to perform after the milkman heard our singing and entered us in the competition. I will leave that story for another time!

I don't remember *ever* taking a family vacation. We milked the cows twice daily, and, at the same time daily, to increase the cow's ability to produce a sufficient amount of good quality milk. The financial pressures lay heavy and constant, keeping my parents close to home.

As the years moved on, the dairy herd that began with a Jersey bull and several cows, grew through the continual arrival of offspring, eventually rendering the forty acres inadequate for feeding them. At that time Dad leased another forty acres to supplement his original land. Of course, the work increased along with this acquisition, until eventually, after Verlin, Marjorie, and Mona were away from home, it became too much. Most of the happenings during this time are not a part of my memory, but ended the time on the farm with an auction, and a ruined marriage.

Note: I grew up on this farm, in the same built-on and modified house, milking the family herd of dairy cows. I attended Vale Elementary School and Vale Union High School with many of the same students that started out with me in the first grade. Though these years on the farm were not easy, they brought growth in responsibility, a strong work ethic, and a sure sense of the continuity of life in the midst of suffering; even chaos. Thanks to God for his immeasurable gift!

Dad's Legacy

In my favorite picture of my Dad, he sits on his horse, Old Jake. Dressed in overalls, light colored shirt to reflect the heat, a wide-brimmed hat, and irrigation boots, knee high, he rests left hand on his spade handle, its blade on the ground. Eyes downcast, he looks bone tired. He is returning to the farmyard from his day spent irrigating sun-baked fields.

Dad on old Jake returning from irrigating.

Dad and Mom carved out their forty acres among the semi-arid rolling hills near Vale, in Eastern Oregon. The trees that grew readily, without regard to the dearth of moisture, were mostly cottonwoods which seeded annually and multipled their kind along streams and ditches, wherever they could find moisture. Sage- brush and Greasewood hugged stubbornly to the desert floor comprised the natural vegetation. Some varieties of sagebrush, though seemingly nutritious for cattle, could cause them to freeze to death in winter, so removing the sagebrush and greasewood was essential.

My dad owned a dairy farm and grew corn from which he made fermented feed called silage. He also grew alfalfa, which was cut, dried and stacked as hay. These crops supplemented what grain he managed to grow, and what he purchased for winter-time feed for the cows of his dairy herd.

Irrigation made it all possible enabling crops, cows and humans to survive the stingy rainfall. On our farm my dad did the back-breaking, bone-aching, never-ending work of plowing ditches, building dikes, and directing water into corrugations—much of it with a spade. When the hours of irrigation were finished, he planted, cultivated, or harvested, according to the season.

Water for the household, except for drinking, was originally obtained from the irrigation ditches, but eventually a well was dug. The pump stood just outside the kitchen door. Drinking water came, before we had a well, from a neighbor's water supply.

My dad and mom migrated from Colorado to the Pacific Northwest in nineteen-thirty-five, two years after the birth of their first child. Verlin had been suffering from dust pneumonia, a respiratory malady caused by the frequent dust storms. The family doctor helped my parents make the decision to move the family in order to save the child's life.

They drove a new car and pulled a trailer. Anything they owned that would not fit in, they left behind. Working harvests north from Southern Idaho to Harper, Oregon, they hired out their services until the Farm Home Administration made down-payment funds available for the purchase of the farm.

Dad taught school in those days. He had first taught in Colorado, building himself a reputation as a teacher who could keep order and teach his classes so well the students were able to win the competitions they entered.

Dad and Mom, during their years in Lone Star, entertained the students each Friday after school dismissal, Dad, singing and playing his guitar, and Mom singing harmonies. Dad played a tuba in Dr. Verity's band, Mom a cornet. That is where they met. They may have continued to drive the twenty miles to Two Buttes after they married in order to stay with the band. I am not sure.

My father continued to teach in Oregon at a country school south and across the creek from our farm, probably about five miles away. He rode his horse, fording Bully Creek, sometimes even in flood stage. He did his farming before and after school, putting in extremely long arduous hours regularly.

The never-ending work, physical exhaustion, and constant financial worries became major stressors to Dad and to my parents' marriage. From the beginning the farm depended on borrowed money which had firm repayment schedules, and the future of the farm depended on those payments being made on time. Dad could never be sure the money would be there.

I remember an argument following one of Mom's trips to the grocery store. She was a fellow worker on the farm. Most of the milking chores fell on her; she recruited her kids to help. My mother denied herself most of what she wanted, and was a real asset to Dad in her use of money.

But Dad's mountain of stress erupted this particular day. Mom had bought some bananas, probably for our school lunches. Apparently, even bananas were a luxury. Dad was upset. It wasn't just an argument. I remember the loud angry accusations, the name calling, and the hitting and slapping. Mom absorbed the accusations and the abuse, usually attempting to share the reasons for her decision, but never being heard.

We children looked on in horror. We were afraid for Mother's safety; and spent our days watching for things that might upset Dad. We witnessed many such arguments. They destroyed any possibility of a close relationship with our father.

One of the earliest memories I have was hearing Dad shouting at Mom during the night after we were all in bed asleep. I have no memory of what was said, but painful memories of how it made me feel. I felt worried, fearful, sad, and insecure, knowing that all was not well between my parents. If I asked Mother what was wrong with Dad, she said. "Your Dad works too hard."

My brother, Verlin, was four years older than I. My siblings and I all looked up to our big brother. I looked forward to double-dating with him. But by the time I was old enough to date, Verlin had gone. Mom watched Dad blaming farm problems on Verlin, and then beating him for small incidents. She called her brother, Barney, and told him of her problem. He said, "I need a son, Marion. Send him to me." And Mom did. His departure ripped a terrible wound into our family, but Verlin had a better life with his uncle, aunt, and cousins in Missouri.

One of the hardest things we bore as children was hearing our dad accusing Mom of hateful things. He called her names like "Bitch," or "Old Heifer." My Mom was a Christian woman with all the ideals and goals of a Christian. She did her best to help and please my Dad, but if he was angry he would accuse her of being unfaithful with men she knew in the church. His ranting would go on and on, it seemed like hours. We worried that Dad talked to people in the community and made these same accusations, though I don't think he ever did. We wondered what people in the community thought about us. We wondered what our friends thought about us, and wondered if we really had any friends.

My brother, Les, just younger than my Sister, Mona, bore a lot of abuse from my father. My memories are clouded as far as detail about what Les's offense was, but in my mind I can still see Dad, Mona and I, and Les, out in front of the barnyard shed. Dad beat Les with a switch, or a stick, Mona and I watching helplessly, in terror. It was more than a spanking, going on and on, as Dad's frustrations poured out onto his son.

I know my Dad loved us. His daily toil to make a success of the farm tells me that. The hard candy he bought at Christmas tells me, as does his attempt to help me with my algebra in high school. He took the family for outings at the Fourth of July or Harvest Festival Parades, and took us as a family to Payette or Fruitland to get fresh peaches or apples, with the intention of treating us, but these trips were too often marred by shouting abuse directed at Mom.

He bought us an American Flyer sled one Christmas, sneaking in and out of the house, playing Santa Claus: "Ho! Ho! Ho! Ho! Ho! Ho! I thought I heard Santa Claus outside! Didn't you hear Santa Claus?" When we opened the door, the sled waited in all its beauty and promise of good times.

I know there should be many more positive memories of my Dad. He was a sweet kind man when he relaxed. The neighbors seemed to think well of him; they traded work with him regularly. I am sad that so much of the best in Dad is forgotten, overshadowed by those difficult years on the farm.

I would like to have watched him in the classroom, teaching so capably. I would have liked to hear him play his guitar, but I suspect the guitar was one of the sacrifices he made to save my brother's life. I would have liked to hear him sing with my mother, but the burdens of the farm dissipated any energy that might have been left for that. I would have liked to be able to really share my heart with him, and listen to his counsel, but my fear and caution shattered that possibility.

About 1965 my Dad came to visit my husband and me in Spokane. That next morning, my Daddy had a massive stroke at the breakfast table. I took him to the bedroom to rest, not realizing that the "seeing double" he complained of was a sign of a stroke. He slept hard for several hours before I began to worry. I could not really awaken him, but knew I must get him to a doctor. I practically carried him to my car, and took him the few blocks to our family doctor, who immediately ordered him transported to the hospital.

Dad remained unconscious for weeks, but finally woke up. We took him home with us to live. One great thing was that my kids got to know their Grandpa Vaughn just a little. My daughter, Barbara, particularly, has good memories of him playing "Tick-tock" and "Suitcase" with her. He seemed to be in his element with little kids, but later on, after they'd grown, he was at a loss.

My Dad's Legacy? He left us with knowledge that life is difficult, but that one can still live it. He left us with a good work ethic; working hard to pay his bills and support his family, he demonstrated it. He left us with the desire and ability to learn and the realization that learning is a lifetime endeavor. He made it possible for us to be in the band; music is a lifetime love of mine. He was always a great advocate if we ever needed anyone to speak up for us.

There are other legacies he left, the chief one being a lack of a male image to relate to in youth. This has left holes in my ability to relate to men in positive ways. It has made my relationship with God more difficult because I had no father figure whom I could always trust.

These words are not written in order to blame my father. He was a human being who had been hurt himself. Mother told me that his own mother, somehow, made him believe that he was unwanted. Intentional or not, what a painful legacy she left him.

I have forgiven my father for the ways he hurt us. And I know God understands who he was, and why he hurt people in the ways he did, and loves him just the same.

Bread Alone

"VERLIN, Mama needs to go milk the cows now. You stay in the house with Tippy. It's cold outside." Marion stroked Verlin's blond curls. "You can read your book and ride your kiddy car. I'll hurry and be back as soon as I can." Marion picked up her little boy, hugged and kissed him thoroughly, and set him down on the couch with his books. She worried about having to go to the barn and leave him, but he was a good child and rarely got into trouble.

Marion left the house, looking back to see Verlin engrossed in his "reading," and headed for the barn. She felt good about getting the bread baked. She had worked hard all morning mixing the bread dough, letting it rise, and baking it. It sat on the kitchen counter now, cooling. The day had been a busy one, but she had crowded the baking into it. They would have bread for a week.

While Mom milked, a drama unfolded in the kitchen. Verlin loved Mom's bread and felt hungry for just a taste. He pulled a chair to the counter and climbed onto it. Standing up he found he could bend over and lick the bread with his tongue, so he licked and tried to bite into a loaf. The loaf scooted away from him but it tasted so good he tried again; the loaf scooted again. Thoroughly engrossed in the bread now, he reached out and picked it up in his hands. He attempted again to take a bite.

The loaf slipped from his hands and went tumbling to the floor where Tippy waited hungrily for his share. The dog dispatched the loaf of bread rapidly, Verlin watching in fascination. *Tippy's so hungry,* he thought. *I'll just give him one more.* So after licking the butter off another loaf, he dropped it down to the dog.

When Mom returned to the kitchen, she immediately missed her bread. In answer to her gentle question, "Verlin, what happened to Mama's bread?" Verlin replied, "Mama, Tippy was just so hungry, he ate it all up."

Mom reported, "I just couldn't get mad at him. He was just trying to be kind."

Grandpa's Girl?

Grandpa Vaughn is leaving.
Grandpa Vaughn, Uncle Maynard, Margie, and Mona

"**M**ARGIE, Grandpa must tell you something; something you don't want to hear. I'm so sorry to tell you, because it will make you sad."

"What, Grandpa?" I said as I snuggled close to my very favorite person, still tasting the lemon drop he had just given me, smelling his pipe. "What do you need to tell me?"

My Grandpa lived just up a small canyon from our farm, and we grew accustomed to his presence and expected him to play with us, talk to us, and comfort us when we felt sad and afraid. My brother, four years older, my sister, two and one-half years younger, and I worried a lot. Our parents' ways of relating to one another were loud and quarrelsome; both Mom and Dad were always tired. We knew money was always short; even at such young ages, we knew. Verlin was nine; I was about five, and Mona, two and one-half.

Sometimes Dad acted like he was going to hit Mama, and we always feared he would hurt her. But we knew we could trust Grandpa. Mother and Grandpa supported our shaky world.

Grandpa moved to Oregon to be near us, knowing that my Dad and Mom carried a load much heavier than they could handle, and hoping he could help. The realities of the pain in our home had proved too much for him.

"Margie, Grandpa must leave. I won't be here any more." A dish crashed to the floor in the kitchen where Verlin was drying dishes. Mona, still too young to understand the loss coming our way, held a sticky lemon drop in her hand, licking it, eyes locked on Grandpa's face.

"No! Don't leave, Grandpa! I need you here!" I cried, jerking my body away from him.

"Grandpa can't stay any more, Margie. Grandpa's going home to Oklahoma. I wish I could take you with me, but I can't."

"Will you come back to see us, Grandpa? Soon?" I begged, inching back toward his embrace. Verlin, standing in the doorway now, dishtowel in hand, listened intently.

"Oklahoma is far, far away; such a long way that I won't be able to visit. I'm sorry, Margie."

I pouted, I cried, I stomped my feet, planted them and held on to him, pulling with all my strength; did everything within a five year old child's power to keep my Grandpa with me. Nevertheless, he left.

During those first days after he left, my thoughts tortured me. I puzzled; couldn't understand what I did to make him leave me. I felt guilty, wondering if I'd been naughty and made him want to go. Lonely, I wandered from room to room, wanting his presence; not daring to believe he had gone. I felt angry at my precious Grandpa; angry that he would go away and leave me, angry that he didn't love me enough to stay, angry that he wouldn't keep my Dad from hurting my Mom.

No one could ever take Grandpa's place. I still hurt when I see the picture taken the day he left for Oklahoma. Mona is grasping and trying to eat a piece of watermelon. Storm clouds shadow my face, and Grandpa wears his grief on his.

Hungry Kids and Cinnamon Rolls

MOM made the best cinnamon rolls! I guess lots of mothers made cinnamon rolls in those days, but our mother made them an art. It wasn't as if Mom had nothing else to do while we were at school. She helped Dad as much as she could with all the farm work, driving teams, helping stack hay, harvesting grain, making silage. Every morning and evening she milked the cows. In addition she regularly grew a garden, canned the produce from it, and made jelly. How she ever found the time to make bread I will never understand, but she did.

How she regularly timed the exit of the cinnamon rolls from the oven concurrently with our arrival home from school is still her secret. We came home hungry after walking one and one-fourth miles to and from the bus. Always we carried books with us, and only slightly less often, a musical instrument. So understand that we were famished children.

Nothing ever tasted so delicious to us as the cinnamon rolls Mom made. The combination of hot bread, yeast, cinnamon, and the wonderful sauce that she created from butter, cinnamon, brown sugar and condensed milk brought joy to our childhood.

As adults we look back and realize what a labor of love those cinnamon rolls were. Thank you, Mom

***

"Mom's baking cinnamon rolls!" Mona shouted. "Let's hurry!" The smells of cinnamon and freshly baked bread filled the air though the girls were still quite distant from the house.

Margie smiled. She shifted her load of books and set her trombone down on the road. They were almost home, and she felt glad. The walk to and from the bus stop seemed longer every day.

"I need to rest a minute. Want to wait for me or go on? Go on if you want. I'll be there in just a few minutes."

"I'll wait." Mona set her books down on the road. "Then we can have our snack together. I can hardly stand it though. Those rolls taste better than candy."

"How does Mom do it? How can she milk the cows, drive the horses during harvest, grow the garden, and can the fruit and vegetables? She does so much. How can she still bake and have snacks for us so often?" I love her so much, and I worry about how hard she works," Margie said.

"I think she likes to do it," Mona smiled. "She's always so happy when she gives them to us, like she's giving us a wonderful present. Ready to go now?"

"Let's do. I'll be glad to see Mom. It's been a long day." The girls picked up their loads and walked the remaining eighth of a mile to the house.

Marion took the last batch of cinnamon rolls from the oven just as the girls walked in. She set them down and came to them, giving each a warm hug. "How was your day at school, Margie?"

"I felt so awful in history class. We were supposed to draw the Trojan Horse. I can't draw. I felt so embarrassed to turn in my paper." Margie's face reflected her embarrassment.

"I'm sure you did your best, Margie. Your best is always good enough. Don't worry about whether your work looks like someone else's."

"Mona, how was your day?"

"I tried really hard in writing, Mama. I just couldn't make those cursive B's right."

"It'll get easier if you practice. Want me to help you later?"

Mona changed the subject. "When can we have some cinnamon rolls, Mama?"

"Just put your things away and sit down at the table. They're too hot right now. We can talk while they're cooling."

The little girls and their mother sat together, laughing and talking. Daddy was still out irrigating and they didn't have to worry.

The Teacher Who Could Teach Pigs

OUR father, Leslie Bland Vaughn, attended a normal school in Stillwater, Oklahoma. He earned his teacher's certificate in the early thirties, and began his teaching career in the one room schoolhouses common before "public" education became available. He secured his first assignment at Walsh in Baca County, Southeastern Colorado. He also taught at Wentworth and Lone Star.

Bland was a good teacher who expected the most from his students and usually got it. He believed all students could learn, and provided ample opportunity for all. He used competitions liberally to spur motivation in his classroom.

Spelling bees—usually at a moment's notice—encouraged students to learn early and study consistently. Bland's students expected him to invite them to the front of the room to demonstrate how they did their homework in math. They delighted in the classroom competitions with flashcards he used to teach math and history facts. Results of district competitions confirmed his effectiveness as a teacher when his classes consistently claimed first prizes.

Mr. Vaughn could be counted on to discipline consistently. The eighth grade son of a current school board member tested him one day, but only once. The boy walked across the classroom on the desk tops, defying the teacher's authority and thinking that he would never be punished because of who he was. Dad called his bluff and turned him over his knee. That boy learned his lesson fast and never challenged the teacher's authority again.

Maybe, somehow, Dad's pigs on the farm got the message, too. Pigs are pigs. If you've never watched them eat, you still don't understand why they're called pigs. They will climb up into the feed trough with all four feet, effectively 'hogging' the food from each other. Dad wanted to change that behavior, and he succeeded by using conditioning. He installed an electric wire along the center of the trough. The most impolite pigs got the most shocks. His method proved simple and effective.

Gooseberry Gobblers

On those long lazy summer afternoons on our farm in Vale, Oregon, life was easy, at least for the younger members of the family. While the elders worked for hours in the fields or in the kitchen, Mona and I, awaiting our growth to real usefulness, were left much to our own devices. We probably should have been weeding in the garden, but in the same vicinity as the garden lived a bush that held quite an attraction for us. After pulling a few weeds—so we could say we had done it—we gravitated toward that gooseberry bush.

Mona picking gooseberries

Gooseberries, during their ripening process, vary greatly in taste. Most of our memories center on that period when the berries appeared quite plump but were still very green. We knew they were extremely sour. Mona and I discovered a very useful property of green gooseberries. They were good for contests.

A Gooseberry Contest was conducted like this. First we picked a bunch of green berries. We carried them to the shady and cool east side of the house. There we sat side by side. We took turns. Mona, then Margie, counted berries. "I've got twenty. How many do you have?" We agreed on the number. Each ate them. "You puckered!"

"No I didn't!"

The winner ate more green gooseberries than the other and did not make that face that usually goes with sour. The gooseberry contests continued until the gooseberries got ripe. Or was it until the day we met the garter snake under the gooseberry bush?

No Bears out Tonight!

Bland and Marion's young children

Another childhood memory from our life on the farm involved an activity that always took place after dark. We had a chase game that we called "No Bears out Tonight."

We chose "It", then "It" covered his or her eyes. Everyone else ran to hide.

No Bears out Tonight!

"It" wandered around the yard and immediate vicinity, singing, "No Bears out Tonight! No Bears out Tonight." Every time "It" came close to a "bear," the bear jumped out to surprise and catch him or her. "It" had to find all the bears. We experienced great fun and fright playing this game.

I remember playing 'No Bears out Tonight' over and over for years. Finally I began to have a re-occurring nightmare in which a bear chased me, and I tripped over a log. This fall never failed to wake me up!

I began to be somewhat afraid of the dark.

I helped with the evening milking which required several hours, and in the winter time, we finished after dark. I left the milk barn walking, but half-way to the house I found myself running for the door, the fear growing inside me. But so far, that bear has never caught me!

Round and Round

ONA and Margie occupied the kitchen this early afternoon. Mom had asked them to do the dishes before they went outside to work an hour in the garden. Their intent was to obey.

While they worked in the kitchen, they turned the radio on. Fibber McGee and Mollie would be fun listening while they cleaned the kitchen. But the radio was in the living room, so Margie washed a dish, rinsed it, and handed it to Mona who stood waiting with a dishtowel. They both rushed for the living room where they could hear the radio much better. The girls stood drying and listening for a long time before they returned to wash another dish. Dirty dishes used by five people would add up to a long job with this slow progress.

As they rushed back and forth between the kitchen and the living room, their actions began to tickle their 'funny bones.' The kitchen and living room shared two doorways. The girls began to circle round and round from the kitchen, to living room, in one door, out the other, and back again, scarcely pausing to get the dishes anymore. Around and around they ran, laughing harder all the time. This continued for about thirty minutes, until Dad opened the door from outside. "What are you girls supposed to be doing?" He asked.

"We're doing the dishes," came our embarrassed response.

"It doesn't look to me like you're doing dishes. Margie, get a switch from the tamarack tree."

This time I got my switch and my spanking. Mona, however, because she was tender in years, squeaked by with a scolding.

Oh, the unfairness of it all! Now Margie is traumatized!

Perils of the Dairy Farm

Our Farm

WHERE there is a dairy, there are cows. Where there are cows, there are cow-pies. On our dairy farm we milked our cows in a "state of the art" milking parlor. Instead of having the cows walking on the same level we did, we had a raised platform for the cows. *Whose idea was that??* The salesperson who sold the system to my parents vowed that "you could milk these cows in your party dresses in this parlor!" Indeed!!

I can't say that I blame my dad for being sold on it. It must have sounded good. He'd had enough of cows' stepping on his foot and going to sleep or switching him in the face with their wet tails.

My mom, Marion, remembers an event where Dad, (Bland), while we had the old milking set-up, was trying to prod a reluctant cow into her stanchion and slipped and fell. Right behind the cow in the appropriate place was a trench that connected to a manure pit outside the barn. And in that trench were the inevitable wet, stinky cow-pies. That was where my Dad slipped and fell.

Mom reports his reaction as "OOOOOOOPS!!!" His next words were, "I never thought *that* would happen to me!"

It's little wonder that he fell for this new—and improved, he assumed—milking parlor and machine.

Disappointment reigned supreme during our first experiences with that new system. Not only had aforethought failed us in not showing us that the cows could take supremely better aim with those wet and cocklebur-infested tails from their elevated position on the new platform. They could also inflict their splatters in extremely more unpleasant places. You can probably guess what happened to the party dress idea.

Dad wasn't the only member of our family to have close interactions with the manure. Outside the barn door was a pit into which all the manure from the barn trench was shoveled. My sister, Mona, had her misadventure while trying to prove that she was a big girl and could do anything that her older siblings could do.

As I remember, Uncle Ross, Aunt Mildred, Richard, and Rosilee were visiting at the time. Mona was probably about four years old. We cousins were having a rare good time together, and engaging in a game of *Follow the Leader.*

I believe my older brother, Verlin, had to be the leader, since older siblings are known to be much superior leaders. So we'll give him the credit. We ran everywhere, following our trusted leader around the house, down to the corner, around the rose bush, out to the gooseberry bush, past that into the garden, on through the sage brush, then back toward the house and the barn.

Before we knew what was happening, we saw him jumping over the manure pit at the end of the milking barn! Verlin sailed over, Richard cleared the pit, Margie had no problem, and Rosilee barely escaped an early burial. But Mona and her four year old legs just couldn't make that jump. Of course, she landed a bit too soon, and found herself waist high in aromatic manure.

Mom and Aunt Mildred, in the kitchen cooking dinner, were surprised by the commotion in the yard, and looked out to see Verlin and Margie on either side of Mona, holding her arm's-length by the fingertips, and crying, "Mama, look what happened to Mona! What can we do?" Mom, always the practical one, applied common sense and turned the garden hose on poor little Mona, who was—more or less—permanently traumatized by the whole event.

Refuge in the Haystack

LIVING was reduced to the ultimate simplicity on our farm in Eastern Oregon. We experienced it when we were disobedient.

Mom, having received such appropriate treatment from her father, Samuel Allen Kilpatrick, knew exactly how to curb our disobedience: She sent us to the tamarack bush—she probably planted It *especially* for this use—to cut our very own switches for our spankings.

Most children will eventually begin to investigate ways in which they can escape the deserved punishment. I was no different.

I do not remember what crime I had committed, and Mom could not remember either. But we both remember one fact; instead of cutting a tamarack switch, I made a run for it. Down through the cow yard I ran, dodging cow-pies all the way.

I ran purposefully to the haystack. Surely, I thought, I could climb high enough on the haystack that Mom would not try to follow me. Thus I would escape the spanking.

I just did not know my mother very well! Here she came, switch in hand, barely noticing the cow-pies; her eyes riveted on me cowering on the haystack. Up the haystack she came, reaching me in less time than I could ever have imagined.

Too late I realized my mistake. Running from a spanking would only make the spanking worse.

Learned: Never run from a Kilpatrick parent with a tamarack switch!

The Girl Who Wanted to Fly

OUR house was non-conventional, to say the least. At one end of the kitchen we sat to eat our meals in a small alcove with a table and narrow benches on each side of it. The benches weren't very long, and when our family sat together there, we were crowded. Impatient kids wanting to get on with their playing sat trapped until Mom or Dad, sitting on the end of each bench, finished eating and went back to work.

Margie, sitting across the table from Mona, wanted out. She sat looking at the ladder in the corner of the room. She wanted to go upstairs to the attic and play with her doll, Lena. Lena would be lonesome; having not seen her for a long time. Lena didn't like to be lonely.

Suddenly, Margie couldn't stand sitting there any longer. She *had* to get away from that table.

"I'm going to crawl under," she said, and with that she squirmed and struggled off the bench and slid under the table. She descended into a forest of legs; She saw Verlin's long skinny ones, Dad's over-all-clad ones, Mom's smaller ones wearing a flowered housedress. Mona's short legs swung tirelessly. Her cheerful voice chirped, "Everybody kick her as she goes by. Everybody kick her as she goes by."

Margie finally wiggled through the jumble of legs and emerged. She climbed the ladder fastened to the wall and leading straight up to the ceiling. She pushed up on the loose square of wood that closed the hole in the ceiling and climbed into the attic.

The attic would have been the full size of the original house, had it not been for the sharply sloping roof's limiting of the space at the sides. The storage/play room was long and narrow. Margie found Lena, her black rubber baby doll, and picked her up. "Shhh! Shhh!" she said. "You're all right."

She walked to the end of the room and pulled open the "door' so she could see outside to the pasture, the mulberry tree, and the Jersey bull with that funny mask on. Daddy called the mask "blinders" but Margie didn't understand why the bull wore them. The door fascinated her. It opened into the south side yard where Mama had her rose bush. But there were no steps leading to the ground. The door opened into thin air.

Suddenly, Margie wanted company. She wanted someone besides Mona. "Mama," she called through the hole in the ceiling. Can Georgie come over and play?"

Marion heard tiredly. "I guess so. I'll call her mother and see. *Father in Heaven, please help me to be patient today*," she prayed. She had picked her green beans this morning, and had yet to put them in the jars, put canning lids on, and cook them in the hot-water-bath.

***

Georgie had come, and the girls were playing quietly in the attic with their dolls, Marion thought. They played quietly for an hour before she began to hear running and jumping sounds. They're having fun, I'm glad.

The first seven jars of beans were in the boiler. Marion sighed and began filling the second batch of jars with the crisp, fresh beans.

Marion thought she heard a scream. All ears now, she listened.

"Georgie fell outside, Mama!" Margie screamed. "She fell out the door! Hurry Mama! She's not moving."

Marion ran out the kitchen door and around to the side yard in a flash. Georgie lay sprawled in the muddy yard, not moving. *Heavenly Father, Please let her be okay. She has to be okay. She's Mrs. Tolman's only daughter.*

Georgie, finally having caught her breath, began to sob with fear and surprise.

Marion comforted her, "It's okay, Honey. Everything's okay now. Can you move your legs and arms? Do they hurt?"

"I want Mama!" Georgie screamed. Her movements told Marion that all was well. "I'll call your mother, Georgie. She'll come over and walk home with you. You're okay, Honey."

"Father, I don't know how she could have fallen that far and be okay, but she is. Thank you for taking care of all of us!"

Then, full of thankfulness, she called, "Come on kids! Let's warm up those cinnamon rolls and we'll have a cup of tea when Georgie's Mama comes."

Kids and Cows and Geese
and Things

A favorite saying of my mother's was, "All work and no play make Jack a dull boy." If working makes us dull, and our parents wanted bright children, couldn't we have become brighter without the work?

Primary among jobs on our farm near Vale during the late forties and early fifties was helping with milking twice daily. We could never skip milking. Milking cows meant no vacations, manure pits, switching tails targeting our faces and clothing, and cows stepping on our feet.

But the milk barn was also the scene of sharing with our mother, hilarity over experiences, blending voices in song, and target practice—fresh milk from cows' udders aimed at open mouths.

The milking chore caused arguments between teenaged sisters. We had an assigned schedule. Each of us milked at least once a day, morning or evening. Evenings brought problems because we had dates and were determined to escape milking on date nights. So we traded nights and lost track.

Those hungry cows mandated the crops grown on our farm; oats, corn, and hay became food during the long winters. The cows provided our only income.

Since Dad was building the dairy herd, there were always new calves. After he started milking the 'freshened' heifer, the calves drank from a bucket. Our job was to teach them how.

"Just dip your fingers into the milk," Dad instructed. "Let the calves begin to suck them, then push their mouths into the pail of milk." At first doubtful, we followed Dad's instructions. With squishy, warm, wet, and toothless mouths, the calves sucked. They learned where that milk was. We loved this job.

Dad had geese on the farm. Those ornery, territorial geese challenged youngsters carrying loads of kitchen scraps to the pig pen, and promptly gave chase, necks strained forward, feathers ruffled haughtily, wings stretched widely, honking loudly.

"I'm scared, Dad," we protested.

He strongly encouraged, "Oh, those geese are not going to hurt you. All they want is to scare you," so we did the job anyway, as invisibly as we could.

Some of the hardest work was in the kitchen. Mom always got the first pickings of the sweet corn. It had to be perfect; not too young, not too ripe, at its peak of sweetness when she preserved her bounty by freezing it for our needs during winter ahead.

"Can't we just freeze the whole ear?" we begged, eyeing the overflowing gunny sacks.

"Takes too much freezer space," Mom said.

Each ear had to be shucked, silked, blanched in hot water and the kernels of corn cut off the cob. A *lot* of cobs awaited us! Endlessly we carved the corn into pans.

"Be sure to scrape that ear and save the "heart" of the kernels. That's where the best flavor hides," Mom told us. We scraped and splattered, scraped and splattered, until we resembled corn ourselves, lacking only butter to provide someone a sumptuous meal.

"We're done, Mom," we reported hopefully, only to be redirected: "Now we'll put the corn into these freezer bags."

Scoop after weary scoop, relieved only by Mom's ever-present sense of humor, a snack of sweet tasty corn, or the unexpected presence of a neighbor, we complied until the job was done. At the dinner table, in winter, we learned the worth of our work.

When Mom finished freezing, Dad harvested the field. Using a tractor-drawn motorized corn chopper, the corn ears and stalks were shredded and blown into a horse-drawn wagon that hauled the corn mixture to a deep pit back of the barn.

The pit was long, straight, and narrow, shaped, ramp-like, from ground surface to deepest, so a wagon could drive in, dump its load, and drive forward and out again.

The Vaughn Family in Vale

Dad dumped the first load at the front of the pit, and drove over it to dump the next load. This is where children came in handy. Dad couldn't afford "hired hands," and used "tired hands"—us—instead.

We could use pitchforks to level the corn, thus smoothing rough descents of the next wagonloads. Finally, days later, the pit now full of chopped corn was packed down —by driving horses or a tractor over it repeatedly— covered with tarps, then dirt, and left to ferment. The resulting silage fed the cows; why it didn't make them drunk I'll never understand. The stuff smelled strikingly suspicious.

Grain harvest brought a dreaded chore. The oats were threshed by machine and hauled in wagons to the barn. In the barn was a small—about ten foot square—room called a granary. Two reluctant children were assigned to this room. There we waited until the wagon arrived.

"Ready?" Dad yelled.

"Ready," we replied, not quite truthfully; dread nearly choking off our voices.

The grain was shoveled into a milling machine and blown into the granary, raising clouds of chaff. Our job was to drag the oats away from the window and make room for more. We itched, we sweated, we thirsted, we tried *not to* breathe, but we did our part, questioning constantly, "Are we done yet?"

The hay harvest was more adventurous. Dad and the boys mowed the hay and raked it into windrows and piles. It was then pitched onto a "slip," a platform that could be dragged through the field by a team of work horses to the site of the haystack.

My Dad had solved the stacking problem by building a wooden contraption he called a derrick. It had long arms and a large wooden "fork" on one end, and cables, attached to the fork, on the other. The work horses were hitched to the cables. After the hay was moved from the slips onto the fork it was time for my part.

During my teen years I drove the work horses to lift the hay fork. Those horses had to move at a perky pace to get that hay onto the stack.

Dad yelled, "Gid-di-up!" I pressed the horses into action. Faster and faster we went until Dad saw the fork reaching the top of the haystack, and yelled, "Whoa!!" We stopped. The hay kept going, and landed, if we were lucky, on the intended haystack. If we were *not* lucky, the obstinate hay landed on that unfortunate person forking hay on the stack—usually, in my day, Dad, or my older brother, Verlin.

When we finished our work, the garden called. It furnished the fresh vegetables we ate and grew a variety of weeds too, large and small, tenacious and tender. Thus we were introduced to one of the necessities of gardening, weeding.

"But it's hot, Mom!" We protested. It was a huge garden.

We tried, we really did, but when a diversion came, we forgot about the garden and picked gooseberries for a green gooseberry contest, or followed our thirst indoors for a drink, or collected the worms we found, or played "Follow the Leader." There were plentiful diversions for children on an eighty acre farm, and so we played.

We loved to play, but needed, for our own good, to work, too.

My mom might phrase it, "A bit of work improves Jack's quirks. All play and no work might make Jack a jerk."

Know what, Mom? I finally get it.

Leslie and Allen, Farm Kids

Imaginative? Or Mischievous?

LIFE was never quite the same on our farm after November 12, 1944. That was the day Leslie Bland Vaughn Jr. came into this world. Leslie, from the early days of his life proved to be a creative dynamo. His younger brother, Charles Allen Vaughn was born in March two years later and proved to be a willing accomplice to Les's shenanigans.

During the time Mother was confined at Brittingham's Nursing Home in Ontario, Oregon for Allen's birth, Les—being too young to stay at home without his mother—stayed with Mom's close friend and neighbor, Violet Baker.

The first story I was told about Les took place when he was brought by the Bakers to see his baby brother. I'm sure Mother had done her best to prepare two-year-old Leslie to welcome his baby brother, and she had done a terrific job—as proved by his actions.

When he saw his little brother and was asked what he thought about the new baby, he said he wanted to sing a song to his little brother. He opened his little mouth and sang in a clear beautiful voice, "Jesus loves me, this I know, for the Bible tells me so. Little ones to Him belong; they are weak but He is strong. Yes, Jesus loves me. Yes; Jesus loves me. Yes, Jesus loves me; the Bible tells me so."

As Mom told the story, Mrs. Brittingham, with tears in her eyes, said, "Vaughn, keep that boy singing!" And Mom did just that.

But singing wasn't all that boy did. He had an incredible curiosity which led him into many activities probably not approved so much. Baby chickens fascinated him, but he did not understand their fragility.

On one occasion while Mom was doing a permanent for Violet, he decided to investigate the baby chickens. He picked them up repeatedly in his young hands, wondering why they didn't do all the things the bigger chickens did. Finally, when several of the chicks no longer stood or moved, he went to find his mother. "Mom, they just don't make chickens like they used to."

"What do you mean, Leslie?" she asked, worriedly. Taking her by the hand he drew her to the baby chickens where she found the disaster she feared.

As he grew, his little brother, Al—his constant companion, and not without imaginations of his own—contributed his talents to the brew. One story, told to me by the owner of the actions, took place after they were several years older.

On our farm, south of our home was a large pasture in which our cows grazed through the days and drank from a pond which was probably nearly a quarter of a mile from the house. This pond was fed by irrigation water; the mix in the pond was made richer by the droppings of the cows as they came to drink. Les and Al found this pond a suitable, even desirable place to swim. Their mother, busy with her many chores around the house, fields, and barn, would have been horrified.

Les remembers swimming underwater and enjoying the sights of hundreds of pollywogs. He remembers trying to teach grown chickens to swim, reasoning in his young mind that if wild ducks could swim in the pond, the chickens should be able to swim too. The reasoning turned to questions after several chickens died trying. "They could only make it two or three times." Les reported.

Another questionable activity Les reports must have happened at approximately this age while Dad was working on the addition to our house that improved the bathroom and added a bedroom for Mona and me. Apparently, Mom was in town doing some business. Dad needed to remove the heating oil from the oil stove and barrels. He drained the oil into our large bathtub and left it nearby.

Les and Al, always looking for something new to do, found the tub full of clear, clean looking oil. Les, dipping his hand into the oil, observed, "It's warm." Together, the two boys decided that they could take a bath and cool off. So they did it, probably for an hour or so.

After these immersions into such undesirable mediums, one is left wondering how these two survived.

This next incident took place when the boys were a bit older. Having observed our neighbor, George Baker, smoking, and thinking him a worthy person to emulate, the two boys thought they should try out smoking.

They found what seemed a secure place out behind the haystack. Never mind the flammable hay. They had somehow obtained a corncob pipe, and apparently matches. They successfully lit the pipe and began to smoke.

Our father, not too far away to smell the smoke or to become quite anxious about his haystack, quickly appeared. "Oh! You guys want to smoke, huh?" He removed the pipe, "I'll give you a real good smoke."

He went to the house and instructed Mom to go to town and buy corncob pipes and Bull Durham tobacco. Preparations completed, Dad invited George Baker to visit.

In Les's words," Dad set us down in the living room, filled pipes with tobacco, put hats on us so the smoke wouldn't go away, and instructed us to smoke."

So they smoked, finding that it wasn't quite as much fun as they had expected. Inhaling all that smoke left them feeling rather unwell. However, the lesson did not take. They both became smokers in later life.

Lest you think Les and Al were nothing but troublemakers during their lives, or that they would presently approve these actions of the past, let me assure you. They both grew into great men who are able and willing to help others in very effective ways.

The Boxing Glove Christmas

WHEN I was in high school during the 1950's, I dated a boy named John Hart. He was around our house a lot, and became friends with my family. Many of the times John and I spent together were in the school gym; he in the boxing ring. He competed routinely, and I watched at the sidelines during bouts, praying that he wouldn't be injured too badly.

John and my brother, Verlin, became friends, and when the Korean War came along and the government drafted young men for a two year stint in the military, John and Verlin entered the service of their country together. This story happened when Verlin and John came home on leave at Christmas time, and spent the day at our house.

Verlin—with John's help, I'm sure—bought gifts for his young brothers, Leslie, about nine and Allen, about seven years old.

"Boys, open your presents," said Verlin. He and John traded winks, and Verlin handed the boys identical packages, the odd shapes clumsily, but thoroughly wrapped.

"What is it? What is it?" asked Leslie excitedly.

"Mine's brown!" Al exclaimed. "It's soft. What is it anyway?"

"We bought you boxing gloves," John volunteered, "like I wear when I'm boxing. Wouldn't you boys like to learn to box?"

"Does it hurt?" Allen asked anxiously.

"That's why they make the gloves thick and soft, to keep you from getting hurt," Verlin suggested hopefully.

"We'll coach you," John encouraged. "Verlin, you coach Allen, and I'll coach Leslie. Let's help them get the gloves on."

The unsuspecting little boys were "coached" and gloved.

Verlin, un-experienced in boxing, said to Allen. "Now Allen, it's important to protect your face with your gloves when you're boxing." No demonstration of technique followed in that corner, the inexperienced coach not understanding its importance.

John, the experienced, told Leslie the importance of protecting his face, and demonstrated, holding his hands in front of his face and peeking around them to see his target.

The boxers entered the ring—well, it was really the living room—Leslie with his hands and gloves protecting his face, Allen, too. OOPS!! Allen's hands are *not* in front of his face, but up over his ears, presenting, as Les said, "a good target." Les aimed for that target with all his energy. He hit Allen so hard that his younger brother flew across the room and into the Christmas tree, knocking it down. Chaos!!

Mom leaped off the couch and ran to the tree. "Allen, are you okay? Are you hurt anywhere?"

Allen, very surprised and a little bruised from his experience with the boxing gloves, slowly stood up. "Just wait till next time, Leslie. Your time's a comin'!"

We put the Christmas tree back up. A few packages looked a bit smashed, a few of the more fragile ornaments were broken, but in short order we had the mess removed and were ready to resume our celebration.

Every Christmas Dad gifted the family with a big can of hard candy. We all dug into it now; hopefully it would restore our spirits and our energy.

Sometime during all the confusion of that day, Dad surreptitiously disappeared. From outside the house came a booming "Ho! Ho! Ho!" Dad, mysteriously reappeared and exclaimed, "I thought I heard Santa Claus outside. Didn't you hear Santa Claus? Let's go see if he's still there."

When we opened the door, there sat the beautiful new American Flyer sled.

This is a precious memory of my Dad, because we saw so little of his sweet tender side; those memories have been blocked for some of us siblings by the more difficult memories of later years.

Another Fragrant Memory

I have recently heard this story from the one who is the owner of it, Les Vaughn, my younger brother. According to Les, this event transpired in the days when he was first coming into manhood, and, as he put it, "Feeling my testosterone." This story is just too good to lose, so, in case Les never gets around to doing his duty and writing it up, I shall do it my way.

Les reported that Dad had just taken the family to a rodeo, probably on the Fourth of July when Vale had its annual celebration. There Les had watched with wonder and amazement while bucking bulls and agitated ponies did their best to remove the cowboys from their backs. Sometime, there at the rodeo, an idea was born. Les decided that if the cowboys could do it, he could too. So he went home and watched for his opportunity.

The opportunity arrived one day when he saw Dad put our Jersey bull into a chute in the barn to de-horn him. This bull was a mean one who had taken after Dad while he worked on more than one occasion. This bull was very likely to be maaaaaaad, since losing his horns wasn't his favorite thing to do.

Les, upon seeing the bull confined in the chute, remembered his idea. "Dad," he said, "I want to ride that bull."

Said his shocked Daddy, "Oh no, Leslie, I don't think you want to ride *this* bull!"

"But Dad," protested Les, "I really *do want* to ride that bull."

Again Dad corrected him, "Les, I just don't think it's a good idea to ride *that* bull. I don't think you ought to try it."

"But Dad, I just really *want to* do it. I know I can."

Dad, seeing that he was losing the battle, finally conceded. "Well, then.

Get on him while he's in the chute. *And don't tell your mother I let you ride this bull!*"

Having won the battle, brave young Leslie mounted his steed in the chute. Dad thought he should try again to discourage the valiant would-be cowboy. He asked, "Leslie, are you *sure* you want to ride this bull?"

Leslie answered, "Let him go Dad. I'm sure."

Dad reluctantly opened the chute, and the bull shot from the chute and ran erratically through the barn, Les clinging to his back tenaciously.

Just outside the barn was a huge mountain of manure and straw that Dad had moved from the barn and corals, and it was wet and smelly. The bull's path led straight to the manure pile.

By now, young Les is wondering about the wisdom of his course of action. Would the bull go straight through that mess?

As he was contemplating what the end of this venture would be, the bull answered the question for him. Just as he reached the pile, he made an abrupt right turn. Les, still subject to the law of inertia, continued unerringly on his way into the pile.

Rather an inglorious end to the adventure, wasn't it? And so typical of those adventures which farm children experience in abundance.

Trombone and Trauma

Y sister, Mona, and I played in the band at Vale Elementary School. Fifth graders could choose their instrument, with the agreement of Mr. Christy, the band director. In the late 1940's that school district provided rental instruments, opening the door for our participation.

Though they struggled to pay the farm bills, our parents gifted us with music. I chose trombone, my long arms a good fit, and two years later, Mona chose clarinet.

I delighted in the new opportunity; it became a passion, a challenge, a joy, and a medium of expression. I didn't understand this then, but my participation in the music program developed my unique talent and personality. Before band, my classmates hardly knew me.

I energetically entered into learning, and Mr. Christy saw my enthusiasm. He challenged and encouraged me. The perceptive instructor invited me to practice with the high school band when I entered eighth grade. He selected me to attend the Music in May conference during my senior year. He gave me special music. "Here, Margie. I think you are ready for this. See what you can do."

I developed a lifetime love for the music, and at concerts during my senior year, I soloed on "Waltz of the Flowers" from *Nutcracker* and "Oh Holy Night, music written in 1855 for a poem almost fifty years old. It had been sung and played joyously for over two hundred years.

Because of my frequent practice, I eventually achieved first chair position in the trombone section. The district had purchased a beautiful new trombone, and Mr. Christy privileged me to use it regularly. My use resulted in its damage.

It happened like this: My sister and I loved one another, but that did not mean a total absence of sisterly friction.

"You've been practicing all day, Margie. I want to watch "Your Hit Parade!" I wanted to practice my music. I played on, ignoring my younger sister's wishes. Mona decided to express her displeasure. She struck out at me with the hairbrush she held in her hand, unintentionally hitting my trombone slide—she meant to hit me—with the hairbrush as I played.

Both Mona and I froze in horror!

"Oh, Margie! I didn't mean to!"

"Look what you've done! I can't even move my slide!"

Trombone Solo

Trombone slides are very fragile. The slide cover is extremely thin; it must move easily and lightly over the slide frame to produce the changes in pitch and tone which are the basis of trombone music.

Both Mona and I knew that some difficult experiences lay ahead. She must confess to Mr. Christy that she had damaged the trombone slide; I, too, must take responsibility for the damage.

Mr. Christy arranged repair to the slide, but reminder of our folly nagged at me daily as I rehearsed with the band. The slide, forever after, hesitated at the dent in third position.

Thankfully, Mr. Christy chose the path of mercy and allowed us to stay in the band. Two wiser girls appreciated the privilege.

The Milkmaid Trio Makes
Its Debut

OUR milk barn in Vale, Oregon hosted all kinds of activity, since we spent so many hours there daily. One diversion we indulged was singing. Mom, my sister, Mona, and I learned we could harmonize, and harmonize we did. Mona sang the lead, Marjorie managed a tenor harmony, and Mom, the low alto.

We sang *I Understand* best, but experimented with all the songs we heard on *"Your Hit Parade"* every Saturday night. Sometimes we impressed even ourselves.

After the milk truck driver, Mr. Atherton, heard us a few times, he registered us to compete at the county fair and told us later. Embarrassed and anxious, but also excited by the possibilities, we went to the fair.

The first time we sang, we chose our old favorite, *I Understand*, and, by some miracle, placed third. Since we got to sing again, we decided to branch out; impress the folks, sing another song. *Joey* was a really cute song about a gal who dated a lot of guys, all of which were immortalized in the song.

The problem hid, therein. We sang great harmony. We just couldn't remember which guy she dated when, and what his particular talent was. We ruined our perfect harmony by the disagreement of names which came out of our mouths.

I guess we forgot to reckon with our nerves while we stood in front of a crowd. We had performed the song perfectly for the cows. Thoroughly humiliated we came down from the stage to hear my observant, thereafter temporary, boy friend say, "Well. I guess we know who is *not* going to State Fair!!"

Better to have tried and failed than not to try at all? Maybe.

The Vaughn Girls

The Vaughn Sisters

WE grew up on a dairy farm forty acres west of Vale, Oregon. Mother took us to worship at the Church of Christ in Vale, about six miles east of our farm. There we met a group of young people like ourselves; farm kids, accustomed to hard work, having little in the way of luxury, but having learned early in life that we needed God in our lives.

In our family, it was Mom who made sure we knew God. I think that in his earlier life my Dad may have gone to church, but in our lives, only a family wedding would take him and that very reluctantly. We never knew why.

We were fortunate to have learned in our Bible classes at the feet of Walter Skelton. Brother Skelton made sure we learned what the Bible said.

He assigned "memory verses." He motivated us to read the Word by giving prizes for "Daily Bible Readers." It was good that we had the scripture in our lives; we needed the encouragements and promises we found there. We carried burdens beyond what children ought to bear.

Brother Skelton gave us another gift; transportation to activities nurturing to us and beneficial to our lives. Quaker Hill camp played an important part. Family camp held there yearly furnished abundant opportunities to meet young people our age. Skating parties— usually held in Ontario—provided fun and opportunities to choose partners for couples' skates. "Singings," led by Lyle Dalzell specifically for the young people, became a popular choice. Our voices blended in harmonies. The large groups of teenagers filled auditoriums. We knew Lyle as a friend. He had given us boat trips at family camp, enforced camp rules, and treated us as friends.

We forged relationships at those singings. We worked together under Lyle's direction to make hymns sound like angel's songs. Boy-girl attractions bloomed, but usually, in Lyle's chorus, sopranos sat with sopranos, altos with altos, tenors with tenors, and bass with bass. Thus, we grew in our singing abilities while engaged in very creative activity. We thought it wonderful fun.

During a potluck dinner before, and after the singing concluded, we socialized. Thus, our friendships grew, along with our musical abilities. In these settings, our friendships with Dick Dalzell, Duane McClung, Melvin Farmer, Jess Armas, Don Brandt, Neva Hoofnagle, Clara, Hoofnagle, Nancy Hoofnagle, and many others, bound us into a unit, even though we lived miles apart.

These young people from Vale, Ontario, Weiser, Caldwell, Nampa, Boise—and many other places in the Snake River and Boise Valleys—forged life-time friendships. In all the years I've since lived, I have never seen such a bond between young people of such widely scattered congregations. Lyle gave us a gift, unselfishly, abundantly, and frequently. It changed all our lives.

These young people were our "best friends"—though they lived in distant places—companions on our journey of faith, and I have never forgotten them.

As young women, Mona and I were interested in all these young men. I had dated a little during High School, but Mona was too busy being Harvest Festival Queen and receiving like honors, to have time for the boys. However, in her heart she held a secret attraction for Dick Dalzell. He was her "first love."

In those days, a "first love" wasn't necessarily someone you ever went out with. Instead, you tried to sit on the end of the pew, hoped he would come and sit by you, longed for him to ask you to skate, smiled at him shyly, and hoped some more.

My "first love" was Ralph Skelton, son of Brother Walter Skelton, our minister at the church in Vale. Since Ralph was a very bashful young man with a beautiful smile, this love interest didn't go very far. But we exchanged a lot of those smiles, and I even named my cat after him. His name was Ralph Arthur Skelton. Since I didn't want to be too obvious, I chose Ralph's middle name, and called the cat Arthur.

I think Mona's interest in Dick actually culminated in a few dates. At least, I have a memory of about four above-mentioned boys visiting our home in Vale on a Sunday afternoon. Dick was among them.

Dick was admired by all the young people. He had a beautiful bass voice—most important—was very handsome, and also very friendly. As the son of Lyle, he already "had it made" with us girls, since we all loved Lyle so much.

Mona, with her heart "given" to Dick could not even consider Gene Linder from Weiser, Idaho, who really admired her. I singled out Melvin Farmer for awhile as a pretty special young man. We heard many years later that the guys all thought "the Vaughn Girls" pretty special, too. But from our perspective, we were just there and not particularly noticeable.

Another thing that I heard with shock many years later was that some of the young people thought I seemed "conceited." It's amazing what shyness can do to people's perceptions! In these days you might observe that I had "low self-esteem," which I did.

Both Mona and I married people from that young people's group. Mona married Jess Armas, a very handsome young man with a Basque ancestry and an obvious spiritual leaning, and I married Vern Skelton, the eldest son of Walter and Lois Skelton, and the brother of Ralph, after whom I had named my cat.

The year of 9-1-1, on September 16, 2001, following the destruction of the World Trade Center, that young people's group—then in their sixties—assembled at a church in Nampa, Idaho for a fifty year reunion which none of us will ever forget. In that time of fear and stress, we united again in faith, lifted our country up to God, sang our love and faith to Him, and renewed those dear friendships we had made so long ago.

PART THREE

Adult Adventures

Author's note: This is another venture into the world of creative non-fiction. The names have been changed to protect the innocent, but this is a story from my past that fits in here. Hope you enjoy it!

Choice of a Lifetime

Margie's graduation picture

MARCY Vellman climbed the wide steps into the Trailways bus. She had graduated in June from the Union High School in Vale, Oregon and today began her trip of nearly eleven hundred miles to Pepperdine College, Los Angeles, California. She'd grown up in Vale on the dairy farm her parents owned. She'd attended school every year with all the same kids, children of area farmers. She knew she was a small-town girl. *I'll be lost in a city. What can I be thinking of?*

She dreaded leaving because she knew she would worry about home. *Will Mom be all right?* Marcy's father, though hard-working, struggled daily with more than he could do. He typically reacted to the physical labor and financial pressure in ways that were painful to the family and to her mother. *I remember times he actually hit her. One of these days he'll hit her too hard.* Marcy felt somehow responsible to be at home, to make sure Mom would be safe. *As if there would be anything I could do!*

Mrs. Howe, Marcy's Social Studies teacher, had continued to encourage her toward college and helped her to secure a music scholarship. Mrs. Howe understood her, Marcy felt, saw in her a young woman who lacked confidence in her own abilities, but who was willing to work hard to achieve her goals. *I'm grateful for her belief in me and her help.*

Arrangements were completed, and in early September Marcy got on the Trailways bus to travel the long miles to Los Angeles. She watched as it pulled away from the hotel, feeling lonely already. Her mother and dad stood apart, her sister two and one-half years younger than she, and her two young brothers stood between them. She fixed the picture in her mind. *It'll be a long time before I see them again.*

Many feelings conflicted her during the long trip: excitement at undertaking a new adventure all her own, uncertainty whether she was doing the right thing leaving the family, doubt about her ability to fit into a new group of city friends, apprehension about whether she could successfully complete the college work, and wonder about whether she could find a job to earn the money she needed to complete the year.

An unknown life loomed before her with all its questions but the excitement of her new adventure won out. *A new life waits ahead of me. It's up to me what I make of it.*

***

"We're approaching Grapevine, the second-highest point on this freeway. This pass is called Tejon Pass, and is over 4000 feet high." The bus driver's voice interrupted the last of the many naps Marcy took during the long ride.

Marcy peered through sleepy eyes and saw what appeared to be blistering heat. She could see waves of it radiating off the land and the road ahead. She realized how hot and sticky she felt.

"We'll be descending into Los Angeles on the Golden State Freeway entering the city from the east. Arrival time is approximately an hour away."

The land lay in hills and valleys covered with dry grass. In the distance she saw groups of trees, oaks, she thought, probably clustered around whatever source of moisture they found. As she looked ahead in the direction she imagined the city to be, the air appeared a hazy blue. Here we are, she thought, smog and all.

Suddenly, Marcy wished she had more detail about the location of the college. She had studied the map and seen that it appeared to be located in a section of the city called Inglewood. But where 79th Street was located in Inglewood, she had no idea. Everyone should know where a college is located, she reasoned, and refused to worry.

About an hour later, the Trailways bus pulled into the station. The tall buildings disoriented her. She asked her questions of a lady at one of the ticket windows and went outside to look for city buses. After waiting nearly thirty minutes in the heat she finally saw an approaching bus destined for Inglewood. She hurried to the bus stop and climbed in.

"I'm going to Pepperdine College," she said. "Can you tell me where to get off?"

"I'm sorry. I don't know where Pepperdine College is."

"It appeared to be in Inglewood on the map. Can you take me there? Someone there will know when we get closer."

After an anxious hour of bus stops with people getting on and off, the driver still hadn't said anything to her. "I'm going to Inglewood," she reminded him.

"We've been in Inglewood for thirty minutes now. I'll give you a transfer for a bus that should get you there. Look for the West Los Angeles bus. Go across the street and wait."

"I'm really a bother to him, and he's letting me know it. Father, please help me find someone to help. I'm so lost." Her feet hurt, and she knew she looked a mess. The strong breeze from the west had done its work with her hair, but she felt grateful for the cooling it brought.

When the West Los Angeles bus finally came, Marcy collapsed into the first empty seat. She repeated her litany. "I need to get to Pepperdine College. I've been riding for hours looking for it. Do you know where it is?"

"Knowing where you're going is your responsibility, not mine."

She had heard things about Los Angeles, the smog, especially. As the day passed she began to feel unwell, her chest burning and feeling heavy. Noticing again the haze around her, she knew why she had these strange new discomforts in her body. Added to the bus situation it was just too much. She struggled to keep tears from her eyes.

I feel so alone. I'm scared. How would she ever find the college? No driver yet had heard of it. So she rode on. Finally, she prayed, and talked to the driver again, and he began to picture where it was this young girl wanted to go. He gave her a pass for another bus and told her where to transfer. *O Father, here I go again. Please help someone know how to help me.* The next driver knew the location of Pepperdine College.

She arrived on a Sunday afternoon in September, 1955. She knew no one, hadn't met even a room mate. But it was Sunday evening, and she knew Christians would be meeting at the Vermont Avenue Church of Christ she had seen as she left the bus. So, not yet knowing where she would sleep that night, she walked back down the Promenade of Pepperdine's campus past a fountain where she saw a small statue—She would later learn that students met each evening here for 'devotionals' and that the statue had been dubbed "Delores."

It was 5:30 when she reached the church, but it was quiet. With relief she found the doors open, walked into the auditorium and sat tiredly on a pew. *Thank you, Father, for helping me to get here. I'll be okay now. People will be arriving in an hour or so.*

About six o'clock she began to hear sounds in the back part of the church, rose, and wandered in that direction. She found two young people in the fellowship room, preparing sandwiches.

Suddenly, Marcy realized how hungry she was. "I'm Marcy," she said to a short friendly-looking girl with black curly hair. I'm here to enter college. I'm from Oregon. Are you a student at Pepperdine?"

"I'm from Georgia, the girl replied. My name's Janine. I'll be a freshman when we register. This is Howard Weeks, my boy friend." Marcy smiled at the tall, stocky, dark-headed boy directing his welcoming grin toward her.

"Do you know how to go about getting registered and into the dorm? I have no idea what to do."

"I have to do that yet, too, Janine said. "I suppose we need to find the Administration building. "Let's have a sandwich first, and we'll go together. Maybe we could even be roommates. Well *almost* roommates. I met a girl earlier and we agreed to room together. Her name is Jan. She's from Idaho. But you can live right next door. We'll be suite-mates. Jan and some of the others should be here in a bit."

"The church is providing food for students on Sunday nights since the cafeteria isn't open," Janine continued. "We can eat here every week. They told us this morning at worship services. Isn't that great?" She handed Marcy a paper plate with a sandwich and apple slices on it.

I'll have friends from the first, Christian friends, Father. Thank you for giving me just what I need.

Marcy, relieved that Janine had such a 'take charge' manner, and glad for the company, replied. "I'm starved. And I'd love to be your suite-mate." *Thank you, Father, for working it all out. I'm finally here. Everything's going to be all right.*

As Jeanine had predicted, more students came in, a few at a time. Jan, Janine's roommate arrived first, and Marcy learned that she was great with her ukulele. An even happier discovery was that Jan came from Boise, Idaho and they had been acquaintances at the youth singings in the Boise-Snake River Valleys in Idaho.

Two guys, both named Dick, entered together and introduced themselves…one handsome, blond, curly-haired and rather short; one tall and gangly with blond straight hair and blotchy skin. Right away Marcy knew they were friends that would bring a lot of fun into her life. At student assemblies they became a popular duo, singing silly songs and playing their washtubs.

A girl named Gloria arrived with a guy named Robert. *Nice looking. Kind eyes.* A tall guy with curly black hair and snappy brown eyes grabbed her attention, and upon being introduced to her said, "Oh! Hi! I'm glad to find you. I'm your big brother, David Barbour. I'm supposed to show you around. We'll look at the campus later this evening. Talk to me before you leave, and we'll get acquainted." In that moment, Marcy lost her heart.

✳✳✳

Later that evening Marcy, Janine and Jan walked up the Promenade eyeing the buildings on each side. Palm trees stood proudly along the asphalt walkway. The campus had a homey feel; some buildings were low, others several stories high. All were made of stucco, a construction designed to shut out the torrid Southern California heat.

They had no trouble locating the Administration building, and none arranging the room selection they wanted right next door to one another. Marcy's assigned roommate was Nanette, a girl she'd not yet met, but she seemed nice when Marcy met her at the room.

After the details were taken care of and they had a place to sleep, Marcy left the dorm to meet David Barbour at the fountain for their walk across campus.

"Hi Marcy," he said. Glad to see I have such a beautiful young lady for a little sister." At that he took her hand, and the couple headed off across campus. As they walked, he identified the buildings, and darkness began to close in. *It must be at least eight thirty.*

Two hours later David led her to his car. We'll sit here and rest, he said, and we can talk. I want to hear all about you, Marcy.

Grateful to have his interest and attention, Marcy began. "I'm a farm girl from Oregon. I'm interested in music; I have been in the band all during high school and am here on a music scholarship. I'm planning a biological science major, and will probably switch my music participation to choral work."

"Whoa! What I *really* want to know is whether there is a boy friend in your life."

Marcy was surprised at the personal question, but she answered," I've had several of them, but none of them are serious interests any more. John went off to the service and forgot about me. Bill lost my interest because of his immature behavior in the car. I write once in awhile to a guy named Clio, but I suspect the writing will be temporary. I'm unattached."

"Thanks for sharing with me. I hope we will see more of each other. Welcome to Pepperdine." And with that David Barbour pulled Marcy to his side and kissed her.

After that first evening, Marcy saw very little of David Barbour, and she found he was the only person she really *wanted* to see. She saw him at church youth group on Sunday mornings, and evenings at the gathering for the meal. But weeks went by quickly, without further interest from him. Marcy watched for him through each long day.

Life in the dorm was a blast. The room filled at night with girls wanting to be in on the fun with the ukulele and singing. Laughing and talking filled the space, punctuated with the sound of *Down by the Riverside* being belted out in enthusiastic harmony. The roommates decided to go bowling, and to add fun and adventure, went in their pajamas. They went in bunches to the Ralph's Supermarket on the corner and brought home snacks for the long hours they would spend studying alone at the midnight hour.

Marcy joined in, but with a heavy heart because David was not there. She began to notice that Nancy talked about 'David' a lot. I wonder... *It couldn't be the same guy. No, it just couldn't.*

College life went on. The fraternities and sororities pledged, and Marcy, along with her new girlfriends, pledged the Kappa Kappa club. Most of the guys from church pledged the Tri Phi's. All the friends were inducted into the two clubs.

Marcy had dates for all the occasions, but David Barbour never came around again. Other than a brief friendly greeting at church there was nothing.

"Come on, Marcy. It's not the end of the world. There are lots of other fish in the sea," Janine told her. "There are lots of guys in the gazebo. Come on. Go with us." So Marcy suffered in silence and grieved her loss. But she went.

The group of friends from church led an active off-campus life. Robert James, the tall, brown-haired guy with the kind eyes, had a car. Usually Janine, Gloria, Jan, Harold and Marcy piled in and headed off with Robert to downtown in their saddle oxfords, or to Griffith Observatory, or Glendale, or up the coast to Malibu where the roar of the ocean surf drowned out everything else.

While they drove, they sang. Robert proved to be a live wire. He taught a song to the group. *"Hotta, hotta, choc-o-lotta, slip a dip o'whippa cream…". Again and again they sang it, laughing together over their silliness, but persisting anyway. Robert said the song had been done on the Toast of the Town TV show by the DeJohn Sisters earlier that year. It became a favorite of the friends.

Many of these excursions followed, until one evening Robert met Marcy on the Promenade. "Let's walk over to the fountain and check out Delores," he said. They arrived at the Fountain just as the devotional began.

"Be still and know that I am God, Be still and know that I am God," the students sang, blending their harmonies. *"Now let us have a little talk with Jesus, tell Him all about our troubles. Does Jesus care when my heart is pained? O yes, He cares, I know He cares."* For an hour they sang, the message of the songs soothing her painful heart.

Later Robert walked Marcy back to the dorm. "Thank you for sharing this time with me. I'd like to take you out on Friday afternoon after classes. I've rented a boat. I have a special surprise for you."

"Oh Robert! Thank you so much! Shall we take a picnic? I'll be looking forward to it." *A date will be a nice change. This guy's a lot of fun to be with. I'll work hard to get my homework finished before we go.*

Friday finally came, and Marcy found herself a bit excited, even though David Barbour was not the young man who would be escorting her. Robert showed up at the dorm about ten in the morning. "I think you'll need a hat, Marcy. It may be hot."

Marcy asked among her friends and borrowed a hat with a wide brim. Setting it on her head, she approved her image in the mirror, her shoulder length hair framing her face. "How do I look?" she asked mischievously.

"Absolutely beautiful." Robert smiled into her eyes, took her hand, and led her to his car.

"Where are we going?" She asked.

"Oh, it'll just be a short drive out Wilshire Boulevard. We'll be there in about fifteen minutes if we're lucky."

Marcy settled comfortably into the seat beside Robert, realizing she looked forward to the day with a good friend.

When Robert finally parked, Marcy could see the city ahead through breaks in the shrubbery, but she was unprepared for the beautiful sight that met her eyes as they walked around a bank of trees and shrubs into McArthur Park. She saw a shining lake ahead, surrounded by luxury hotels hugging the shoreline in the distance. They cast their reflections into the placid water. The palm trees interspersed among the buildings added their images and colors to the picture. *Perfect. I've never seen anything more beautiful. Robert's bringing me here says that he really appreciates beauty and he's giving me a gift.*

"The boat ramp is down here," Robert said, taking her hand and leading her toward the lake. She saw swans on the shore, two larger birds with five smaller ones trailing along behind, parents and babies, she supposed. *How neat to have the swans a part of our day.* They stopped to watch the busy family feeding.

"Did you know, Robert…about the swans?"

"Yes, Marcy. I wanted to share them with you. I read about them in the Los Angeles Times. The parents' names are Rudy and Susie. The babies are the first that have been hatched here for over ten years."

"How wonderful that we get to see them! Do you think they'll come into the water while we're boating? Wouldn't that be exciting?" Marcy looked around again at the placid, verdant, glistening scene. She was touched by the bounty. "Thank you, Robert."

"Let's get the boat and check it out."

Robert led her to a small row boat tied to the dock. He held her hand as she stepped in and sat in one end, and then picked up the oars, sat, and rowed a short distance into the lake, stopping among the lily-pads where they could still see the swans. "There. You have a ringside seat!"

They sat silently, drinking in the peacefulness of the scene. The swans busied themselves eating on the shore until finally one of the parent swans called the brood, and they headed for the lake. One by one they swam into the water, closer and closer to the boat, until finally Marcy could almost touch them. "What a lovely gift this day has been, Robert. Thank you for including me in it."

"I wanted to do something special for you, Marcy. When I read about the swans in the paper, I knew it had to be you I shared them with. I think you're a very lovely girl. I'd like to date you seriously."

"Oh, Robert, You're so sweet. What a beautiful day it's been. I love being with you, but let's wait a while and see whether things work out, whether we'll want to become more committed. Where's that picnic lunch? Let's eat."

And so, Marcy had changed the subject. She had not allowed Robert to express his feelings or told him she'd like to see him again. Instead she'd remembered David Barbour's dark eyes and curly hair and continued to hope for attention from that disinterested young man. It never came.

As the year progressed, she learned that her roommate, Nanette was, indeed, dating David Barbour, and in late spring she saw Nanette wearing the sparkling diamond he had given her.

Though Robert continued to be her close friend, he never again invited her for a date alone with him. Though Marcy had many days to reconsider the words she had spoken, and perhaps, wish them away, she had no opportunity to speak to him again regarding the feelings he had revealed to her.

But the day was not without reward. She had returned to the dorm with a different attitude, believing that what Robert had said was true; that she was special. She felt special. She would remember this lovely day all her life, and wonder what her life would have been had she made a different choice.

Margie's Family Begins

JUNE of 1956 found me leaving Pepperdine College after one year of study, a broken heart, and many new friends gained. I had a job and should have kept it, but I had been away from home for a year and needed to see my family. Banking on being able to get another job in Vale which would enable me to return to school in the fall, I returned home.

I was excited to be going home for another reason. Our minister in Vale was Walter A Skelton. His son, Vern, had just been discharged from military service and would be spending the summer in Vale working on the Skinner farm, and I had 'set my cap' for him. Vern stood tall at six-foot-four inches, had a warm, welcoming smile, and taught very interesting Bible classes. I considered this guy a highly desirable young man. So I returned home, and before long Vern invited me to accompany him on a trip to Fruitland, Idaho, where he would be preaching for the church. Of course I accepted the long-awaited invitation. I created a beautiful new dress for the occasion, soft yellow, fitted bodice, slightly scooped neckline. The rest is history.

(The job in Vale finally materialized, but not until August— too late to save money for school. School would have to wait, so I accepted the job and worked at the Idaho Power Company as receptionist and bookkeeper.)

Through the next year we dated, and in August of 1957, Charles LaVern Skelton (Vern) married Marjorie Laverne Vaughn in a beautiful candlelight ceremony where the groom forgot his vows and struggled to get the bride's ring on her finger.

By the time we were married, Vern had been living for some time in Spokane where he had secured a new job with the Washington State Highway Department. Because he took a few days off so we could get married, we had no time for a "honeymoon," but spent the days he had off traveling to Spokane. We loaded so many wedding gifts in Vern's brand new Hudson Rambler that we sprung the trunk when we tried to close it.

Mr. and Mrs. Skelton

Vern had secured a place for us to live: a studio apartment—no kitchen, bed in the living room arrangement. We moved in with our three electric fry pans, five casserole dishes, and our trunk-full of gifts. I did most of my cooking in an electric fry pan or on a "hot-plate," and even learned to bake a pineapple up-side-down cake in the fry pan. We didn't starve, but neither did we enjoy a large variety of food. I knew how to make All-At-Once-Spaghetti, a Hunts tomato sauce specialty recipe. That was our company dish; when paired with a green tossed salad we dined sumptuously. We entertained the Bill McCoys as our first guests. Bill and his wife Bertha were young-marrieds like ourselves, but a little further along. They already had a little boy, Mark. Bertha loved to laugh. That's why we enjoyed them so much. They did the entertaining.

Skelton Wedding, 1957

I also knew how to fry chicken, and I remember clearly the first time I did it for Vern. His first comment was, "This chicken is sure greasy." Wrong thing to say! Young cook at this point is already convinced of her inadequacy, and thus, very emotionally reactive! I cried and refused to talk to him for days.

"But I like greasy chicken. I wasn't criticizing your cooking. I thought I was saying something nice." I finally let him convince me, and forgave him.

While Vern and I lived in this studio apartment, we visited often with our landlords, Jim and Helen Taylor, who lived just downstairs. They were a Christian couple with an eight year old son, Mike. We played a lot of *Pinochle* and *Rook* together, and became very good friends in the months we lived there. Helen shared her oven generously when I asked.

"I'd like to bake Vern some cookies, Helen. Would you mind if I used your oven?" While the cookies baked, we shared our lives.

Vern and I shared the Asian Flu in that apartment, both at the same time; the achy, vomiting-variety lasted day after day, and we lay together in a double bed with a spring and mattress duo that dumped our aching bodies toward the middle. Imprisoned and suffering, we crowded helplessly against one another wondering if it would ever pass. This may be the beginning of Vern's often repeated maxim, "This too shall pass." Since we had no couch, no alternative place for either of us existed; we were too sick to sit up!

It may have been that flu that convinced us to seek another place to live. Or it could have been the discovery of our first pregnancy. We looked reluctantly, since the rental of $35.00 monthly fit our necessarily frugal budget.

Vern spent a lot of his time in those days standing on the highways flagging traffic. That first May the temperatures were in the low 100's, and he stood out on that hot asphalt eight or more hours per day! An exhausted man came home every night to an emotional expectant mother.

We looked for another apartment only to learn by trial and error that we really didn't *know* much about looking for apartments. We moved into the first place before realizing, too late, that it didn't have a sink in the bathroom. Another mistake put us in an apartment which had perhaps one electrical outlet per room. The rent got higher with each move.

Six mistakes later, we finally met Bud Fitzsimmons, a Realtor who was also a Christian. He had to do some fancy financing, and we had to make two payments every month for a year, but he did get us into a cute little house at 4223 North Calispel, not too far from where he and his wife, Joy lived. We were also within a few blocks of Walt and Margaret Fetch who had two children when we first met them, but birthed Tracy, a son, about the time our Doug was born.

Both of these families became our very close friends. With the Fetches we shared our family experience, and I, daily phone conversations with

Margaret. With the Fitzsimmons we shared a love of A Cappella hymns, spiritual songs, and singing. We joined them often in their home just to sing.

Doug, our first born, came along just twelve months after we were married, on September 5, 1958. It was during this pregnancy that I was diagnosed with Type One Diabetes. Douglas was born on my sister, Mona's birthday while Vern paced the floor of the waiting room and almost wore out the asphalt on the street just below my hospital window. Doug claimed the status of first grandchild for both sets of grandparents.

Doug and Tracy—latest son of the Fetches—were soon playing together often and becoming great playmates. All of us were so proud of him, and as he grew into a quiet, helpful, and gentle child, we gave thanks.

His brother, Gary was born on June 16, 1960, amid a great deal of worry and stress. Apparently, little Gary's body had been trying to produce enough insulin for his mom. When he was born, he had significant respiratory problems, as well as one giant insulin reaction, and his life was in danger.

I was devastated. *Look what I've done to my baby. How can I ever forgive myself?*

We feared, and the doctors warned us of the possibility that we would lose him, but God was gracious, and our second baby boy, after two weeks in Deaconess Hospital, lived; a definite answer to prayer. Gary's temperament was so different. He shook his crib, and threw his bottle; perhaps protesting his difficult beginning. As he grew he was all action and no rest, but he was well, and we were thankful.

I delighted in baking for my children and husband. While I stirred up cookies, the little ones played in the cupboard, pulling out pots, pans, and lids. They made such a lot of noise, there was no fun like the cupboards, they thought.

I made it a practice during my motherhood years to continue attending functions like our ladies' Bible classes and all the church services. I never believed that such a blessing as a child should be allowed to become an excuse for not making the effort to attend worship services. Car-seats were non-existent then. I laid my babies on the front seat beside me, or they sat beside me or they stood behind my shoulder. Thankfully we were accident-free.

Winters in Spokane were frigid with lots of snow, so I soon learned to put the shovel in the trunk before departing on my adventures. I was thankful many times for that shovel!

Well! It's time for a girl, isn't it? But when our third due date came, and our baby was of the same 'pattern' we accepted him with thanksgiving because he came without health problems.

I should mention that my pregnancy with Tim was very stressful for me. I worried that the baby I was carrying would have the same problems Gary did at birth. I spent a lot of time crying and praying. I remember reading one of Catherine Marshall's books, *Beyond Ourselves*, during that time, and that through her encouragement I gave the outcome of my pregnancy completely to God. And God was faithful. Tim came into this world a healthy baby boy. Oh, what quiet relief it is to trust in God!

Our lives continued and our children grew. We attended the North Jefferson Church of Christ, both of us teaching Bible classes and enjoying the friends we made.

We looked longingly at baby girls. The congregation was quite large, but it finally came to our attention that a couple in the congregation had adopted a baby from Korea. This is probably when the adoption option began to play in our minds. I had uncles and aunts who had birthed multiple babies of one sex in a row. Tim represented our number three, and we didn't believe it would be smart, given my health, to keep trying to get our girl.

So when the opportunity presented itself, we jumped at it. Vina Hall, a Christian lady who was ministering in the country of Laos had learned of a baby girl who needed a home and was in danger of being sold into prostitution. Vina had sent the news on to her friend, Joyce Anderson, who was a member at Jefferson Street Church of Christ. Joyce knew we wanted a baby girl and lost no time passing the news on to us.

At the time we learned of her availability for adoption, Nang Lei was three weeks old. Vina Hall did us the service of taking her into her home and caring for her about nine months while we completed all the paper work and required home-study.

During the home study, we had a close call. Gary, in first grade and in a new school, bit the teacher when she tried to pull him into an activity he was uncomfortable with. Of course the social worker learned of this and wanted to interpret it as Gary's objection to the adoption. We, knowing how eager he was for his new sister, did some very fast talking and convinced her to approve us.

We had chosen the name Barbara for our daughter, but Vina advised us to keep her Laotian name until we had her out of Laos, so she became Nang Lei Barbara. Vina sent wonderful pictures of "our" little girl and the two little girls she had adopted. We pored over the pictures and longed for the day when she could come to us.

However, in Laos, as Vina told us, they have a saying, "Bo pen yan," meaning "Tomorrow will do." Unfortunately, that philosophy didn't bode well for an efficient adoption process, but finally, when she was about ten months old, we brought our baby girl home.

The church had a missionary in the country of Thailand named Parker Henderson. Vina knew of him, and contacted him for help in bringing our little girl to us. Parker knew of a young man, Virasak Viristikul, who wanted to attend Oklahoma Christian College, but couldn't afford the airline fare. So Vina made the arrangement through Parker to have Virasak act as "nurse" to our daughter during the flight to Portland, Oregon. In return, we would pay for his airline ticket, plus an amount for a stewardess to help. Had Virisak known Nang Lei would cry nearly the whole distance, would he have agreed to help us?

We—Grandpa and Grandma Skelton, Grandma Ritchie, Helen and Lee Phillips, my brother Les, and Nang Lei Barbara's new family—met the two very weary travelers at the Portland airport in February, 1967. We were living in Vancouver by the time all the paperwork was completed and Barbara could come to us.

I felt petrified as we drove to the airport and as we walked out to the gates. For months I had been worried. I had heard of stranger anxiety. Wasn't Barbara about that age? But when I saw the tired travelers, I impulsively held out my arms, and our Barbara Lei held out her arms and came to me. I cried. What a wonderful answer to my prayer that she would know me and love me!

Her Dad tried to wait patiently for his turn to hold her, but little Barbara would not leave me. "The competition was fierce!" he later reported. Her older brothers jumped up and down in excitement, wanting to touch her.

We had a near tragedy that day at the airport. Our active little Gary's excitement caused him to forget the care needed in crossing streets, and— running excitedly—he almost ran into the path of a car. Thankfully, his Uncle Les saw him, grabbed his clothing at the last moment, and stopped his entrance into the street, preventing the tragedy.

Little Barbie, exhausted by all the changes and by her long trip, slept in my arms all the way home, and, in spite of many bedtime routines, slept on all night long. We had borrowed so much trouble, thinking she would be terribly upset by the change. Our worry was in vain.

She brought us pure uninterrupted joy. Our family doted on her, and finally had to threaten to put a sign on her: "Please don't tell me I'm cute!" Her big brothers thought she was theirs, and competed for her attention.

Barbara saw everything around her. I remember one particular trip to church when she jabbered repeatedly, pointing to an airplane flying through the sky. Could she remember that she had flown on one? She always loved to talk. Her Grandma and Grandpa Ritchie took her with them in their car and reported later that she talked to them all the way to their destination.

From the first, we took Barbara to church with us at the Andreson Road Church of Christ in Vancouver. Of course she was all eyes, loving to see all the people, and loving their attention to her. But once the services started and she had to sit quietly, everything changed. Her restlessness and impatience with that situation caused her to take many trips to the cry room with her mama.

Our little family was complete. We had our little girl and three wonderful little boys. I enjoyed being a mother, and chose not to get a job away from home. Though the children were a full time and sometimes very demanding job, I felt happy and fulfilled. I rejoiced in the children and in my wonderful, kind, non-critical husband. From this point in my life, I look back at those days and believe they were among the happiest of all.

Young Skelton Children

A Crocodile Story

OUR family's stories of misadventure would never be complete should I leave off this story, so I shall tell it, even though it leaves a lot of doubt about my sanity, my artistic ability, and my family's performing aptitudes.

The event being here recorded took place back in the late 1960's, probably about 1969. We lived in Vancouver, Washington, and worshipped regularly with the Andreson Road Church of Christ where we developed many close and lasting friendships. I mention the church, because it was a plan of the church leaders that was a cause of our downfall, but I must take the rest of the responsibility.

I was a young mother with four children and desirous of creating many happy memories and family times. I had read in numerous self-help books and magazines about the importance of family fun, and I believed we could use some. Thus, I acted upon my belief.

The church leaders announced that—in the interest of Christians having more opportunities to get to know one another—they planned a talent show. This announcement stimulated great thoughts and much consternation on my part.

I was not under the illusion that any of our family had great talent to display. I had played the trombone for eight years during my school years, but had no trombone, so that idea was dead. Vern and I had sung together with other people to make a quartet when we were going together, but I am an alto and he a bass. That is only half a quartet. Besides, I wanted our whole family to get involved and have fun doing something together. Finally I had an idea.

My children, ages about 10, 8, 6, and 2 had lots of Disney records; sound tracks of musicals that were so popular then. They—and I—played these records constantly because they stimulated and added fun to our daily lives.

On the Peter Pan record was Captain Hook's song, "You Should Never Smile at a Crocodile." Bright idea! Our family would pantomime this playful song. The four kids and their dad would have the easy parts and be the scenery. I would be Captain Hook and "sing" the song.

What gave me the idea I could keep a straight-enough face to act that song? Experience? No. Acting talent? No. Confidence? Well, I just thought I could do it.

So I got busy. The sewing machine and I were fairly good friends at this point in my life so I made vests and pirate hats for the children and a Captain Hook jacket and hat for me. Here my imagination failed me.

How would I ever create a crocodile costume? I started by buying *lots* of very green fabric.

I must confess that I started cutting and sewing before I did my crocodile research.

I sewed lots of huge *dragon* zigzags into the fabric to run up the spine of the wearer who was to be my husband, Vern. I fit a long tubular body onto the zigzags, fit it to the potential wearer—maybe he didn't know he was performing until the last moment, or maybe he actually trusted me in those days.

I still needed a crocodile head—Remember that the creator of all this is just a grown up version of that fifth grader who dissolved in tears over her sadly inadequate version of the Trojan Horse—My crocodile head started as a brown grocery bag, was painted green with tempera paint, and given slits for the eyes. I hoped 'the crocodile' would be able to see. As it turned out, this version of a crocodile head was sadly inadequate, too.

The night of the "talent" show came. After a hasty afternoon practice together as a family and many protestations from that reluctant and demurring crocodile, we made the trip to the church and awaited our turn in the limelight.

Sadly enough, our turn did come, and we gathered on-stage and started the music. But, hardly had "Captain Hook" begun his song when the crocodile—badly blinded by the fact that his glasses could not perform their duty through the slits in the 'baggy' face and further hampered by his cumbersome costume—was stepping on the pirates.

Captain Hook, badly distracted by all the unexpected happenings, had lost the story of the crocodile's smile, and the music played on and on, leaving him and the pirates behind.

I won't say at *that* moment I felt amused, but the laughs we as a family have shared in the retelling have been numerous and restorative. I doubt *I* would ever do it again, and I know at least one crocodile that's fed up with performing. *Forever!*

Dad and the Broiler Pan

UNHAPPY day it is when the head cook gets sick and Dad has to step in!! This memorable event in our family happened in Chehalis, Washington on a Sunday afternoon.

It had been Margie's habit to prepare Sunday dinner before driving to Centralia for the church service. The choice for Sunday dinner was usually a beef roast with potatoes, carrots, and onions cooked along-side.

On the particular Sunday under discussion, Margie chose to vary the menu and broil steaks after our return. Unfortunately, she was seized by an unexpected illness, and upon our arrival at home, went to her bed, first giving brief, hasty instructions to Dad for broiling meat. Margie rested on her bed, blissfully unaware of the cooking methods being utilized in her beautiful kitchen.

Dad, who had no previous experience with broiler pans or much of anything else related to cooking, correctly placed the steaks on the slotted lid of the pan. He then placed the lid on the top rack of the oven, and the pan on the shelf below, directly under the lid holding the steaks, he thought. He turned the oven on broil and cooked the steaks, feeling very pleased with himself. He sat the children down to dinner and joined them in consuming the steaks of his labors. Then he felt free to pursue his ever-present work diaries.

Upon Margie's eventual return to the kitchen, her eyes fell upon many unfinished chores, but none could equal what she found when she looked in the oven for the broiler pan. White congealed fat hung in profusion from the top rack to the broiler pan below, and where the descending fat had completely missed the pan it fell all the way to the floor of the oven. In all her history of messes, the one she faced was the worst.

She thought twice before ever getting sick again.

The Santa Claus Gifts

WHEN money is a little shorter than the month and the shopper just a little more than exhausted strange gifts can appear under the tree.

One Christmas season, inspired by an idea for "Santa Claus Gifts"—or gifts you would hate to give if anyone knew you gave them—I came upon some decals in the Woman's Day magazine. Being the mother of three teen-aged sons and having an overly serious husband—sometimes at least—the thought which came to me was more than I could resist.

After a trip to the bedroom bureau drawer yielded a clean pair of under-shorts for each son and one for their father, I got out my iron and 'branded' those shorts with beautiful poinsettia decals.

After wrapping the creations carefully and labeling them "From Santa Claus," I placed them innocently under the tree in a stack to be delivered simultaneously to all.

What a wonderful bedlam and turmoil of anguish, horror, embarrass-ment, and glee—mine—when all opened their "Santa Claus Gifts!!"

My second son expressed it all perfectly: "Mom, You've ruined a perfectly good pair of shorts!!"

Funny. I don't remember those shorts ever seeing the light of day again.

The "I Don't Feel So Good" Sunday

As the parents of teenagers in the late 1970's we had some rules. One of those rules was—in my husband, Vern's words—"As long as you put your feet under my table you will attend church." Though occasionally meeting with some resistance, compliance was definitely the easiest habit for our kids to form.

As with most rules, though, even this one was made to be broken, at least in the eyes of our second son.

One Sunday morning that second son said, "Mom, I just don't feel so good." Unsuspecting mom replied, "Then perhaps you should stay home. But if you're sick you need to stay in bed!"

So the family departed without second son, drove the considerable distance to Centralia, enjoyed the Bible classes and the worship service, and returned home.

All looked normal....except...wait! The second car, our old Plymouth was missing from the driveway!! We must look into this!!

Upon entering our home we found sixteen-year-old Gary, but he was not resting. He sat dejectedly on the edge of his bed, his eyes downcast, his chin hanging. Upon questioning him, the truth came out: He had taken the car and driven it along an old road that left our cul- de- sac, circled through the woods and came back out near our house. The guilt-ridden car —or perhaps the driver–– managed to stall in the woods on that rainy, rainy day, trapping young second son in his attempt to deceive. Not knowing how to repair the car, he was forced to confess his perfidy.

The result? Suffice it to say, one very chastened and smarter young man. There are other chastisements than conscience. Whether he partook of another I leave to him and his father to tell.

Turkey Drumstick Disaster

IN 1976 we made another of our moves, this time to Chehalis. Our new house was close to woodlands and had a beautiful U-shaped kitchen. Payments were higher, and our first son, Doug had just gone away to college. Bills were everywhere!

Some of my money saving meals began with turkey drumsticks. They could usually be purchased for under a dollar a pound. I first stewed them, and then prepared them in various ways. The meal might be turkey and dumplings, turkey grape salad, turkey tortillas, or soup. The following calamity befell my dinner preparations one day.

I had recently started working for the Lewis County Assessor's Office. My job entailed a lot of detail and required deep concentration. I picked up the property deeds from the County Auditor's office, got out appropriate plat maps, interpreted the legal descriptions—sometimes struggling to understand them—penciled in the new owner's name, located the correct record book and recorded the details there. I was also responsible to greet taxpayers who came in with questions and to help them or refer them to the correct department. It was hard work, and though I worked only afternoons, I typically came home exhausted.

I always liked to do at least a little of the cooking before I went to work. So on this particular day I put some turkey legs on the burner to cook. I wanted to bring them to a boil before I left, and since I was running late, I turned the burner on high. Several distractions later I left for work feeling great satisfaction because I had started preparing the meat for dinner. I did not realize my mistake. I had not turned the burner down under the turkey legs.

The kids got home before I did, and I soon received a frantic call that interrupted my struggle with a difficult property description. "Mom, when we got home smoke was coming out the windows, and when we opened the door, the whole house was full of smoke. It stinks!"

"Turn off the burner! Don't touch anything else! Go outside and wait for me. I'm coming right home."

I dropped everything and started for home, remorsefully realizing now what I should have remembered when I was leaving home.

The Skelton Family. Back Row, Left to Right: Gary, Vern, Tim, Doug. Front Row, Left to Right: Barbara, Marjorie

Somehow I managed to get there safely. When I drove into our cul-de-sac a horrible stench filled the air. Regret and embarrassment erased what was left of my composure. What must the neighbors think? They couldn't help knowing what was going on.

What a gut-racking attack to the senses greeted me as I walked in the door! Smoke filled every nook and crevice of our home. A horrible overpowering stench assaulted my nostrils. What a revolting sight! On the front burner of the stove sat what used to be a stainless steel sauce pan. Inside it the turkey legs—bones and all— had become forever a part of their container.

Thank God for Home-owner's insurance! We called a company named Service Master. The walls and ceilings had to be washed and repainted. The carpet and floors had to be cleaned. Windows needed washing. They even attempted to clean the air. When all this was done, the odor remained. "The odor should disperse gradually," the foreman said. Disbelieving, I watched the cleaning crew drive away, my stomach churning. I started washing clothes and blankets.

The time for the kids to go back to school came. Apparently, as fate would have it, Barbara picked out clothing that hadn't been washed. She came home complaining. "No one would sit by me, Mom. They told me I stink!"

Of course, Barbara gave full credit to her mom! I'm sure neither of us ever lived free of stink in the memories of those kids at school again!

We finally, however, did eliminate the stubborn odor from our home. Amway had some wonderful little lemon-scented air cleaner fans. We used several of those, and extinguished every last bit of that smell. All that was left was one very chastened and more learned cook.

Imperfect Angel

The "Great Green House" refers to a ceramics supply store which sells "green ware," but is not the actual name of the store. "Green ware" is molded and solid in form but still unpainted and unfired. It is extremely fragile.

This is a story about two lives, two sisters, Margie and Mona; two angels, Tootie and Fluttie; imperfection, and love. It is a story about the love of sisters and the love of God.

MONA and Margie enjoyed several special days together in October, 1988, when Margie paid a long-awaited visit to her sister. The amount of time they could spend together had diminished over the years while they raised their children. Parenthood demanded a lot of time and money. Now that the children were grown the sisters could, at last, indulge in this visit even though many miles separated them.

During their latest visit they had gone shopping in Salem, Oregon, where Mona lived. Mona, being the guide on this trip, had led them to "The Great Green House," a supply store for artists involved in ceramics. Mona was one of those artists. There they had found Tootie and her twin sister, Fluttie, beautiful little angel sisters who, though they were unfinished, were busy praising God, and the shoppers brought them home to Mona's house.

The angel sisters had expected to become instantly beautiful when they left the "Great Green House." Instead, they waited in a box in Mona's dark basement with other green ones like themselves, longing for Mona's attention—they had been chosen to live at Margie's house a long time ago when

Margie discovered them at the ceramics supply store. Destiny had imprisoned them in that store until someone fell in love with them. That someone was Margie on that long-ago visit. Now they found themselves waiting again.

The long years went by, and a flood came into the basement. Tootie crushed her toe accidentally, and got wet, and broke her beautiful trumpet. She couldn't seem to do anything right, and she looked so pathetic that Mona felt frustrated and delayed the restorative work over and over again, saying, "This isn't the right time." Sad as that made Tootie, she didn't give up hope but waited patiently for her restoration. She hopefully expected that someday she would again make beautiful music on her trumpet.

During Margie's October 1988 visit with Mona, the sisters re-discovered Tootie and Fluttie waiting patiently for their beautification, and those who found them loved them. Tootie thought *she* might be ignored because of her imperfections, but even she escaped the dark box and found herself in Mona's hands waiting for restoration.

Margie, the novice in ceramics, worked on Fluttie, the perfect little flute-playing angel, giving her blonde hair, a beautiful light blue dress, and white wings. Mona, the most-skilled in ceramics, assumed the intricate care Tootie needed.

"Margie, we can put Tootie's trumpet like this," and Mona showed Margie how the straight trumpet would look, "or we can make it bent, like this."

Suddenly Margie realized Tootie *must* have a bent trumpet. Her own life seemed such a failure. She struggled in her relationship with her husband who was precious to her, but non-communicative. She had failed to bridge the chasm between them in all the years they'd shared, and the ravine between only grew deeper. She and Mona had been talking about life's challenges and God's love, and Margie now saw the meaning of all that had been said...for her own life.

"Her trumpet should be bent, like my life," she said. "She will be like me, imperfect, but still loved."

Many hours of planning, laughing, crying, and sharing followed. Lo and behold, when those hours ended, Tootie's shoes were repaired, and her horn, though bent, still made beautiful music, for she knew she was loved even though she would never be perfect.

Mona lavished many more hours of tender care upon this not-so-perfect angel long after Margie had gone home, and by Thanksgiving Day Tootie was ready to travel to Margie's house to receive her adoption and to see Fluttie whom she hadn't seen for such a long time. She knew that her mission in life would always be to bring hope to all those mortals who, being so conscious of their imperfections, are tempted to give up hope of attaining their Heavenly Home.

Because of the love she has been shown, Tootie will never cease to play her encouragement to all who will take time to hear. Every Christmas she will join Margie's host of angels rejoicing over the love that has been poured out for mankind.

She will always remember those long years when she waited, doubting that anyone still loved her, and she will know that she was wrong to doubt. She will remember the joy of being discovered in that lonely black box and chosen to receive the artist's careful love and attention. She will know that all the waiting was not in vain, for she rejoices in her new home. And most of all, she will remember that not only the perfect are chosen, but also those who *long* to be beautiful for the Master.

Balloons the Colors of Happy

THE phone rang in our home in Washington State where we had lived for about six years. My husband who was doing some "temporary" work on the east side of the state was on the line.

"They need me over here, he said. "I'll be starting work permanently here next week."

In total shock I saw all our dreams for our much loved home shattered. "But you promised we'd stay here! When we bought this house and all your rhododendrons you said we wouldn't move again."

Suddenly frosty, his voice interrupted me. "I work for the State of Washington. The economy and the State's early retirement option have created vacancies that must be filled. Those of us who are still working have to fill them."

What could I say? No apology for his broken promise followed his pronouncement of plans for our family. We were moving again, leaving our church and all our friends, leaving the home where we had allowed ourselves to put down deeper roots. Just as the rhododendrons were later uprooted, we were torn again from our environment of love and put into a strange community where we knew no one. We were able to survive these moves mostly because of our church family which always welcomed us in. It was not so easy for our daughter.

"Dad, I don't want to move. My friends are all here. It's my senior year. I'll miss out on all the fun if we move because I won't have friends there!"

"It's decided. You'll make new friends. Now, that's enough!"

In February of her senior year we left our lives in that home behind. We bought a house on the east side of Wenatchee and registered our daughter at the high school.

Barb met a girl her age in Youth Group at church; Sherry became her companion at school, but the friendship proved uncomfortable for Barb. "She flirts with every boy she sees. She embarrasses me." Other friendships came, but slowly. Barb ignored the ball games and other school activities, not feeling a part of the school, and chose to spend her time with a boy, a friend from church too old to be a member of the student body at the high school.

Barbara and Marjorie at Mother's Tea

When she brought home an invitation to the Mother-Daughter Tea, I insisted we go.

"I don't really see any reason to go, Mom. There's no one who will miss me."

"Honey," I said, "This is a chance for you and I to do something fun together. I'd like you to take me."

"It'll be boring, Mom, just drinking tea and eating cookies we don't need. It won't be fun for me."

"Darling, please do this for me," I said. "I'd like the memory."

The memory is a picture. My daughter is standing. She has Asian skin coloring and beautiful black, longer than shoulder-length hair, softly waving around her face. I am sitting close to her wearing a corsage presented to me as a guest of honor. Both of us wear smiles pasted on at the last minute for the photographer. He has surrounded us with balloons the colors of happy. But we were not happy that day. Amidst the sounds of laughter, cheerful voices, soft music, and the clatter of dishes, we were silent.

When I see the picture I want to cry; cry for my daughter's unhappiness during her senior year, cry for the lost opportunity to be happy together; cry for the barriers between us then, cry for the pain that lay ahead.

There is, too, much to rejoice in. Though Barbara spent several years in prison, it was a healing time for her and a building time for our relationship. Her release over two years ago became a new beginning for her life.

Incriminating Attentions

OUR relationship began in the farming community of Vale, Oregon the year I left Pepperdine College. We first met at the Vale Church of Christ.

A tall, handsome young man stood before me, looking slightly unfinished. Sleeves of his blue plaid shirt ended above knobby wrists; shirttail, skimpy for his height, dangled partially outside his pants' waist; his jeans stopped above ankles sporting green socks inside well-used tennis shoes. His legs, astonishingly short for his long torso and 6'4" frame, contributed to a lumbering gait a little like an ox. His brown straight hair fell across his scalp and drooped over his left forehead. The smile on his lips sparkled in his brown eyes imprisoned under wire-rimmed glasses resting on a wide nose.

His unpolished appearance did not discourage my interest in the tall, intelligent, young man with the friendly smile. Drawn by his spiritual qualities, ability to teach Bible classes, and deep bass voice, I dated him. That unpolished farm boy "cleaned up nicely." Following his proposal of marriage and my acceptance, Vern secured a job in Washington State, and left for Spokane, seriously abbreviating our opportunity to know one another. We married the next year.

Lack of time together during our engagement deprived us of knowledge we needed for decisions about marriage. We learned after our wedding how different we were, and how difficult our time together would be. My birth family was emotionally expressive; his was dominated by a father who permitted no emotional expression, by children, or wife.

Our expectations were very different, I wanting an emotionally intimate relationship, he a quiet, non-demanding one. When a problem arose,

I wanted to talk, he, to avoid. He retreated to his car and went exploring, leaving me, frustrated and angry, at home. Since insecurity was one trait we shared, this lack of resolution troubled both of us greatly.

By taking correspondence courses and night school classes, Vern demonstrated his industrious spirit and completed his engineering degree, adding to his Bachelor's degree from Abilene Christian College. At the Washington Department of Highways he graduated to supervisory and management positions.

My husband proved responsible and dependable, both as provider, and employee. He possessed a kind and thoughtful habit, never too proud to help wash dishes,

"Just don't ask me to cook!" he said. In his younger days, when he had to prepare his own meals, he lived on scrambled eggs, and was once caught trying to cut a cantaloupe with a razor blade!

I loved being Vern's wife. I was always proud to sit by his side hearing him sing, admiring his Bible teaching, or enjoying his great sense of humor, but our inability to problem-solve drained our relationship and bred resentments in him. He had been trained to bottle-up his emotions. Bitterness grew, dominated his spirit and stole his joy in our relationship. He escaped our troubled marriage by devoting more hours to his job, robbing his family of his presence.

***

From my kitchen window I watched my husband as he came home. I noticed his gait, lumbering and tired. I saw his face, eyes lowered, mouth crimped in a straight tight line, brow furrowed with cares I could vividly imagine. Things had not been going well in our marriage. Good intentions often resulted in misunderstandings and hurt feelings. Tonight, I thought, I have to do something to encourage us.

Dinner waited: roasted chicken, baked potatoes, green tossed salad, and a mixed fruit dessert; I hoped Vern would enjoy the meal and our time together.

Early this Friday morning I had been happy, knowing that he would be home tomorrow.

I had found him sitting in his chair, reading the Wenatchee World. I asked if I could sit in his lap, and he made room for me. I sat down, hoping for love and attention. He riveted his attention on the TV, gave no hug or smile to welcome me, leaving me devastated. I missed the smile, remembering how it had sparkled in his eyes as he gladly received me into his life so many years ago. Things had gone horribly wrong between us these last years.

"Can't you put your paper away and look at me?" I hinted. My overture was ignored. I saw him clench his jaw, and suddenly felt unreasonably angry. I struggled to stand, and rushed away from him, feeling rejected, unloved, and neglected.

This evening I had to try again.

"Tell me about your day," I invited as we sat at dinner.

"Oh, not much happened. I've been studying the plans for the new bridge over the Columbia. It's to be built in twenty years or so." We visited about the bridge.

"How are you feeling tonight?" I asked, hoping he would share his heart with me.

"Okay," he replied.

"I have an idea that I think might make both of us feel better," I said, knowing that the conversation was ending.

"What?" He asked, peering doubtfully at me.

"We've been having a hard time recently," I began. "I would like to be able to please you, and thought if you would write down five ways I could show my love to you, it would help me."

"No. I don't want to do that. I would be sorry in the end." His face was stony and cold.

"Not if you express your requests positively," I pleaded.

Irritably he grabbed a tablet that lay next to him, and proceeded to write quickly, and angrily.

When he had finished, I heard, "There, I did it! And now I'm going to tear it up and throw it away. It's not productive."

Unwelcome feelings assaulted me: Insulted. He had chosen to make something negative from a positive effort. *He is determined to throw roadblocks in front of my attempts to improve our relationship.* He looked at me with eyes of distrust rather than love. *He is unreasonable and unforgiving. He is unkind and selfish. It all feels so hopeless*!

"Father, You can look down and see my heart, and Vern's. You know my grief and my anger, my hurts and my emptiness. You know his frustrations and disappointments. You, the epitome of Love, love both of us with an understanding and patient love. Comfort us both right now. Give us wisdom.

I spent some of the most rewarding, and most miserable years of my life with this man who is the father of my children. He gave me life's greatest gifts in them.

A Letter, April 17, 1992

DEAREST, I am truly sorry for all the unease and discomfort I have brought into your life. You have been the center of my life for so many years. All my joys and sorrows have revolved around you. It grieves me greatly that I have brought so much pain to the one to whom I wished to bring so much joy. If I could erase it all, I would, but it is there, between us, ruining the joy we should have in one another, destroying the spontaneity of the relationship we once had. I can only ask your forgiveness.

I am thankful to God and to you that you have finally expressed your feelings. I have never viewed myself as a person with a bad temper, but I am trying to look at that possibility. It is difficult. The times when I have lost control have come from so much pain that it is hard to be objective in looking at it. But with God's help I will look at the possibility you suggested. I am sorry for my initial defensiveness. That, too, I must unlearn.

I am sorry, too, for communicating to you in ineffective ways, ways that caused you to feel put down, or talked down to. That is never my desire, only a bungled attempt to share my opinions and feelings with you. I am sorry for making you feel "lectured," or "corrected" or not listened to. I am working hard to learn better ways of communicating. I can't do it without your feedback.

I know I am not the authority on anything, and I am sorry if it feels uncomfortable to you when I express my opinion. Please forgive me for the mistakes I have made in the past, and those I may make in the future. I am trying to change, but the change won't be an overnight one. Please help me.

Life is difficult in this place we are in. It is difficult enough when two people who love each other are sharing the problems and working through them together. Going it alone is very much more painful. I pray that you will choose to forgive me, and work on our marriage with me. If not, I will find reason for living, difficult though that may be.

You are my husband, and I am committed to being your wife and trying to make you happy. Please forgive me for not being perfect. God is perfect. Man is only an imperfection at best.

I want your love and commitment to me. I know from my feelings that you are not feeling love for me right now, that the road ahead looks bleak, and rather hopeless. I pray that you will lean hard on One Who's strength is perfect when our strength is gone; the One Who will carry us when we can't carry on; the One Who can strengthen our weakness. I pray that you will, through Him, find the strength and desire to renew your commitment to love me in sickness and in health, for better or for worse.

If you will make that commitment and take that risk, I can promise you that through God's power working in us both, turning our weaknesses into strength, the end of our marriage can be better than the beginning.

Always,

Margie

Author Note: *Though Vern proved unwilling to make the asked-for commitment, and though our marriage ended in 1994 after thirty seven years, we have both taken the path of forgiveness and are trying to forget the pain we caused one another. We enjoy one another's company at family holiday occasions, thus trying to make our children's lives easier.*

Vern remarried in late 1994 or early in 1995. I married my husband, Clio on Thanksgiving Day, 1996.

PART FOUR

Grandchildren

Memories from Grandma's Bear Hug Journal

YOU, my grandchildren— who are no longer children— are so very precious to me. I feel that somehow you have grown up without us really knowing one another, and that grieves me greatly. I'm so sorry to have let so many years go by without knowing you better. I'm not sure why, or what happened to all the birthdays I would have loved to share, and didn't.

I want to share memories in this writing. I've forgotten so much of what happened, and am very thankful for the memory-jogging clues I left in such places as journals. If I've forgotten something that you remember be sure and remind me about it.

Phil, you were our very first grandchild, both in the Skelton family and the Vaughn family. We were so excited by your arrival. Your folks made a trip to Chehalis for Christmas that year to introduce us. Of course they had shared lots of pictures *before* Christmas! Your Grandpa and Grandma hugged you as much as they possibly could. You were the best Christmas present of all.

It wasn't too long before we couldn't stand it any more and made a trip to Southern California to visit you. By the time we could come you had grown into a little boy. You were fascinated by Grandpa's shoes. I remember you constantly put your little feet into them and tried to walk. Not much success there but right away you showed us you had big dreams.

Joshua, you came next in April of 1986. Your Grandpa and I lived in Wenatchee by then. He had climbed the job ladder and now functioned as a supervisor and manager. I had taken a real estate class fearing that when

Barbara left home I would find myself at loose ends, so I was working, too. You arrived in April, our second grandson, and before we knew it we had *four* grandchildren. Kristine came along May 5 just one month after your birth, and Ashton followed on May 17th. We traveled to Texas to meet you when you were about a month old and Kristine was brand new, and had probably just returned home when Ashton came along.

I feel many regrets as I write this, and one of them is that we didn't get to welcome Ashton and Jeremy and Kayla into the world as soon as we would have liked to. And Ashton, you were born right here in Washington! In another world we'd have enough money, enough time and enough energy to do all the things we wanted to do. Never doubt that we were delighted to have our second granddaughter! The same goes for our third and fourth grandsons, you Jeremy and Mitch, and our third granddaughter, you, Kayla.

Kristine, I don't think you remember this, but when you were about eight months old your parents lived with us in Wenatchee—right after they graduated from ACU while your Dad was looking for his job, about eighteen months, I think—This was before Mitch came along. I enjoyed having your family there so much. You loved to play with the hose while I was gardening. You would imitate what you saw me doing, for instance watering the half-barrel of flowers I had on the corner of the patio. You've probably seen the picture of you and the upside-down watering pot. It never fails to make me smile.

I never tired of watching you eat. Do you remember the pictures of you eating the roasting ears? You attacked that ear of corn in every conceivable way, and from every direction. And spaghetti! Wow!—More smiles!—There wasn't a clean spot left on your face.

You loved rhubarb, too. Even though it was so sour, you would suck on it for hours. Remember the picture where you are standing in the rhubarb plant? Never too much of a good thing!

I'm not so sure your parents enjoyed that time in Wenatchee. Though we had a full carpeted basement for them to live in, we had no furniture; there was no chest of drawers for clothing, no chairs. There were plenty of comfortable beds for your family. It was warm and dry, and we had plenty of food, but that comprised about all the amenities. Kristine, your mom tried to keep the clothing organized, but you were an enthusiastic dis-organizer in those days. Your parents could never find anything. Your grandparents couldn't even *think* about buying furniture. I know your parents were so relieved when your Dad was hired at Boeing and you could get your own place to live—with furniture!

More Memories June 1992

KRISTINE and I read about *Lyle's Birthday Party* and colored pictures together. As I colored my picture of a little girl with an umbrella walking in the rain, I sang a song: Just Walkin' in the Rain. Later I heard her singing it, and came in to peek over her shoulder. She was looking at my picture. I told her to remember how much Grandma loved her when she sees the picture. Do you remember, Kristine?

Later, Kristine brought a small pamphlet of religious poetry to me and wanted me to read it to her. I read one or two poems and put it down, thinking it was too "old" for her. She said, "Read the rest." This happened several times. I was afraid I would bore her. She definitely *wasn't* bored. Do we have a Budding Young Poet here?

Mitch was a joy, but still a little bashful with Grandma. It was such fun to watch him and all the others paddling around in Barb's swimming pool. Mitch almost fell asleep in the water, but wouldn't let us take him out. Grandma and Mom were watching him "like hawks."

One other time, Mitch, your family was at our house in Wenatchee. Your mother was helping me in the kitchen. We had a small bathroom just off the kitchen, and you ventured far enough from your mom to go in there. I had stored some Comet in the lower cupboard, not accustomed to having babies around. You got Comet in your eyes. Your mother and I held you over the kitchen sink and rinsed your eyes for a long time. You screamed on and on. I felt so guilty for leaving the Comet where you might get it! I hope you never had any bad effects from that accident.

A more pleasant memory for you will be all the times we made home made iced cream. I had a freezer in those days, and I used it often in the summertime. One of my favorite pictures of you, Mitch, is of you sitting on the counter with an eager look on your face while I made iced cream. More smiles! I wonder where that freezer is!

Phil and Ashton, do you remember the time we roller skated down by the Columbia River in Wenatchee? Many preparations went into that.

First I went to a sports store and checked into roller blades which I knew nothing about. I tried a pair on and then tried to skate on them. The young ladies in the store didn't quite know what to do with the older lady that insisted on doing something she'd never done—right there in their store. I wobbled from the back of the store to the front, one of them on each side of me, and then decided I'd better stick with the kind of roller skates I was familiar with. Besides, they wanted about $90.00 for those roller blades. Then they tried to sell me wrist guards, ankle guards, and knee guards. Turns out that what I needed when I started to skate was a head guard. I remember several hard falls when I started skating again—at the skating rink on *their* skates—I banged my head on the floor at the rink several times. Were you ever there when that happened? It's nice I survived that! Anyway, I remember the skating at the Columbia Riverside Park with much pleasure. We had a lot of fun.

You will probably both remember the St. Patrick's Day your family spent at our house in Wenatchee. I remember that we sure had a lot of green food for breakfast. The cooks thought they were surprising each other. I sneakily made green oatmeal and green muffins. Many voices protested when I put them on the table. Then I got the milk out of the refrigerator and started to pour it on someone's cereal. The milk was green, too! Surprise! The joke is on me now. I think Phil and Ashton have a very sneaky mother! What fun we had.

***

Remember the woodchucks down by the river, and how we visited them and even fed them?—Kristine, you loved them, and weren't even afraid— Joshua, you and Jeremy, were present for that outing. Kayla, you were just a baby, then. I remember you lying on the floor by the dining room table wrapped in a blanket, and sleeping, or peering out to see what was going on.

Do you all remember the Christmas when we made our individual gingerbread houses? As I remember it, all the girls were into being creative and all the boys wanted to *eat* the shingles and trees, and wreaths—candy—that should be going on the houses. Even Moms and Dads got into the action.

No one wanted to take their houses home, so I took them all. A friend of mine came over to my house and we finished decorating all those minimally decorated houses. I kept them for years. In January when I went to Texas to see my Texas grandchildren I took a kit and we made a *big* house together. What did you kids do with it? I'll bet I can figure it out.

Mitch and Kristine, you came to visit me quite often in Kent, and every Christmas when the gingerbread houses were out I noticed a bit more of the candy disappearing. I smiled and hoped you enjoyed it. I finally threw the houses away when the graham crackers started disintegrating. But I *didn't* throw away the memories!

***

Then there was the Christmas, maybe the same one, when I spent Christmas Eve with Phillip and Ashton. We made Macaroni Angels together. We got into the 'recycle' box and played, making trucks and things out of toilet paper rolls, film cartridges, small boxes, whatever we could find. When you finished with your truck, Ashton, it had eyes and nose and a bow on its ear! I hope you kept it!

We made Macaroni Angels at your house, too, Kristine and Mitch. That same Christmas I played Santa's elf at your house and helped wrap all your Christmas gifts. I even took a bite out of Santa's cookie, privileged character that I am. Bet you didn't know that!

I remember one day that Ashton's Mom brought her part-way down to my house in Kent; I drove north and she drove south and we met. Ashton came home with me. Kristine and Mitch came over, too. We spent the day scrap booking. Mitch, you weren't particularly interested in scrap booking, but you were a good sport, and helped *me* make a page. Ashton and Kristine jumped right in and each did their own creative pages. Ashton, I got such a kick out of your page, the spray can, and all. And Kristine, as usual, you displayed your artistic bent. I enjoyed so much getting to see what your imaginations created. That was probably about 1995.

Another thing we did together in Kent—probably another time—was Dough Art. Do you remember making names and flowers and worms and all kinds of imagined creatures with me? Then we baked them in the oven. I think you all *ate* yours. I made the word "Peace" with two little birds sitting on it. I saved it as a memory of our day. It fell off the wall and broke several months ago. That made me so sad.

Ashton and Kristine also made greeting cards with me, and turned out some pretty great cards. We recycled old cards, and used waxed paper and my iron to make them pretty fancy. Remember? I still have a huge box of old greeting cards and the directions. Want to do it again?

I so wish you, Josh, Jeremy, and Kayla, could have been here for *all* of these activities, but we've had some of our own times together. I'll share some memories I jotted into my journal. I hope you enjoy reading them.

Visit With the Texas Grandchildren: 1-8-92

FIRST Day: Today I enjoyed lots of frustration trying to find things—your mom was at work—but that frustration was definitely overshadowed by the time spent making macaroni "angels" with my grandchildren, Jeremy, Kayla, and Josh. The angels are very different, but charming. We did lots of improvising as I began to run out of supplies. The walnut head I had planned on substituting definitely was *not* angel material! It ended up as a wrinkled old lady. She will be Claire's treasure.

I have enjoyed the children!

Tuesday: Thank you, Father, for all the good visiting time with Verlin. After one cancelled flight and a disappointing trip to the airport, we finally got him collected. It means so much to have him come and visit me, especially at this time. He borrowed the money from Everett., and looked for ways to give it away all the time he was here—having Claire pick up a bottle of Tums and not taking back the change, well over $15.00; taking us out to have hamburgers after church; the vanilla bean ice cream he was so crazy about couldn't be distinguished from any other vanilla ice cream; the $20.00 he gave me to buy Tim and Claire a wastebasket for the kitchen. Thank you, Father, for the family you have given me.

The grandchildren are so special. Yesterday we "played" for a little while, making puppets out of paper bags. We used buttons and lace trim, and fringe and magic markers. Grandma had a good time, and I think the children did, too.

I want to try to take the best advantage of the time I have with them. I want to make memories. Perhaps today we can have fun with bread dough; we'll bake their names and make bunnies and bears. *Father, Help me to be creative and fun to be with. Help me not to be frustrated over all the trouble I have finding things, but to laugh. Help us make the most of each moment in this day and live the moments in view of eternity.*

The children and I created a "Stuff Box" from a very nice Cheetos box that had out-lived its first purpose. You can do wonders with tempera paint, glue, fringe, and buttons. Sorry I don't remember the details any more. It's 2006 now!

Friday, 1-15-1992: Today I go home, Father. The dough "names" turned into bunnies, bears, beavers and frogs. Jeremy couldn't wait to begin. Kayla watched for some time before she was willing to put butter all over her hands and get involved, and Joshua, who *"hates butter"* would not consent to have it on his hands. He said he would put *oil* on his hands, but *"not butter!"* The oil we just couldn't find, so Josh became purely a watcher on this project.

We got the wastebasket bought: a great big tub with a lid. It works great. The $20.00 also bought a laundry basket, a replacement pitcher for the one without a handle, and a set of Rubbermaid storage bowls, all in powder blue or various shades thereof.

We also bought white T-shirts, and yesterday we decorated personal T-shirts for each one of the kids. We even remembered to take pictures to save the memories. *Father, Thank you so much for this time I could spend loving my grandchildren.* Thank you, Texans, for the pictures. Your mom must have framed them for me. In the picture you kids wore the T-shirts we painted, and the frame said "I love you, Grandma." That picture has been in front of me at the kitchen sink for all these years.

January 4, 1993

AN unexpected invitation came inviting me to Texas to "baby-sit" while Claire starts her new job. Fees will be paid by my dear son and his wife. With difficulty I turned loose of the real estate business and went, bearing with me lots of ways to play with the kids—Remember, I brought a gingerbread house kit, and we made it together?

On January 16 and 27 I had visits with my grandchildren on the phone. Kayla told me both times "I have a new Leo the Lion—our previous gift to her—Jeremy said he didn't miss me, but Claire said he is asking when they can move closer. Josh is still very immersed in the Nintendo. It was a challenge to get any of them away to come and talk to me.

You don't remember this, Josh, but this grandma spent some time holding and loving on you right after you were born. Grandpa and I came to Texas just to meet you. That experience gave us a special bond. I thought, and still do think, that you are pretty special.

Josh, Jeremy, and Kayla, I wish you could have been here for all the times the others were with me, and at the same time wish Phil, Ashton, Kristine, and Mitch could have shared the times we had together in Texas. I realize how blessed we were to have each one of those times.

I never knew my Grandparents. Grandpa Vaughn lived close in Vale for a short time, and then moved away to Oklahoma. I never saw him again. I met my Kilpatrick grandparents when they were very old when we went for a short visit to California. From my cousins who lived near them I heard stories about how Grandma Kilpatrick made each one of her grandchildren feel that they were her very special grandchild. It sounds like they were wonderful grandparents.

JANUARY 4, 1993

I'm so thankful

for all the times
I've been able
to be with you.

I just, somehow,
thought there would
be more of them.

July 4, 1993

I visited with Doug and Gary's families, and then brought Kristine and Ashton home with me: We ate at Burger King, went to Century Twenty One and did "floor time," went roller skating down at River Park, went home and played in the sprinklers, went swimming at "Auntie Barb's" house, watched "Snow White and the Seven Dwarfs, went to church, and made homemade iced cream. What a busy day we had! In the evening when you got lonely, we cried together. Gary and Suzy came to retrieve you, my lonely little granddaughters. I felt very disappointed that you didn't know me well enough to feel safe.

I wish there were more entries in my journal, and more memories. Each of you is an adult now, and is busy with your own schooling, job, and friendships. I think of you all a lot, hoping that there will be more times we can share. That means I am hoping you will make time to come and see me. My door is *always* open. Kayla, you and I have a *lot* of getting acquainted to do. I have really missed the contact with my Texan grandchildren so much.

I have been doing a lot of writing since October of 2003. The family reunion in Albuerquerque got me started. Most of the writing has something to do with family. I am trying to leave some ways for all of you to know me and the family better. I hope you will want to read what I have written, and hope it will fill in some of the holes in our relationships. I am also hoping we can spend a good bit of time together in the next short years while I am able to do some things with you.

Goodbye for now. Please know that I am always loving and being interested in you. I don't always get done all that I want to do for you, for many reasons. Please forgive my omissions and my imperfections. Take care of

July 4, 1993

yourselves. Every day is full of important choices. Decide to make the right ones. I would like to hear from you if you would like to write or call. Please do. It would mean so much to me to have you in my life more often.

Always, I will love you,
Grandma Skelton Eldred or Grandma Margie

GREAT GRANDMA MARION AND GREAT GRANDCHILDREN: UPPER LEFT TO RIGHT: CLAIRE SKELTON, TIM'S WIFE, WITH CHILDREN KAYLA, JEREMY, AND JOSHUA. NEXT PICTURE: KRISTINE SKELTON (GARY'S DAUGHTER) AND ASHTON SKELTON, DAUGHTER OF DOUG.

Marion and great grandchildren

PART FIVE

Clio and Me

Why Is the Little Robin Lonely?
How We First Met

"I'M so excited," I told my sister, Mona. "Camp is always so much fun! There are always a lot of neat boys I've never met, from everywhere imaginable."

My sister, just two years younger than me, and not quite so easily interested in boys, responded, "The part I like best is campfire. It's so much fun to see people acting silly, or to hear them singing. I hope I can be in a skit this year!"

The summer camp, usually held at Quaker Hill Camp, McCall, Idaho, was the highlight of our summers when we were teenagers. Because we lived on a dairy farm, summer *family* vacations were non-existent. Mother made sure we attended camp.

We usually traveled the two hundred miles to camp in someone's truck bed, standing and feeling the breezes in our faces, or sitting and sweating against the side boards of the truck, singing or joking with our church friends.

The exposure of this mode of transportation left us lacking in polish of apparel and grooming for our arrival but high in anticipation of the fun to come.

We arrived after several hot hours in transit, registered, and disappeared into the girl's dorm for quick repairs before checking out the lake, or investigating who might be at the ping-pong tables. As I was outside the dorm brushing my teeth in the open air, unprotected from intruders, one arrived.

"You seem to be foaming at the mouth," the tall young man with curly hair commented, eyes sending a smile my way. Supremely surprised and embarrassed, I whirled back into the dorm, face red as a June strawberry.

That was my first meeting with Clio Eldred, but certainly not the last, and certainly not more embarrassing than our other meetings.

The next time we ran into each other, he suddenly began to whistle; not a wolf-whistle, but a whistle embellished with warbles and trills, and he was whistling a song I knew: the Lonely Little Robin. Again I suffered embarrassment in the extreme; turning my back and walking away I decided this guy wasn't the kind of challenge I was ready for. My plan? Avoidance!

Clio and Marjorie, circa 1996

But no matter how much peeking out the dorm door, or pre-planning of my route, I seemed somehow, to be where he was, get caught at the ping-pong table, or find him sitting beside me at campfire. Every time Clio saw me, his whistles burst forth, always trilling about the lonely little robin. Extremely disconcerted, I tried vainly to be friendly, but also very clear about my intentions.

In the end, the ping-pong table was helpful to our eventual friendship. Mona and I were accustomed to playing a lot of matches at home. Clio had an equal exposure, and challenged "the winner" repeatedly. We had found something we could enjoy doing together. We chose a friendly truce, no matter who the winner was; and even began to meet purposefully at the ping pong table.

Before camp was over we could usually be found together, playing, going for boat rides, or sitting together at campfire or the evening devotional service.

When camp ended we planned to write one another, but before too many letters were exchanged, that contact ceased.

But this is not the end of the story.

"This is not the "unvarnished truth, but the truth with a lot of varnish" (Quoted by Ramona Scarborough as one of her mother's quotes; this may be applicable to this story. Forgotten conversations are re-created by the author.)

Meet My Husband

CLIO remembers that his parents took his cousin, Roger, and him to Quaker Hill Camp in McCall, Idaho, several years in a row, giving them opportunities to meet other young people in the church and to receive additional teaching from the Word of God. As parents Merrill and Anna provided much in the way of stability and encouragement, teaching the importance of paying rigorous attention to Bible teaching. Clio describes his Mom as tender, loving, and anxious to please his Dad. He also believes she may have been over-protective of her children's, and perhaps her own, health.

When Clio was a teenager, a friend, Merle Bunn, taught him the love of photography, as well as advanced skills of adjusting the meters and choosing the subject of the picture. After Clio received a nice Kodak camera from his parents, he could often be found behind the camera, coaxing his subjects into the perfect poses. At least one of his landscapes won Best of Show at a community art show held in Clearfield, Utah. The honored picture was taken at a beach party at Birch Bay near Bellingham, Washington. It now hangs in our living room. Clio is very proud of his photography collection, with good reason.

Clio had always wanted to sing, so sometime during his high school years his parents provided voice lessons. According to Clio, his first teachers didn't quite know what to do with him or how to help him. "They gave up on me," he says, adding that they didn't believe he would ever reach the skill level he would need for solo performances; a goal firmly entrenched in Clio's brain.

In 1954 Clio entered school at Abilene Christian College with the intention to study accounting in order to prepare to take over his Dad's fuel business. He completed that degree as well as a minor in music. During the five years he was at Abilene and working in Montgomery, Alabama, he studied with over twenty voice teachers. Some had little to give, some more. Clio was determined to sing.

He must have been very busy, because it was at Abilene that he met Alice Heck, who became his wife in December of 1957. Their first child, Celice, was born in 1959, on March 17. Clio remembers that Celice's birth was a difficult one, and that he waited for hours and hours at the hospital while Alice struggled unsuccessfully to give birth. The young couple had chosen a reportedly "good" doctor and put their faith in him; but Alice remembers being partially conscious during the "C" section which followed. Clio had waited at the hospital most of the night with only brief and infrequent reports from the doctor. He finally left for the church where he worked knowing there was nothing he could do, only to be retrieved by a phone call from the hospital.

Later he learned that they had almost lost Celice during birth; Alice's small 120 lb frame not being able to accommodate Clio's baby, Clio being 6'3" and about 175 pounds. Celice, partially deprived of oxygen, needed intensive care for a time following birth.)

Clio said, "She was one of the prettiest babies I had ever seen. Her features were lovely, framed by a head of blonde hair, and she was on her knees before we ever left the hospital." Precocious, too, it seems. Sounds like a proud daddy to me!

Alice had been working as the church secretary up to this time, but stayed home to care for Celice after her birth. Celice was about three months old when Clio contracted polio.

On Clio's first job following college he worked for the Montgomery, Alabama, Highland Church of Christ as youth leader, associate minister, and song leader. While Clio enjoyed his work there, he felt something was missing, and remembers that during this period of time he asked God for a challenge. He was still working at the Montgomery church

He contracted Polio in June, 1959. His initial treatments after his fever was gone were primarily physical therapy, however, after several days, the therapists noticed that his skin was turning blue and he was placed in an "iron lung." This machine did all his breathing for him for eight days. It was a month before Clio was able to feed himself again, and six weeks later he still needed therapy, had no job, and had a wife and baby girl to support. At this time, the polio foundation, then called "The March of Dimes," made special arrangements for Clio to fly back to Bellingham. His parents took Alice and Celice into their home while Clio entered the hospital for several months of intense physical therapy. After that he continued out-patient therapy for over a year.

Clio proved a challenging patient. The doctors predicted that Clio would never be able to walk, drive, bicycle, or sing again, since so many muscles had been damaged by his bout with polio. Clio, never one to listen to negative feedback, ignored the dire predictions and prayed. "Father, please restore my strength enough that I can serve you in whatever way You choose."

Clio and Alice, putting their faith in God, kept insisting that the doctor order a body brace for him. The doctor, at first, refused, but when Clio kept gaining strength through lots of water therapy, finally ordered the brace. It covered from shoulder to hip, with joint-stabilizers to hold him erect. After Clio had the brace, lots of time spent walking in the parallel bars strengthened him even more.

Clio's determination to walk eventually paid off when he learned to walk using two canes. When he began to wear the brace and walk, he lost no time in imagining other previous skills he needed to regain. He was soon convincing his friend, Bob Ellsworth, and his wife, Alice that he could drive. He had seen many adaptations during his therapy. Now he made a few of his own. Clio's right leg muscles were impaired so he could not lift his foot to the brake. Clio found a broom handle, cut it to the right length, and stuck an old phonograph needle into the brake pedal to keep the handle in place—thus creating his own version of a hand brake—and drove his car out on Chuckanut drive and home on the freeway.

However, his adaptation was not adequate in the doctor's eyes. He insisted on a professionally installed hand brake before Clio could drive. So the hand-brake was installed, and the doctor gave his permission. In spite of the objections of therapists, parents, and friends, Clio took his driver's test and passed it. He says, "Alice was the only one who would ride with me."

Alice also proved to be a "willing?" accomplice when Clio decided he could learn to ride a bike. He says she drove along behind, at first jumping out of the car to help him over hills. They eventually moved on to a bicycle-built-for-two. Bicycle conquered, Clio fixed his eyes on buying and learning to ride a motorcycle. Ira Pirtle, a long-time church friend, rode with Clio during the first motorcycle ride, braking and helping to support the bike at stops.

Clio's Dad was also very supportive. Clio eventually became self-sufficient as long as the bike was right side up, and rode about 120,000 miles on his cycles. All those miles, however, were not trouble-free. Clio can tell many hair-raising stories about his misadventures during those rides.

When Clio was able to work again, Columbia Christian College hired him as a choral director and teacher. He stayed at Columbia for two years before deciding to enter the University of Oregon in Eugene and study voice performance— At the university and as a part of his voice performance study regimens, he was finally privileged to sing bass leads in oratorios like Messiah, and Elijah. I have been blessed by hearing his performance of Elijah. Clio did a masterful job, one anyone should be proud of. These performances continued throughout the 1960's.

The choice to study voice performance gave Clio pause because his father would be disappointed if he did not join him in his coal business. Clio had faced the fact that his physical limitations made it impossible to meet the physical demands of the job. Also, he now realized that teaching at a Christian college was exactly what he wanted to do and what God wanted him to do.

After Clio received his Masters Degree in Voice Performance and after he and Alice parented a new baby boy, Cyle, he accepted a job at Magic Valley Christian College, Albion, Idaho, as choral director and teacher. Clio put heart and soul into this work with the young people and in 1967 was chosen by the students as *Most Inspirational Faculty Member*. This honor reinforced his conviction that he should teach. He remained in his work at Magic Valley until the school closed in 1969, a huge and lasting disappointment to Clio.

The school's closure necessitated a move, and Clio moved his family back to Bellingham where he secured a job as music teacher in the middle school. He remained in this position for a year, until health problems again forced an interruption to his plans. Problems with his back necessitated a spinal fusion following which he needed a body cast all summer. In spite of this situation, Clio made plans to enter the University of Washington to study for his Doctorate in Musical Arts. He could attend school only part time as a compensation for his reduced strength. Even the lightened schedule challenged him; however he remained to finish his course work, and worked for Seattle Community College during the last year he studied at U W. He taught private voice lessons, music theory, and sight singing to students who loved him. The dean was impressed with Clio's teaching and with the rapport he built with the students.

Alice had gone to work when Clio entered the University of Washington, and she worked on the campus. This began a time of much turmoil for the Eldreds, and ended with divorce and separation of the children as well. Celice stayed with her mother, and Clio took Cyle to Idaho, avoiding the obvious difficulties of raising a son in the city.

Once in Idaho, Clio found jobs scarce. He found no openings, so then moved with Cyle to Ogden, Utah, where he believed there would be more opportunities. Many applications later he remained jobless, so he began to use his voice entertaining in restaurants.

A friend, Steve Eaton, opened doors for Clio with Ron Watkins who had his own recording studio in Ogden. It was here that Clio recorded his first sound track, singing new songs by song-writers and friends, Steve Eaton, Andy Haight, Larry Kennedy, Mack Davis, Don Hildenbrand, and others. Clio persuaded Nancy Goldsmith, then living in Idaho, to move to the area, and Clio and Nancy recorded the original Amazing Grace tape, featuring Clio and Nancy, the two singing all four parts a cappella. The recording included an arrangement of a song by Brother J.C. Bunn: *A Wonderful Savior*. At least one other song by Glover Shipp, *Be Thou Merciful* was arranged by Clio and included on the tape. Clio has gifted this tape to many, but not sold it. Clio entertained in restaurants for years, but found his music earnings insufficient for his living costs.

Clio says, "Throughout these years of growth, learning, and rearing a family my thoughts kept returning to the teachings of Christ concerning Judgment Day as described in Matthew 25:31-46: *Come ye who are blessed of my Father, inherit the kingdom prepared for you from the foundation of the world. For I was hungry and you gave me something to eat; I was thirsty and you gave me drink; I was a stranger and you invited me in: naked, and you clothed me; I was sick and you visited me; I was in prison and you came to me.* "These thoughts, ingrained in my heart and mind, became a driving force, compelling me to enter the prisons and lead men and women to Christ."

In the beginning of his prison ministry Clio sang songs which had messages that were positive, and used his guitar. One of his favorites was World of Love. He visited and sang weekly or monthly, as he could. After several years of ministering in the Northwest, he learned in the early 1990's of a prison ministry in Texas, and made the decision to move there and contribute to that ministry.

During a visit back home, circa 1994 Clio learned through a mutual friend that a long-time friend, Marjorie Vaughn—maiden—was single again. Memories of Quaker Hill Camp returned, and Clio made the decision to stay in the Northwest, and "see" Marjorie. In November of 1996 they were married in Clio's daughter, Celice's home in Seattle.

Marjorie had never performed in singing before, but before long Clio had encouraged her to accompany him to the prisons where she added her harmonies, and even occasionally her planning, to Clio's presentations.

By this time Clio was volunteering at the Washington Corrections Center in Shelton. His long-time volunteer status there eventually gave him the opportunity he wanted: to teach Bible classes. He was placed in the receiving units; there were four of them. Each inmate coming into the prison system went first to Receiving 1, then R2, R3, and R4. Clio found these men to be very receptive to Bible truth and began to tell other Christian men about the opportunity.

Eventually, Bobby Lumpkin, and John Johnston, having been introduced to it by Clio, committed to prison ministry. John also taught in the Receiving Units. Bobby Lumpkin continues to minister at Shelton today. Many men were buried in baptism through the efforts of Clio and these men.

Clio was eventually offered a position as choral director at Shelton, and actually received wages for the time he spent with the chorus. However, his Bible classes occupied most of the time he spent, and he received no pay for them.

The prison superintendent's permission to baptize by immersion came with difficulty, but finally, Clio's persistence and God's intervention made it possible for a period of time. However, after several years in the R units there were often multiple baptism requests per week and, eventually. the officials at the prison decided that it just caused them too much trouble. Clio was told that the prisoners could be baptized after they reached their new location. Shortly after this a misunderstanding ended Clio's permission to volunteer at Shelton.

A wiser Clio began to look for other prison locations where he could minister. He was first given permission to enter the Monroe facility every 5th Saturday of the year for the purpose of coordinating a music program for the prisoners. Then he uncovered an opportunity at the Federal Prison at SeaTac where he would be allowed to teach Bible. The chaplain at SeaTac has been very pleased with Clio's influence on the prisoners, and baptisms have increased. Clio now has several hours every week to teach Bible.

When Clio and Marjorie were married, they lived for the first six years in her Kent apartment. Marjorie worked first at a Life Care nursing home, then at Farrington Court, a retirement home, then for Auburn School District. Clio attempted to find a teaching job, but either because of his disability or lack of recent work history, he did not succeed. Instead, he poured his energies into the prisons.

During the years in Kent, Clio also began to entertain at retirement homes around the area. Marjorie and Clio had worked together a bit by this time, and had a large number of songs to which Marjorie could add her harmonies.

Those were pleasurable times, and seemed to be enjoyed by most whom we entertained. While we lived in Kent, Clio borrowed a tape recorder, and he and I did our first and only recording, He played his guitar and sang, and I lay on the couch —to help me breathe correctly—and sang harmony. Despite an incorrectly adjusted recorder, some of our songs came out pretty well.

At this time Clio was still using his two canes to walk, and a "glide-about"—a chair with handles he could push to move around the apartment. Because the outside steps had handrails he was able to navigate them. The neighbors, and anyone else observing his manner of moving up the stairs, lived in terror of the day he would fall, but the only time he ever did fall on the steps, he landed on his slick, padded, jacket and slid and bounced his way to the bottom. Though there were sore muscles as a result, there were no broken bones.

However, this event and the continually rising cost of the rental caused Marjorie to start looking for another place to live. Their limited funds soon brought her to the realization that the only way they could buy a home would be to buy a mobile home. Clio raised immediate objections until he saw Golden Valley, a development for manufactured homes located near the wilderness and in the vicinity of Bonney Lake and Buckley.

Then the Eldreds were able to start looking for their home. They bought a Marlette doublewide with a pod, containing about 1900 square feet. They had their home set up in August of 2002 with ramps to the doorways to enable Clio's movements in and out with a wheelchair. Clio added their names and the date to the wet cement in their sidewalk

The new home brought its own set of problems. The carpet which had been installed became a problem when Clio's difficulty walking up the ramps encouraged him to use his manual wheel chair. The ramps, intended to simplify his entrance into the house were difficult; lacking rails, being quite lengthy, and a little too steep. The manual wheel chair moved laboriously on the carpets. But in spite of disappointments, they felt happy in their new home.

By February of 2003 the need to bring Marjorie's mom to live with them became obvious, Marion moved in with Clio and Marjorie. She lived with them until January, 2006, when she was taken from them during a gallbladder attack and attempted surgery. Marjorie's older brother died October of 2006. In December, Marjorie suffered a heart attack, was diagnosed with Coronary Artery Disease and Congestive Heart Failure, and spent about two weeks in the hospital after a three-way by-pass.

In May of 2007, Clio fell, bringing on a heart attack. He had several dangerously blocked arteries, and the surgeon wanted to do open heart surgery, but feared that Clio would not be able to resume breathing. He opted for a very risky angioplasty. All was completed successfully, but the extended time in bed left Clio very weak. He required about two weeks in rehabilitation. Recovery after the rehab took a long time.

In 2005 Medicare had provided a power chair for Clio when his neck and shoulders began to deteriorate from the wheelchair use. It gave Clio the relief he needed while he was at home, which was significant relief. However, the power chair could not be loaded into his means of transportation, a Ford Escort Van, so when Clio arrived at his destinations, he was forced to ask help, usually from strangers, to get his manual chair unloaded and to his car door where he could transfer into it. Eventually his doctor's office asked him to always bring someone along who could do these things for him. The Monroe Prison, concerned about inmates who always tried to help Clio, actually suspended for a month his right to enter the prison for ministry, until he could "bring a helper" with him every week, or bring his power chair.

These developments came in late November, 2007. Initially, Clio began to call the churches, looking for men who could accompany him regularly. Marjorie, who had required a three way by-pass surgery in December of 2006, felt unable to accompany Clio, or do the lifting required for the wheel-chair.

Agreement to become involved in Clio's prison ministry was slow in coming from the men contacted, so Clio committed himself to raising the money to buy the van he needed to transport the power chair, the chair which would enable him to continue the ministry. Again he used his phone to

MEET MY HUSBAND

contact hundreds of people, looking for those who would like to be involved in continuing his ministry.

In the process of contacting his acquaintances, Clio called Joel Coppinger, a past friend whom he had known during his time at Magic Valley Christian College. Joel's family owned a van which had been used by his mother. It was equipped with a wheel-chair lift, showed low mileage, and appeared suitable for the adaptations which would enable Clio to drive it. Clio focused on raising the money to purchase the van, which was for sale for approximately twenty thousand dollars.

Marjorie viewed the project rather hopelessly, seeing the size of the financial commitment needed, but Clio began to receive commitments of money to help. The first sizeable commitment came from the Orchard Street Church of Christ: $2000.00. Only ten commitments of that size would be needed.

Clio felt energized by this commitment, and continued his phone calls, telling people he needed the van by the end of December, the time when he hoped to begin re-entering the prison. Help began to come, usually two or three hundred dollars, with an occasional commitment of a thousand. By late December, Clio had received promises for funds amounting to about $11,000, including some funds which had been promised specifically for adapting the van once it was purchased. At this point a huge blessing materialized. The Bellevue Church of Christ, whose minister, David Shaner, had accompanied Clio into the prison several times and was enthusiastic about what he was seeing, announced that their congregation would match the funds Clio had raised* At this point the giving of thanks began, and plans were put into place for Joel to bring the van to Washington. God had rewarded Clio's hard work and faith, and provided him with the means to continue his prison ministry.

Joel delivered the van to Puyallup on New Year's Eve, 2007. Clio and Marjorie attended the church's New Years watch party, had their introduction to the van, and Clio accepted an invitation to speak to the church there. In addition to Clio's report on his ministry, Joel Coppinger reported on his World Bible School ministry, and Jeremy Jackson reported on a church

*Accurately, Ed Kartic gave This news To Clio.

243

planting which he led on the South Hill in Puyallup. It was a great and encouraging evening.

On Thursday, Clio and Joel went to Bellevue to complete the purchase of the van. Clio complained that he was catching a cold. By Saturday morning, January 5th, Clio was ill, having difficulty breathing. Despite a trip to the emergency that morning, the hospital sent Clio home where his problems only increased. Sunday morning, January 6, doctors at Tacoma General Hospital diagnosed him with double pneumonia, and admitted him to the Intensive Care Unit. By Wednesday doctors invited Marjorie and the family to a family conference where treatment issues and life support were being discussed. The doctors felt it possible that Clio would need a ventilator before morning. They asked our permission for a process which had no guarantees but numerous very frightening risks.

The thirty to forty percent odds that Clio would be able to breathe on his own again frightened the family; additionally, the risk that his vocal cords could be injured rendering him unable to sing troubled them.

By this time, Clio, too ill to make his own decisions, left Marjorie, with the support of Cyle and Celice, his children, to make his choices for him. They felt overwhelmed trying to make the decision they felt he would have made. After much conversation, prayer, and struggle, they knew that Clio, being a fighter, would want to give life support a try.

During that night the call from the doctor at the hospital came. Clio, no longer able to breathe alone, would probably go into respiratory failure and die without the ventilator. The decision having already been agreed upon, Marjorie gave her permission with the qualification that, as Clio had previously requested, it would be for a period of no more than a week.

Thus began a week of no communication with Clio; the unknown loomed like a specter; the family members did not know whether to prepare for Clio's continued life or for his death. Nagging questions plagued them: Why would God provide a van for Clio's ministry, and then take him home before he ever used it? Why didn't the emergency room personnel recognize the pneumonia Clio struggled with and begin treatment at the appropriate time? Why didn't the doctors change the ineffective antibiotic sooner? Would this be the last week they would be able to share with their husband and father? They held tremulously to time that week.

Inevitably, the week drew to its end. The routine breathing "tests" the medical personnel had been doing brought no conclusions, one day looking hopeful and the next day looking grim. On the last day of the week the family still struggled in the extremity of the situation.

That evening, Cyle and Marjorie talked on the phone, not knowing what to expect. Marjorie said to Cyle, "I want to put a "fleece" out there. Couldn't God either make him decidedly better, or much worse, so we would know what His will is?" She didn't know God would answer that "almost" prayer, but the next day, the last day of Clio's week, He did.

The test which doctors gave to Clio while the family struggled through another family meeting showed Clio's ability to breathe. The doctor decided to remove the ventilator. The family felt suddenly doubtful, suddenly hesitant, thinking perhaps another day would give Clio a better chance, but the medical personnel had their orders, and sent the family to lunch while doctors and nurses took him off the machine on January 16, 2008. None of the things the family feared happened.

As of this date, March 14, 2011, Clio continues his ministry. Another unit at Monroe opened its doors for his Bible studies. Three additional men joined the ministry because of his encouragement. Baptisms continue to happen. Two prisoners enthusiastically began the Sunset School of Preaching Bible study course, churches in the area having purchased the materials after hearing the need from Clio. God is good and enables His servant to continue up to this time. Praise His Holy Name.

An Invitation to Prison

"THE fifth Saturday of May is coming up," my husband said. "I have asked ten people to go along. You and I will make twelve." So began my involvement for the musical program Clio coordinates several times a year at Monroe Correctional Complex.

Actually, Clio had started planning months ago. A former student of Clio's, and an accomplished choral director in his own right, Wenatchee resident, Larry Henderson, had agreed to save the last weekend in May for Clio's ministry. He planned to spend the night with us on the Friday before the performance, squeeze in a practice that night, participate in the practices and performance on Saturday, then go on his way back home. We love and appreciate him for his talent, his generous heart, and all the help he gives to Clio, helping build his website, sending out his Newsletters, and participating in so many other ways.

Several weeks ago we visited in Burlington, Washington where we attended a morning worship service. My husband—always thinking ministry—after presenting his report, asked if there were singers who might be willing to go into the prison with him.

"The Todds sing all the time, and they sound good," he was told. After the morning service Clio made it a point to locate the Todds; Roger, and his two daughters Sandra and Carolyn. They demonstrated on the spot what they could do. Beautiful a cappella harmonies filled the auditorium. They promised to help Clio with the program.

Several of the other performers who agreed to go had gone into the prison previously: John Calhoun, a great guitar player, has helped us several times and earned recognition by his contributions. Calvin Carter, whom we met at the Orchard Street Church of Christ in Tacoma, plays guitar and sings. He always contributes great new inspirational songs.

Rather unremarkable singers comprised the rest of the group but all showed compassion for those behind bars and willingness to be involved with us.

Clio involved several first-timers in this group. His constant recruiting of new people spreads concern and compassion for people behind bars. Some of these new people will minister to those in prison in the future.

Little did any of us know on the day we agreed to go what our commitment would mean: Clio had decided that we would learn to sing a difficult piece of choral music that he had learned in the past at Abilene Christian College; *The Pharisee and the Publican* by Heinrich Schultz. He had also set his heart on doing *The Battle Hymn of the Republic,* also difficult and also a choral arrangement. Not only did we have to cope with the distances people lived apart and the difficulty of planning practices, now we had strange hard-to-read music to learn. We had few times to practice, and huge challenges.

I judged that we'd never learn this music properly, or even well enough to attempt it. I think I resembled Eor the Donkey of Winnie the Pooh with my negativity.

We suffered and struggled through several practices, never with the full group together, and made very little, if any, progress on the music. I thought better of my agreement to take part in the venture.

Finally, on the last Friday evening of May when Larry arrived, the Todd girls came down to practice, and the four of us, Clio, the Todd girls and myself, with Larry's help, made enough progress to visualize our success on at least the first half of the *The Pharisee and the Publican*. When our voices began to blend and harmonize, and as we learned to sing the music as it was written, we rejoiced at the beauty this difficult music held. We began to look forward to practicing on Saturday afternoon and singing during the program.

On Saturday morning Clio did not feel well and feared that his recent pneumonia might be returning. He realized he needed to stay home in bed, but because of the eleven people planning to go in with him and because his absence would mean no program, he pushed his body to go. He did an amazing job of singing in spite of the way he felt, but toward the end of the program we could see the stress his body was under. Words started getting in the way of words, and the group singing with him had to guess what would come out of his mouth next. By the time we finished around 8 pm, Clio, obviously ill and near collapse, felt feverish, and could no longer hold his head up. We knew he could not drive and made arrangements with his son, Cyle, who had come in for the first time, to drive the van home. Thankfully, after Clio was home and in bed resting, he improved rather than relapsing to the pneumonia we feared.

Approximately twenty inmates stayed with us for several hours that day. Larry Henderson sang several very beautiful songs, including "Who is this King of Glory?" and spoke special words of encouragement. Calvin sang several solo pieces, and invited the Todd girls to sing with him on several songs they knew. He also spoke to the inmates. The Todd family sang several moving hymns new to the rest of us, including "Enter In." Larry, Clio, the Todd family, and I performed "*The Pharisee and the Publican*," singing a cappella—without accompaniment by instruments—at our concert in the prison. Friendships grew among the singers; another by- product of Clio's prison ministry.

I visited with several inmates following our program. They attended because they appreciated Clio and his Bible classes. "I think he must have the whole Bible memorized," one of them said. "I'm waiting to be baptized until David Griner can come in and do it," said another. David visits the prison regularly, only one of many men whom Clio drew into the ministry. All prisoners spoke appreciatively of the men that work with Clio, or in his stead. We heard their statements with gratitude and offered our encouragements. Remarkably, we look forward to the next fifth Saturday of the year when we will again accept the "invitation to prison."

Meatball Madness

NOT considering my past 60's body and mind, my full-time-plus job, or any of the many other demands on my time, I readily agreed to help bring food for the wedding. Thinking I would plan ahead, do the job in pieces, and simplify the preparation, I volunteered to make meatballs. Meatballs have never been a specialty of mine, understand, however we had eaten some wonderful meatballs at Farrington Court, the Retirement home for which I work. My plan was to get the recipe from Bill, the cook. From there on it would be easy.

On Monday, before the wedding on Saturday, I asked again for the recipe. Bill delivered it to me promptly: 15 pounds of hamburger, 1 and ½ pounds bread, ½ pound celery, etc. I could see the difference right away! Since I had no scale at home, I would be obliged to do a special kind of grocery-shopping trip and weigh every ingredient except thyme, basil, and eggs.

I made the shopping trip on Thursday, and that evening started chopping onions, garlic, parsley, celery. Then I measured in thyme, basil and pepper, and stirred the mixture thoroughly. Feeling very smug and well-pleased with myself, I refrigerated the fragrant mixture, thinking of the easy job I would have next evening: adding the meat.

Friday evening, the day before the wedding, I emptied three five pound rolls of lean ground beef into my largest pan—oops—into my largest pan *and* my dishpan. I then divided the vegetable mixture and put half into each container of meat. *Then* I read the recipe again. "Sauté onions, celery and garlic in olive oil until tender."

As you will understand, this reading produced consternation as I realized that all my early preparation had produced unforeseen complications. Clearly I could no longer follow recipe directions. I must improvise.

I painstakingly retrieved as much of the chopped vegetable mixture as possible from its resting place in the meat, and sautéed it, parsley spices and all. Reasoning that the parsley and spices should *not* have been sautéed, I pondered this dilemma: Should I add more parsley? More spices? Realizing that the fresh green look of the parsley (which was forever lost in the sauté pan) was very important, I decided to chop more parsley and stir it in.

The spices, however, I hesitated to add again, fearing the unknown result of too much thyme or basil. That decision made, another dilemma presented itself: The recipe called for no salt. Beef stock was listed in the ingredients, but had been crossed out for some unknown reason. How much salt should I use to replace the saltiness of the stock?

I chose a mathematical solution, pulled out my Betty Crocker cookbook, found a meat-loaf recipe, and ultimately decided I needed ten teaspoons of salt. My exhausted brain did a trip of its own: three teaspoons in one tablespoon. Use the tablespoon, and make the measuring easier. So I pulled out the tablespoon and proceeded to measure three tablespoons of salt into *each* meat mixture.

At that point my husband interjected: "Was that tablespoons or teaspoons?" The appalling realization of what I had done burst upon me, and I erupted into wails and tears. I had added eighteen teaspoons of salt to my meat balls that needed only nine, ruined fifteen pounds of hamburger, and wasted all my energy and work.

Despair and Discouragement reigned as my husband and I dipped salt and bread crumbs out of the two containers until we could retrieve no more. Then, resigned to the inevitable too salty conclusion, I stirred in more bread crumbs, removed a small portion from each container fried it, and executed a taste test. Wonder of wonders, both batches of meat passed the test!!!

Wonderful welcome relief now complemented the exhaustion that had set in. All I had to do now was form the meatballs. Bill had loaned me a small ice cream scoop for that purpose.

How many times would that small scoop go into these two very large mixtures of hamburger? Eight large cookie sheets and three and one half hours later I had my answer: About one hundred eighty times. The baked meatballs filled my large crock-pot and my electric fry pan plus a bowl which I put away for Clio and me.

The next day following the wedding a lady came to me and said, "My mother makes the best meatballs I have ever tasted. I'll have to tell her I finally met someone who makes meatballs as good as hers." I wanted to reply, "I must tell you a very long story about my method." I *wish* I had just said "Thank you."

PART SIX

Ah Life!

Gifts from my Garden

"**M**OM, why do you have such a big garden anyway? The work is hard, and hot. Why do you do it?"

Why do I have a garden? The answer to my fifty year old son's question isn't short. I must share in intimate detail the rewards that come in their own time and of their own accord.

Entries from my journals help tell the story:

"During the night I was restless. Finally I arose and wandered into the living room. As I glanced into the night I saw the luminescence of my fragrant white lily, bountifully in bloom. I was deeply impressed. Later, as I went about my tasks, I thought about the picture I had seen, the light in the darkness.

As I remembered the lily's beautiful fragrance, I recalled a song about Jesus. He is the Lily of the Valley. Like my lily, He stands tall, first among men: He is Immanuel. Like my lily, He lends lovely fragrance to our rather humdrum lives. Like my lily, He is beautiful, worthy to be admired, an inspiration for mortals. Like my lily, He is light for our lives as we walk in this world of tears and pain."

For many years I have found comfort and release in my garden, and many times have written my joy. My sister, Mona, first stimulated my journaling with her support and inspiration:

"I brought you a present, Margie, several presents," she said one day about fifteen years ago. Her mischievous smile warmed me. "I was just looking around my house and I found these. They had your name on them." She handed me eight blank journals, including one with a teddy bear on the cover. "This is your 'Bear- Hug' Journal," she said. "Write the things that make you happy, and be thankful for what you have."

I have written my thankfulness:

"Winter is 'visiting' again this morning. My thermometer beyond the window reads thirty-two degrees Fahrenheit, but it is much colder. Frost lies like a silver blanket over the grass, the mountains of blackberry vines in our back woods, the red barberry bush standing in solitary splendor. God uses frost to put my garden to sleep."

"I, too, need a rest. Frost's icy blanket turns the leaves of my Popcorn Vibernum a dark beautiful red. The new flowering cherry tree shouts at me in glorious vibrant orange, 'Good night, Good night.'"

Another Winter Entry:

"I am amazed at the infinite varieties of wonderful plants and flowers. I love creating my garden. But there is so much to choose from! I find myself making lists and filling out order blanks and wanting to see 'for real' everything pictured in the catalogues. I love the lilies, the rhododendrons and the tulips and daffodils that bloom so early in the spring."

"Thank You, Father for giving us such excitement and so many beautiful colors and forms. *I* am amazed, but nothing is a wonder to *You*. You created the Garden of Eden, the most beautiful garden of all!"

I received a nice surprise one December:

"Yesterday I saw Spring coming. We were in Seattle, and the bulbs were beginning to peek through the ground, the camellias were capering tentatively on their bushes. I felt encouraged and entranced. Thank You, Father, for Resurrection. I enjoyed the frost-painted landscapes, but I'm looking forward to the 'coming of the green!'"

Another May arrived at last:

"What a picture! The Popcorn Viburnum is in full bloom, and the neighbor's red rhododendron snuggling next to it is rejoicing too." I saw the first blooms the day Clio, my husband, entered the hospital with pneumonia. A whole month later, the blooms waited to welcome him home.

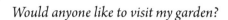

Would anyone like to visit my garden?

Our front garden

"The daylilies are opening, new ones every day. The blooms are large and lovely: orange, gold, red. I can hardly wait until there are dozens someday. I would love to share them with you."

August's rewards:

"The phlox are so delightful. I wondered a lot before I ordered them. I was afraid the stalks might not support the weight of the blooms. They've been blooming for weeks, all shades of pink, red, and white, too; bountiful blooms greet us when we look out our bedroom window."

"The blackberries are ripening, plump and pretty. I look forward to putting a few in the freezer. They make my tropical Jello extra tasty. I also want to freeze some of that exuberant zucchini for bread at Thanksgiving time."

"I took a bouquet of fragrant Stargazer lilies to church this morning. What a joy to share them. They went home with Amy."

And then comes the harvest:

Yesterday was Labor Day, so this lady acted appropriately and labored in the garden. The vegetables and berries invited *Eat me, eat me!*

"The squash harvest was prolific: The extras went into a box. Desperate phone calls went to neighbors whether we knew them or not. Success! One neighbor offered to take the whole box!"

"The blackberries hung heavy on the vines. I picked a gallon and put them in the freezer. The beans filled a big kettle; they and the strawberries embellished our dinner. These small labors reminded me of the harvests you bring faithfully to those who plant, tend, and reap, Lord. Thank You for giving us Your bounty."

More journal reflections:

"Especially, I love the garden, Lord. I am not surprised that you chose a garden to place your first family in, or that You wanted them to tend it. What a perfect place to feel Your presence, to be reminded of Your love by the vibrant colors You placed there. What a perfect place to learn responsibility, and the results of shirking it. Thank You for giving us trees and shrubs, vines and flowers."

The garden encourages creativity. The garden provides respite and restoration to the weary of heart. The garden blesses the earth and brings joy to men. What a gift is a garden!

Why do I want a garden? Don't you see, my son? It is the garden that makes me rich.

***

Holey Moley Desperation

A T Christmas time this year we had one of the best snowfalls of our seven-year history in Golden Valley, Buckley, Washington. The 'White Christmas' resulting was the stuff fairy tales are made of and lingered for several weeks, transforming our woodland setting to a dazzling show of frosty wintry white. From the safety and warmth of our family room we gazed, wondering at the beauty of the change God had wrought in our own backyard.

Our woodsy back yard

HOLEY MOLEY DESPERATION

One morning during my leisurely inspection of our winter-wonderland, I was jolted into reality. Under the snow in the middle of the lawn Mt Vesuvius was rising! This sight brought horrible recognition and realization: The moles were busy, even in the middle of the winter, even *under* four inches of snow! What an unwelcome sight. It destroyed my peace of mind and mushroomed my guilt over work that I wasn't doing in the garden! It was winter, after all!

Moles, a common pest in the Northwest, drive most gardeners to near-neuroses, as evidenced by the number of remedies on sale at the hardware store, written up in gardening magazines, and passed by word of mouth by anyone who has found 'the answer' to the destruction they cause.

Our friend, Bob, was the first to attempt our rescue from the pesky little varmints which pushed up mounds, continued along my brick-lined beds evicted bricks from their hard-won homes, and uprooted any plant unfortunate enough to be in their path. Then they wreaked their havoc in my beautiful green lawn. The mess they created seemed near impossible to repair.

When Bob couldn't abide the mess in our front yard any longer, he went to the hardware store and bought a generous supply of smoke bombs. In order to use the bombs, he had to dig down into the mound, find the direction the mole had gone, and send the smoke into the actual run. Bob courageously tackled each mound, hoping he had found the run. As he demonstrated the process: one lights the fuse, hurriedly sticks the bomb down into the run, frantically tries to cover it with dirt, and runs, hoping not to gas one-self along with the mole.

After several sessions of smoke-bombing—the moles were usually excited into increased frantic activity—Bob had another idea. This time he brought along a hair dryer, and after hooking it to electricity, digging into the moles' run and inserting the bomb, turned the hair-dryer on, thinking he would make this long story short. The hair dryer moved the smoke through the runs, all right, as evidenced by the geysers of smoke arising all over our yard, and even over at the neighbors! However, we saw no evidence that the moles were bothered. Instead, we heard in our heart of hearts, the moles asking one another, *Have you tried that new flavor of tobacco? They were giving free samples today. Did you miss it?*

Eventually, while doing my garden shopping and reading, I discovered a product called a Mole-Chaser. Hopefully, I ordered *two* of them since both front and back yards were bountifully blessed with moles. This miracle of someone's imagination was supposed to send out vibrations that were *hated* by moles; consequently, the moles would just stay out of your yard. Sounded good! Directions were to bury the Mole Chaser upright, so that meant a considerable amount of digging through our rocky soil; no small job—The device was about a foot tall—The magic didn't work well in our yard. The moles snuggled close, reporting to their peers, *They've put in two new massage parlors! Check them out!* The batteries died, and I forgot exactly where I buried my Mole Chasers; they are now trying vainly to compost.

My daughter sent me a remedy suggested to her by a frustrated gardener behind prison bars. The lady told her that she had gone to a golf course where she had never seen any moles, and that the gardener had told her the secret was to bury broken glass in the mole runs.

I inserted seltzer bottles into the runs, broke them with my crow bar, and waited, feeling very smug about my new knowledge. The theory was that if moles cut themselves they won't heal but will bleed to death. If my seltzer bottles murdered any moles, I never knew it. What I did see, over and over again, was a new mound where the old one had been. These new mounds were brazenly decorated with glass, now on the surface in my lawn, as if those moles were taunting me. *Ha! Ha! Ha! Fooled you again!* My second son could occasionally be seen bending over my flower bed or lawn, removing the glass so his Mom wouldn't get cut.

Another trick—I actually tried this—I found in a garden circular. It stated that Juicy Fruit Gum was very popular with the moles. It *must* be Juicy Fruit. The theory here was that when the mole tried to eat the gum, it would become stuck in his digestive system, and he would die. So I went into my yard and garden armed with a large package of *the* gum. As for every other mole-chasing tactic, I had to dig down into the mole run. Then I un-wrapped the gum, chewed it, and threw it into the run, for good measure including mole poison—maybe *that* was my undoing— I always have difficulty following directions *exactly*—and covered all with dirt. The moles must be wearing new gumballs on their noses or blowing bubbles with the gum; they still romp nonchalantly through my garden.

My neighbors finally took pity on me. Anyone who would believe *all that* was seriously in need of help!

My next door neighbor, Dick, came over with his scissor traps. He set them, repeatedly; the moles must have misunderstood the purpose of the traps; perhaps they thought it some kind of puzzle to play with, or in. Only one of my resident moles met his Maker through Dick's traps, even though Dick was diligent and fastidious about covering each trap with a bucket to keep out all the light.

Tom was the most skillful trapper. The difference in the way he set the traps was that after the trap was in the run, he would be sure to put dirt back into the run on either side of the trap to hide it from the moles. Thanks to Tom, I have two or three fewer moles to make my life difficult.

But the moles still come, and I continue to search on and on, looking for the perfect way to *escape* this holey moley desperation!

Tornado in our Back Yard

I opened the van door and felt the wind grab it from my hand. The empty bottle of vitamin water I had just finished flew out of its depository in the door and, wind-driven, fled down the street. The wind moaned; a strange roaring rumbling sound. It frightened me.

We were home after a day of weather surprises. Seeing the sunshine as I ate breakfast, I had dressed in a skirt and light sweater, not anticipating rain. I left my coat at home.

Rain had complicated our freeway drive to Seattle where we habitually attend Fellowship Church of Christ on Sundays. When we arrived, Clio insisted on giving me his blue patriotic blanket to cover my head and shoulders as I hurried to the door in pelting rain.

The trip home after we had eaten in Seattle was easier, the rain not beginning until we had finished our shopping at Lake Tapps Top Foods and driven Buckley-Tapps Highway to our home in Golden Valley. Another weather surprise greeted us.

I rushed, key in hand, for the house through a brief hard hailstorm, opened the door, and ran straight through to the back windows where I could see the Sunsetter awning over our deck whipping and bouncing. "Oh please, Father," I implored, fearful that we would lose the awning.

Suddenly all was quiet. I walked out the back door onto the deck, looking around at the disorder the wind had created: Plants rolled around the deck and patio in their pots, statues blown onto the deck, a small table lifted and thrown into my Weigela bush, and its two chairs upset onto their sides.

Ahead of me on the lawn I saw a pot blown onto the ground, and past it, on the grass near the back garage door, a huge tree branch ripped from its trunk, confronted me. The leaves were unfamiliar, and I could not immediately identify where it had come from. I walked around the garage to the front yard, and found our neighbors arriving in our driveway. Clio sat in the van.

"Are you ok?" They asked. They told us that they had seen a black funnel cloud surrounded by lighter matter swirling in from the west, and all the trees back of our house and the next-door neighbors' whipping violently.

They pointed out a tree back of our house in the woods, and said, "There's where your branch came from. We saw it come down, but couldn't see where it landed."

Numerous large branches near the top of that tree were torn away; others remained, still nakedly reaching for the sky. A deciduous Alder to the east was stripped of most of its leaves.

As we walked around my back yard we discovered more damage. The Cosmos I had started from seed had been standing tall. One white plant had been beautifully in bloom, its daily diet of sunshine apparently more adequate than that of the others. It was split down the middle and lying on its side. All the Cosmos in the back yard were damaged.

We walked together into our next door neighbor's back yard. Most of their sunflowers that had stood taller than the house had been ripped from the ground by the storm.

Friday afternoon I ventured into the woods to see the touch of the tornado. Some trees, denuded, stood out prominently and were surrounded by thick layers of branches. Our path through the woods was buried thigh deep in the tornado's debris.

It happened so fast, and was over so quickly that there was no time to think. Now that the tornado is past, I can only be thankful that we were spared the kind of damage some others suffered: A barn up on Buckley-Tapps Highway was destroyed; gas pumps apparently up-rooted still lying in the rubble. At a plant nursery in Enumclaw numerous greenhouses were stripped of their protective coverings, plants were up-rooted and nursery stock upset. One family's home in Enumclaw was struck by a huge falling tree, and one family's camper was overturned.

Tornados are rated for strength. Our tornado was rated 0 to 1. One Enumclaw man saw trees and their root systems spun in the ground like a top. I'd really hate to see a 5.

The news tells me tornados come to Washington State only once every two years. I think that's often enough!

It's Dr. Seuss's Birthday!!

MARCH 9, 2004

And it's his 100th birthday at that!! From my desk at the rear of Mrs. Korlann's first grade class I observed Mrs. Korlann on Monday getting the kids ready for the big day on Tuesday.

The chief method for preparing the class was a very tall and colorful "Cat in the Hat" stovepipe-type hat set deliberately upon said teacher's head. I really enjoyed seeing some fun brought into the classroom; and it was almost too much for me to handle, especially on Tuesday morning—the day—while I was getting dressed. I wanted to have some fun too.

But how? Well, I guessed, I would need lots of color, so I chose my red pants and my blue and black striped shirt. Now what? I needed a hat. I decided to borrow mother's little black hat with the bow in front. But was one bow enough? I found a colorful red, white, and orange scarf and tied it around the brim of the hat.

Then I found my pin which read, "The secret? Find an age you like and stick to it!" and pinned it on the back of the hat.

I applied very dark red circles of rouge on each cheek. I still wasn't satisfied. I added knee socks into which I tucked my pant legs.

When I looked into the mirror, I asked my husband, "Am I really going to do this?" He spoke confidently; encouraging me to follow my first impulses, to whatever destination. So I did.

I arrived at the school uneventfully, considering. The secretaries in the office, distracted by their jobs, didn't notice the arrival of such a strange looking character. Mercifully! Mrs. Korlann, also suspiciously busy upon my entrance into her domain, read on. The children sneaked looks at me, but for a long time said nothing, keeping their distance.

The first child to comment said, "Who are you?"

"Mrs. Eldred," I said.

"But who *are* you?"

I had to admit it. "I'm from Dr. Seuss land," I said.

Guess Who Dr. Seuss

The children repeated this question as I moved from one classroom to the other.

One little girl came to me and said, "I think your hat is just bee-oo-te-ful. I like the scarf."

"Thank you, Honey," I said. "I'm glad you like it."

As I was departing after an interesting morning watching people's responses to my appearance, a third grade teacher, Jacki—the teacher who consistently commented on how professionally I dressed—stood in her door-way. She stopped her conversation with the person she was talking to and looking sweetly at me, said, "Tell me why you are doing this."

I told her it was Dr. Seuss' birthday, and that I had surely enjoyed getting dressed that morning. She stepped back, and beckoned me into her classroom where I modeled my Seuss-land outfit to an appreciative and surprised audience. This ended my day very satisfactorily; I continued to my car. The pedestrians and the drivers who wondered at my appearance were kind enough to keep quiet.

I had a wonderful time with the whole experience on Tuesday, so I started thinking about how I could costume on Wednesday. Not many new ideas, except that I kept thinking about the little girl's comment about the scarf. Wednesday morning I was ready to be creative again. This time I chose a tiered denim skirt and a red plaid blouse. I added bows all over the skirt, blouse, and the hat from the previous day. I made bows on my cheeks. I even chose a name: Hattie Bowbinsky Lewinsky.

That accomplished, I wondered how I should answer the rest of the children's questions, and came up with a little poem, a very bad one, but that's ok; I never got to use it. Not once. *Not Once!* Not one child asked me who I was. The adults politely ignored me, too, probably thinking, *That poor lady has lost her mind!*

One teacher met me outside the school and helped me feel just a little better. "You look wonderful," She said. *Kind lady!*

By this time I was getting a little tired of my costume, so when I arrived home, I removed the multi-bowed hat and gave Mother her breakfast...Yes, she *was* sleeping till I got home.

About this time, Clio arrived home from his trip to the airport where he had picked up a friend, dWayne, and invited him to spend the night with us. When Clio arrived, he sent dWayne to the door with some of his things. When dWayne knocked, I ran to the door, completely forgetting my appearance.

Poor dWayne! He reported later, "I thought, there for a moment, that Clio had married a crazy woman!" I guess this appropriately described my state for the last two days. What do you think??

There She Goes Miss Inquisitive

MY daughter, Bee is a great employee. Really!! But you may wonder after you read this account of one of her days in the office.

Bee had been working for Tacoma Community College for some time. She had proven her dependability, independence, initiative, and even mechanical prowess. She had handled student registration for the school independently and competently numerous times, freeing her immediate supervisor, Mibbie, for family activities she had missed out on for years prior to Bee's employment in the Education Office. She had mastered a brand new copy machine, even learning to program half dozen jobs at once.

But there was one task she had never completed: She had never changed the toner cartridge in that copy machine. Oh, she had watched Mibbie change the toner numerous times, but she had never handled the job herself.

The day dawned like any other, and Bee showed up at the office early, as was her habit. Mibbie was there, but when the copier announced its need for toner, Bee, feeling very confident, decided to handle the job herself. She removed the old cartridge capably, and picked up the new one. Imitating what she had observed the office manager doing, she raised the cartridge overhead and waved it from side to side in undulating movement. While in this process, she noticed something she had never seen before, and wondered if this particular part of the cartridge might explain how the copier held on to the cartridge. Curiosity getting the better of her, she reached up with one hand, still holding the cartridge over her head, and pulled on the obstruction, releasing a shower of new toner powder down into her face and hair, all over her pink sweat suit, all over her shoes and stockings, and blacking every surface in the room she was in. Big mistake!.

Bee describes her next actions. "I plaintively cried out, Mibbie, Mibbie!!" When Mibbie came to the door, Bee said, "Whatever you do don't come in here. "I'll clean it. I'll clean it all up! It was my fault!"

Being the kind person she was, the office manager did not leave Bee alone to clean it all up. She got on the phone and called the janitors: "Education office stat. Miss Bee needs assistance cleaning up toner. Stat!"

Thus the news of her predicament spread into larger circles where it could be properly circulated, much to her chagrin. These same janitors told her the next day, "We spent three or four hours cleaning up the mess you made!!

By this time all the bosses in the office had heard the ruckus, and showed up on the scene. They wanted to get the guilty party out of there before she did any *more* damage; placing her between them, each taking an arm fastidiously, they began to lead her from the room. Step by step the toner incident grew as black toner footsteps followed them all the way down the hall, and out the door.

It just so happened that it was time for the office meeting. All employees were required to be there, so the managers escorted Bee into the almost overflowing room in the next building and seated her in front, there to wait until they could better take care of the situation.

For at least an hour she contemplated her New Year's resolutions there in full view of her office peers: "I will *never*, under *any* circumstance, change the toner in that copy machine or any other! *Ever*!!"

The First Square Dance

I found it. I didn't know I was searching for it, but sometime in August or September this year I stepped out of my comfort zone. It happened at a picnic. Our neighbors had built a fire pit down the road at the edge of the forest. The occasion was our neighborhood's fall get together. For the program, square dancers had been invited. We were all eager to observe their demonstration of expertise in the art.

I sat comfortably on a bench beside several neighbors and my husband and watched the dancers. I watched with special interest because square dancing had always looked like great fun. It looked pretty complicated to me, and I had been content with *wishing* I knew the art, wishing my husband was not in a wheel chair, wishing for the frolic and fun that it could bring to my life.

I was in for a jolt. Each member of the visiting square dance team came out of their "square" and chose a partner. I was one of the chosen.

His name was Neil, a very attractive and friendly man. He walked to me and held out his hand. "But I've never square danced," I protested. "I won't know what I'm doing!"

"That's okay," he said. "We're going to teach you."

So I took his hand with much trepidation and walked with him to a circle that was being formed.

"I've never done this before," I reminded him again.

"The caller will tell you exactly what to do," he smiled and reassured me.

"All join hands, circle to the left," came the instruction.

Well, that's not hard. The caller, Greg, went on to instruct us how to "alamande-left" and "dosado." He taught us who was our partner (on the left) and who was our "corner" (on the right). Then, staying in the circle we practiced listening and following directions. We danced through two sets. My breath was short and my legs trembled, but I felt somewhat successful in my adventure.

I asked lots of questions of the instructors (callers) that day. I was told that each lesson was $3.00, and that new moves were added at each lesson. I thought I could learn one or two new moves in one night. So when September came, I started lessons.

Every Tuesday night at seven we gathered. New moves were added almost from the first—and not just one or two. As long as we stayed in the circle, I felt confident. But almost immediately the caller directed us into "squares." After all, it *is* called Square Dancing.

No longer did we dance only with our partner and our corner. New moves changed the identity of both partner and corner. I "turned through four" and got completely lost among hands reaching for mine. I was supposed to do the "Grand Square" and make my "own little square." My confusion set in.

At each lesson I dreaded the moment when we moved into "squares," a group of four couples; "head" couples and "side" couples. The night soon came when we went immediately to squares. *This is going too fast for me.* I protested. Everybody told me to "not worry. Just have fun."

The caller started announcing "student level dances." The first was to be held on Friday night, December 4th. The same night of the announcement we were taught four or five new movements, all of them complicated, and told that now we were at "level 30." We were strongly encouraged to attend the dance. There was to be an ornament exchange and a potluck at 10:30 pm. We were told we could wear any skirt or outfit we wanted, and told how much fun we would have.

Finally, I decided to go. A fellow Golden Valley friend who was also taking lessons but had previous experience dancing convinced me, told me how much fun I would have, how glad the other square dancers were to have students there, and offered me a ride. I went.

Most of the women at the dance wore square dance attire, knee length bright colored skirts or dresses with voluminous petticoats. I was in my red A-line plaid skirt and black sweater, *Christmas attire*, I thought. A few other women joined me in my rebellion against the "outfit:" one wearing black pants and a blouse.

I didn't have much time to worry about my apparel. Neil, an accomplished square dancer had coaxed me to the dance, saying he would be my partner, then remembering that he had to take tickets at the door, but there he was, inviting me onto the floor. That was where the *fun* started.

The music was familiar: "It's beginning to look a lot like Christmas;" the music drew us in, all singing, and then the calls started. As before, the 'circle left' was easy, but I soon learned that many of the things I could do on lesson night now confused me. The dance moved faster, with no pauses between calls, and added to the music's distractions, the calls became more than my challenged brain could process. Then came the calls of movements I couldn't keep straight, even on lesson night: Grand Square: There was no connection I could see between the movements being made by the dancers, and making my own square. I was lost at practice, but there is no word but frustration for what I felt at the dance. If I *heard* the call it took far too long to register in my brain and order my movements.

My befuddled presence in a square was a complication to be dealt with, and everyone was guiding me, "go here," "alamande left," "dosado," repeating to me the last call. Square dancers are kind, fun-loving people, but I felt sure I had really tried their patience that night, disarranging their squares, disconcerting their calm. *Who's worried about their calm? What about mine?! Why, Oh Why did I go against my intuitions and attend the dance?*

As I thought about the reason, I figured it out. *I'm here to learn. Staying home would be like staying home from band practice because I hadn't learned the part, or taking riding lessons and never getting on a horse afterward. The dance is part of the learning process, a necessary transition to competency.*

So I continue the lessons. I go to the dances. I am learning to have fun in the journey. In the midst of the learning and the confusion, I found a perfect way to exercise, one that I don't have to do alone; consequently, one I will continue.

PART SEVEN

Introduction to My Siblings

The Little House That Grew Up

MY sister, Mona, and her husband, Jess, live in a quiet neighborhood in Southwest Salem, Oregon. Years ago they purchased a large older home there, and over the years have creatively worked to keep it maintained. Historically it has been shown that any small maintenance job will take hugely more time than expected and allotted for it. Their experience proved it true so very many times in that house, around it, and on it.

However, the best illustration of this traditional wisdom showed itself in what happened when the family of an older neighbor put their mother's house—across the street from Mona and Jess—on the market. The offered property, small in comparison to Mona and Jess's house, proved tempting. The possibilities of renovating the old house intrigued them. Maybe they could rent or sell the improved property. They purchased the house.

I had expected that they would fix what needed to be fixed, paint what needed to be painted, replace carpets and curtains, and be done with it. But very different plans developed.

Mona and Jess have two sons. The oldest, Tony, worked in construction, and possessed some know-how as far as house-building goes.

My mother used to say "Your eyes are bigger than your stomach!" I believe Tony's, or *someone* else's, eyes were bigger than their stomach. When I visited some time after their house purchase, I felt amazed at how the project had grown. Foundations for a huge new addition sprawled over the back yard. The original house had all but disappeared.

Since then Jess, Mona, Tony, and some of Tony's friends have faced a huge project. Coming inspections dominated their lives. They worked, doggedly, to put that house back together. They enjoyed sleepless nights over it, laughed over whatever calamity was currently happening and cried with frustration over the project that never ended.

This project severely taxed the creativity of the creator in my sister which inspired beautiful tole-paintings, ceramic projects, furniture re-buildings, and re-finishings. Her reach for perfection in everything she completed goaded her and frustrated her when necessary economies and differences with her co-workers arose. I admired her ability to make the compromises graciously.

The little house grew into a very big house with many bedrooms and bathrooms. The workers rejoiced when they passed the electrical and plumbing inspections and saw completion down the road. Many hours remain before the realization of Tony's dream, but I think that when the builders complete the house they could probably host the Kilpatrick family reunion in it! Or nearly.

Mona

OOPS! I FORGOT THE DOG!

IN late August one of my cousins, Don Williams, had his eightieth birthday. This occasioned a large family gathering in LaGrande, Oregon. After a lot of consideration, and after my brother, Les received an invitation to bring his guitar and do a program, we remaining siblings decided to make the trip to LaGrande for the festivities.

From my home near Buckley/Bonney Lake, Washington the trip would take nearly eleven hours of travel time, so I elected, with my sister, Mona's approval, to drive the distance to Salem, spend the night with her and her husband, Jess, and continue on to LaGrande the next day, leaving the driving chore to Jess.

As we began to settle in for the night at my sister's, some decisions remained to be made. Chief among them, "What should we do with Bearly," the aged and beloved dog who has been part of the Armas family for years?

We considered every choice: Perhaps Tony could come home and either pick Bearly up or stay with him for the weekend. That choice evaporated when Tony, his brother, Jeffrey, and some friends revealed their plans to make a rock-hunting trip to the desert that same weekend.

Well, then: Perhaps we should just put Bearly in his cage and take him along to LaGrande with us. A call to the motel where we had our reservations answered our inquiry: "Not in *that* room!"

Pressed into her least favorite choice, Mona called Tony's friend and asked the question: Could Barely possibly come to their house for the weekend? "I'll check with my mother and call you back," came the non-committal answer. About ten o'clock the call came giving permission to bring the aged poodle over in the morning.

Early the next morning while Mona and I made final preparations for the trip, Jess decided to deliver the dog and its paraphernalia to the friend's house. When Jess departed, he stayed about ten minutes, not long enough to complete his mission, we thought.

When he came through the door, Mona and I heard the rattle of Bearly's collar and wondered why Jess had brought him back. Had something happened to the arrangements Mona had made?

Jess answered all our questions when he reached the kitchen. "I forgot the dog," a red-faced Jess confessed, sending Mona and I into gales of laughter. How does one forget the primary reason for his trip? Chalk it up to another "senior moment" I guess.

***

Musical Inclinations

L ES Vaughn, local singer and imagination behind the popular Open Mic. Show at the Naked Winery in Hood River has a couple of stories to tell about his service in the U.S. Navy during the Vietnam War; how music played an inevitable part in his life, even in very different circumstances. If we ask, he may even tell of the beginnings of the show that has had its home at Naked Winery in the Columbia Gorge for over two years now.

One story he told centered on laundry time at Nimitz Naval Training Station near San Diego, California in 1961. Outside the buildings stood massive rectangular concrete scrubbing tables sixteen feet long and four feet wide. Thirty men faced one another across those tables. Each man spread one clothing item at a time on the table and scrubbed it with a brush until he rendered it spotless and it could pass next morning's inspection. Then he went on to the next item. When he finished the scrubbing he still had to run each item through massive wringers, shake out as many wrinkles as possible, and hang the items separately and neatly on the clothesline, tied there with a perfect square knot. Laundry could take a long time.

One night Les stood at the scrubbing table dreading the monotony of the chore ahead of him. "I started scrubbing with a rhythm in my motion and a song in my head." He smiled when he heard a solitary voice start humming. "Do you have words for that song?" He asked. Two more voices joined in with the words, *This Little Girl of Mine…*" The beautiful harmony he heard moved Les to add his own voice. A quartet formed in that moment.

"That Whitey, he can sure sing," his new black buddies stated. The other guys in the laundry room stopped their scrubbing task just long enough to dub the singers "The Company Twelve Four."

Then a strange thing happened. One guy approached them. "You guys sing. I'll wash your clothes." The phenomenon kept repeating itself. "You guys sound good, man. I'll do your wash. You just sing." Soon the four singers had no washing chore left to do, so they just sang.

From that day on, the quartet entertained and the others washed their clothes; the dreaded task became one they all looked forward to. The singers avoided the worst task of all, too. Tying their wet clothes on the line in a perfect square knot wasn't fun to do.

Opportunities to sing multiplied, and the quartet sang most nights. They became known throughout the company.

Their time at Nimitz drew to a close. About two weeks before their deployment date, the company commander contacted the men in the quartet. "Each company will have one act in our talent show. Your company has chosen your quartet to perform."

"Okay. That sounds like fun. We'll be practicing."

Over five hundred men attended the talent show. The quartet sang two songs, *Whadda Chow Choo Choo* and This *Little Girl of Mine.* The listeners cheered wildly. The quartet felt happy and proud when they walked away with the prize; a three foot tall trophy.

Les spent his remaining days in the Navy on the U.S.S. Ticonderoga. He habitually played his ukulele and sang every night He enjoyed many fans until a disgruntled seaman wanting sleep threw his ukulele overboard.

But don't think, for even a minute, that the lost ukulele ended Les's performance in music. Today he plays, sings and writes his songs in the Pacific Northwest where he earned the respect of the community. His experience at the Naked Winery in the Columbia Gorge explains why.

The Columbia Gorge is a popular tourist attraction, particularly in the summer. People come to Hood River to wind-surf on the Columbia River, hike the Cascades, enjoy fabulous scenery like Multnomah Falls, and listen to their favorite music. Any summer night people wander the streets looking in the windows of the many curio shops and checking out the music around town. On any given night three or more bands perform. Per Les, "Hood River is like a little Nashville."

Les has a musician friend named Ted Matzen. His home overlooks the beach just north of San Diego, California. Each summer Ted comes to The Dalles and spends several months playing music with Les. Both men possess very high musical standards and a real respect for one another. They choose to become musical partners.

In June of 2008 after Ted arrived in The Dalles, he and Les drove the ten miles to Hood River to look up the owner at the Trillium where they had previously performed.

As they left the concrete and asphalt of Interstate 84 they were welcomed by the picturesque streets of the small town about fifty miles east of Portland that is perched on a mountain side and overlooks the Columbia River. They drove past red brick multi-storied buildings and like-styled buildings of white stone and saw no parking space. They circled the block again, passed the Naked Winery, and saw one space in front. They grabbed the space as it seemed to be the only place anywhere to park. They could walk the block and one-half to the Trillium. Suddenly remembering that he had heard that the Naked Winery might be considering live music, Les understood the empty parking space as a lead to follow.

"Hey, Ted, let's check this out. I heard they're talking about having music here." Ted and Les entered. "Do you use live music?" Les asked the tall slender man tending the bar.

The man he spoke with identified himself as David Micaelec, a co-owner. "Well, no. We never have. But we've been talking about what we might be able to do."

Les had an unknown ally on this day. He had performed an impressive variety of Johnny Cash songs the previous week at a place just down the street called Double Mountain Brewery. Unbeknownst to him, the co-proprietor of Naked Winery had heard him. The performance had gone very well; Les, a single act that night, had interacted a lot with people in the audience. His performance impressed David Barringer of Naked Winery

Les held out his hand. "I'm Les Vaughn. This is Ted Matzen. We'd like to play here."

"Les Vaughn." Dave repeated. "I've heard that name before."

"I performed at Double Mountain Brewery last week; I played a lot of Johnny Cash."

"Yes! David's wanted me to look you up! You're hired! How much do you charge?"

Les Vaughn

"We usually ask for $100 per man for three hours."

"You're on! Are you booked on July 4th?"

"Sounds like we are now, huh Dave? You won't be sorry."

That was the beginning of Les's involvement at Naked Winery. He and Ted played together on Friday nights there all through the summer. When September ended and Ted went back to San Diego, the owners wanted Les to stay on and perform alone.

Les motioned to a near-by table and chairs. "Could we sit down while I tell you what I'm thinking?"

"Sure!" The proprietor summoned a waitress. "Would you please bring us some iced tea, Anna."

Les accepted the cool drink with gratitude. Summers in the Gorge could be toasty, and that constant hot wind really dried a man out. He took a long drink. "I've been in the Northwest for a long time, and actively involved in the music scene for a lot of those years. I know most musicians in this area, and most know me. I can bring you a lot of variety. What I'd *really* like to do is an 'Open Mic.' program. I think it would be good for the community and relieve a lot of frustration among musicians out there that have to work full time in other jobs to feed their families. They practice diligently but have no place to play, no outlet for their talent."

"But how do I know they'll be good musicians? It doesn't take many bad ones to drive the people away."

"They will have to believe they're good. If they can't tell me that, I'll send them home to practice."

"Well. I guess I'll have to trust you on this one. If you'd rather do the Open Mic. than the single, we'll give it a try. How does Monday night sound?"

Les walked to his van. He felt good as he thought about his plan. He would spread the word to musicians in the community that they would be welcome to participate in the program. "I don't care how 'good' you are, but if you're bad you will get just one song." Usually, each participant would be allowed three songs. Eight or nine singers could perform in the three hours.

The plan caught on. Each Monday night more people showed up at the winery. The proprietors opened another wine-tasting room, then another. Business grew, and with it, Les gained popularity. If someone wanted a new guitar, he knew Les could advise him on the best sound out there. If he wanted help, he knew where it could be found. Those young musicians in the community felt real gratitude to Les for providing a place where they could gain recognition as performers.

Les has seen much of the growth he hoped to see among the musicians.

"They came at first as strangers. They are becoming friends. Some came as 'tolerable' musicians; through their constant practice and performance they have become skilled professionals. Everybody is helping everybody." Les says. "They share their talents with one another now."

As of March 2011, the "Open Mic." programs are still featured every Monday night, with Les Vaughn as host.

The proprietors at Naked Winery? They have promised Les a job there for as long as he wants it. Their business enjoys new status in the community and new people to serve every Monday night. And they are making money.

***

On the Precipice

AL Vaughn left Leabo Electric in The Dalles, Oregon shortly after six on a Thursday morning in November 1996. He had a full day ahead. The wiring he planned to install that day would require a full day's work if he was feeling well, but today was not one of those days.

Al was a Vietnam Veteran, drafted into the army in August 1967 where he served in an artillery unit, one year of that time in "Nam." Since his release he had bought a house in Texas, sold it for a great profit, and invested those profits in the farm he now owned near Maupin, Oregon.

Al in front of his shed project, 2010

He worked at the Mill in Tygh Valley from 1973–1990, where his talent and expertise around machinery had propelled him rapidly into supervisory positions. Those talents did not help him when the company folded, one of many such closures, in 1990.

Al, suddenly without work, faced a tough decision; to look for a job or go back to school. He chose the education route but also worked as an electrical apprentice, a part of the program he entered. When he finished the course, he owned a journeyman electrician's degree and a lucrative job with a local electrician.

As Al pulled into the driveway at his appointment, a country address to which he traveled long miles of unfamiliar winding roads, he began to realize the folly of being on the job today working with electricity. His head pounded, his cough irritated him constantly— to say the least—and he felt weak and listless.

When he arose this morning, he had known he was ill, but hating to disappoint the customers who expected him to finish their kitchen today; he pushed himself out the door in spite of his aching body. Now he doubted the wisdom of that choice.

He removed his tool box from his van, carried it to the door, introduced himself, and asked directions to the kitchen. There he tackled the job he came to do. As he worked hour after hour, he noticed weakness creeping into his body, becoming more and more insistent, until finally his hands began to tremble.

"I'm sick. I've got to go home. I'm sorry; I don't think I can even put my tools away."

With that, he stumbled to the van, struggled to open the door, and collapsed into the seat. The weakness in his hands and arms steadily grew, challenging his ability to hold on to the steering wheel as the slow miles disappeared behind him. By the time Al reached town he knew he could not stop at the shop to drop off the van or pick up his car. He would not be physically strong enough to get in the car again. He could not drive home to Maupin, forty-five miles away. Thankfully he remembered that his mother, Marion Ritchie lived in town. He would go there. Mom always knew what to do.

The trembling controlled him now. He lurched to Marion's door, and rang the bell. Al remembers almost nothing of the next few hours. He remembers Marion putting him on the couch and rushing to the kitchen where she produced some chicken broth, then came back to him and sat spooning broth into his mouth, hour after hour through the night, hoping to increase his strength. She called his wife, Kathy, telling her Al was critically ill, and urging her to come, even though the weather had turned nasty with freezing snow and wind.

Early the next morning Kathy and Marion had Al at the doctor's office. Al no longer had strength or coordination to sit upright. Al remembers telling Kathy at the doctor's office, "If I have to sit here in this chair even one minute, I will be sprawled on the floor."

The nurses took him to an examining room, but when the doctor entered and saw Al trembling violently he told Kathy, "Take him to the hospital right now. Don't wait. He *must* be seen immediately. Don't stop for any paperwork. We can't wait for an ambulance."

Kathy desperately followed directions, insisting on immediate treatment. The rest is history. Al received the treatment he needed and was saved from the failure to listen to his body that almost cost him his life.

The doctor told him amazing things several days later when the crisis had passed. "See this table. It is your life. You were right on the edge, ready to fall off. If you had come to the hospital thirty minutes later we could not have saved you."

The doctor' diagnosed Bacterial Pneumococcal Pneumonia Stage Five.

Al's recovery required about a week in the hospital, lots of rest, and my sister's presence of mind to make sure he started phyto-chemical food supplements when he began to relapse.

Al and Kathy are the parents of an adopted daughter, Alexandra, who gave them their first grandson, Dustyn, in April 2010.

PART EIGHT

Goodbyes

Where's Your Driver's License?!!!

Mischievous Marion

SHORTLY after my mother came to live with us in Buckley, Washington, I decided that a shopping trip would be in order. Not having shopped with Mother for a very long time, but having observed her difficulty in getting around, I had the bright idea of putting her on one of those fancy shopping carts to be found in most department stores.

"Here Mom, this cart will make everything easier for you. The store is so big that walking would be very difficult."

Mom's version: "Margie took this country girl to the "Big City" and being so very kind and thoughtful, she deposited me in a motorized cart with push and stop, pull and go handles to use as needed."

Mom settled herself in the seat. This was no ordinary cart, as we soon found out: The lever that would enable the driver to stop was to be pushed forward instead of, as most brakes are set up, being pulled back. This fact alone should have been sufficient warning for us, but alas, we were a bit slow to figure things out.

"Mom, if you want to stop you *push* the lever *forward*."

We started off up the aisle. Our first stop was to be Vision Optical, but 'stop' was not what the cart wanted to do. Perhaps it had never been educated in the fine art of mind-reading. Instead of *stopping* when *we* thought stop, it wanted to *go*! The first casualty was a display in Vision Optical. Mom ran directly into it.

"Oh! I'm so sorry. I'm so sorry!" My face flushed scarlet, I apologized over and over. Thankfully the display contained nothing breakable, and since it was of cardboard, moved ahead instead of capsizing.

The amused clerks helped repair the damage. "How *else* can we help you?" We needed only to have Mom's glass frames straightened. This being accomplished without further mishap, and being very chastened, we headed over to the grocery department.

By this time I was questioning the wisdom of putting Mom in the cart, but it was too late, and we continued the shopping, almost without error—if you can discount my jumping in front of the cart every time we needed it to stop." Mom! Mom! Stop!!!"—until we headed for the check stand. Once there, Mom ran the cart into the check-out counter.

"I'm sorry, oh! I'm so sorry." Almost purple with embarrassment, I continued to apologize. It should go without saying that all this was very stressful; it was with considerable relief that we recovered Mom's light aluminum walker and retreated through the front doors of the store. The following is *Mother's* account of the day's activities, written on the day following the event, 3/3/2003.

"I *wanted* to believe that she had confidence, that she was doing me a big favor. That thing was motorized, and set on a high speed. As if that wasn't enough, she put herself in front of me and that motorized cart; then, every minute yelled, "Mom! Mom! Stop!" The foot traffic in the store was certainly getting a free moving picture show. We did a lot of laughing, and whether or not we wanted attention, we certainly *got* a lot of it. Our audience was laughing, too."

PS: "Marjorie just heard me read this piece of literature, and accused me of persecution. The next time you hear of me, I may be wanted for "adult" abuse!!!"

Woops!

SUNDAY, August 28, 2004.

I returned today from a visit with Barbara, for which I had to travel to Spokane. Since I was not home this morning, Mom had needed to dress herself for her trip to church.

She greeted me with joy when I walked through the door, home at last. I sat down beside her, and we talked. Smiling, she told me of the help she received from "Clio's relative," (Kelly) after arriving at church. She reported, with a twinkle in her eye, that she had gone to church with her dress on backwards and wrong-side out, and that Kelly had taken her in the bathroom and helped her change it.

Horrified, I exclaimed that Clio was supposed to watch for those kinds of problems since they didn't need to be advertised. Mom replied that she had the problems, and didn't guess it did any good to try to hide them! What an uplifting and honest attitude toward aging. I hope I can and will replicate it.

We Lost Our Mom

ON Sunday morning, January 15, 2006, our Mother passed into eternity after a struggle of ten day's duration. All the family who could come visited her in the hospital: Mona and Jess, Les, Al, and Marjorie's sons, Doug and Gary.

It all started when, on January 4, Mom experienced a gall-bladder attack. The vomiting was continuous. We took her to emergency; they released her to home. We visited the referred surgeon; he readmitted her. The gall-bladder surgery took place on Friday, January 6. The next day Mom was alert and even witty at times. By Sunday, however, she was struggling. Bile kept building up in her stomach and causing her to vomit again.

That day, while Clio and I were at church and Mona was with Mom, she aspirated bile into her lungs. The next day she had aspiration pneumonia. It took two days for the antibiotics to clear her lungs, and then she had a good day. However, by the next day the doctor told us that her lungs were clouded again. This time it was "hospital pneumonia." He said that the bugs that cause hospital pneumonia are very resistant to antibiotics. From then it was all downhill.

By the time Mother left us we were all begging God to take her and relieve her from her suffering. She died about eight o'clock Sunday morning.

Mom's memorial services were in the Dalles, Oregon, on Saturday, January 23. We know that some of you wanted to come, and that the time and distance were just too inconvenient. Thank you all for loving her, calling her Mom, and making her feel at home in our gatherings. We would like to spend a bit of time on Sunday morning, January 29, during or after services, remembering her. Thank you all for being our family in Christ. You mean a great deal to us.

The Beauty of Holiness

Last Gifts Mom Gave Us

JANUARY 20, 2006

We are on our way to The Dalles for Mom's memorial and burial. I am thinking about the many gifts Mom gave us during her hospital stay, even during some of her worst suffering.

On her last night on earth Mona, Les and I thought we would sing to her. Mona started singing "I come to the Garden Alone." Les and I joined in, and suddenly we saw Mom's lips moving, and heard her singing in strong voice, along with us. How beautiful that she used the very last of her strength to sing about her savior! I shall never forget those moments.

During the Memorial, Mona told the background. On the day after surgery Mom seemed to be doing well. Les was telling her how she was going to get well enough to be "running around Margie's garden."

The next day—Sunday—while Mona was alone with Mom, she reports saying to her, "Mama, Les says you will get well enough to run around in Margie's garden. I don't know if that will be true, but I do know that you are eventually going to a very beautiful garden."

Then Mona began to sing the song mentioned above. Even though Mom was to have a very difficult day in which she aspirated fluids into her lungs, she sang along with Mona. That song became our expression of faith in those difficult hours, ending in the event mentioned above.

Mom gave Les and me another reason to smile during the early part of that same evening. We were trying desperately to keep all the fluids that were coming up from going back down and into her lungs. I held a tube that was supposed to siphon it all out—it was a miserable failure—and Les was giving me urgent directions where to hold it in her mouth.

Suddenly Mom reached up, surprising her anxious attendants, and pushed the tube out of her mouth. She said, "Les, we're going to make a doctor out of you yet!" In spite of everything, we couldn't help laughing.

Les tells another story which I did not witness. Mom's doctor was in the room with Les bringing him up to date on Mom's grave condition. Mom was quiet, apparently sleeping, when the doctor told Les that since Mom would not be able to overcome the many challenges she had, that she could have anything she wanted from that point on. Mom reached up, pulled off her oxygen mask, and said, "I want some fried chicken!"

"It took that surprised doctor a moment to recover from the unexpected. Then he said, "What would you like with that, Mrs. Ritchie?"

"Coleslaw," Mom retorted. Do you suppose fried chicken and coleslaw will be her daily fare in Heaven?

Les made three trips from The Dalles to Puyallup/Buckley, while Mom was in the hospital. When he came into the hospital room, probably on his second trip, he was giving Mom a close hug and kiss, when she remarked on all his whiskers, probably something about how they tickled.

Les asked, rather sheepishly, "Well, Mom, don't you like my whiskers?" Mom's reply sent us all into laughter. She said, "I think Clio has enough whiskers for this whole family!"—Clio, my husband, insists on letting his hair grow long, and sports a long beard, too.

Al's precious last memories involve seeing Mom on her good day after surgery.

Mom was sitting up in bed, relaxed, her eyes closed, head leaned back against the bed, a peaceful expression on her face and her much red-underlined New Testament open in her lap.

We enjoyed many laughs together, before Les and Al decided they needed to go back home. Al said goodbye to his mother for the last time.

Memorial Service Memories

JANUARY, 22, 2006

The service went together beautifully. Mona and Tony worked on a picture board; they mounted pictures on a tri-fold display board.

Jess worked on a power point presentation of pictures telling Mom's life story. This was played prior to the service while people were coming in and being seated.

Les brought his sound system and a CD player. We had known right away that he should be the soloist, and that he wouldn't be able to sing that day. Gary served as the activator of the CD and the track selector. Les sang *Amazing Grace, I'll Walk with You*—written by Les—and *Peace in the Valley*.

I took along Mom's Kilpatrick/Kelley genealogy book, our family story-book, and some of my scrapbook pages.

Flowers were sent by Fellowship Church of Christ, Dallesport Church of Christ, The Indermill Family, Gayle and Ed Eddy—Margie's classmates for all twelve years she went to school in Vale, Oregon, and Ted Matzen— Les's good friend and music companion. Our family chose a beautiful casket arrangement of daisies and pink carnations, and a floral cross of the same flowers. Mona and Jess bought roses and cyclamen, also a mixed bouquet of freesia and baby's breath.

Jess Armas, our dear family member, coordinated the service, and shared wonderful thoughts about how Mom's suffering paralleled and helped "fill up" the suffering of Jesus.

The last portion of the service was an opportunity for everyone to share their memories of Mom and the ways Mom had impacted their lives.

Chuck, George Ritchie's son, told of a "double date" he and a new girlfriend shared with Mom and George before they were married. Chuck says, "I was flabbergasted when Dad made me and my date sit in the front seat, and he and Marion sat in the back seat. Sure ruined my date!"

Bill Ritchie told how he found his life companion as a result of Mom's marriage to his dad and Margie's encouragement to Betty to write to him while he was in the service.

Al, too, shared his memories of when Mom and George were dating and the sparkle that came back into Mom's eyes when George began to show an interest in her.

Bill, Chuck and Al all shared how much our families blended and bonded. Bill, Chuck and Phil were all welcomed as sons by Mom, and they all love her dearly.

Al shared that George always told him that he got "a double blessing" when he married Mom because she led him to the Lord—Mom said repeatedly to me, "I couldn't do anything wrong in George's eyes."

Mary Bales shared how Mom loved to teach Bible classes and how she taught the young women "how we could make those relationships with our husbands better."

Mark Proctor told me how Mom and Erma Couch had convinced him to study the book of Acts with them and then watered and cultivated the seed until it grew.

That story reminds me of Chuck Grant, the neighbor across the street whose wife Phyllis was coming to Mom's home Bible study. Chuck inquired whether he could come too—even though he would be the only man—and when he received an affirmative answer, did come, eventually learning the truth and becoming a Christian—Mom, during her stay with Clio and I never quit thinking and praying about Chuck.

Another side note: Reuben Phelps, baptized as a result of Clio's Prison ministry and integrated into the Orchard Street Church of Christ, was always a recipient of Mom's warm hugs and encouragement. Reuben, when I told him of Mom's death, said, "I'm going to miss all those hugs."

That Mom was not perfect was proven by several stories. Jess described his experience with her plum pie—the pits were still in it— her chicken stew—the bones were still in it.

Jodie, a granddaughter, told of being at Mom's house for dinner, when Mom served a casserole. Her husband pulled out a green twisty tie! Now how did *that* ever happen?!!

My sister-in law, Carol, told of a time when Mom and George visited in their home. Carol remarked that she would really like to have blond hair. Beautician that she was, and always willing, Mom proceeded to give Carol what she wanted. As Carol tells it, "The only trouble was that I had used a red rinse on my hair. It turned out pink!"

After these stories, I must add a word or two of defense for Mother. Most of the time, no such disasters happened, either in her kitchen or in her shop. Long after she had closed her beauty shop, many of her customers continued to come to her home for their hair-do's—and for a good listening ear.

Loving Absence

My oldest brother, Verlin became a very special man in my life, and I want you to know some of what I know about him. Though he lived far away after I was thirteen years old, I remember many positive ways he affected my life.

Verlin cared for me when Mama was out in the barn. Four years older than I, he could get Mama when needed, and filled an important place in that regard. He played with me and taught me, and helped me learn my first words. He taught me how to put milkers onto cows and helped my unpracticed efforts to feed the baby calves. He guided me on the first long walk to the bus stop and protected me when I needed protecting. As I grew he changed from merely brother to hero.

During my earliest teen years, Verlin left Oregon and our home to live with an uncle in Missouri. With only brief, occasional visits at home he entered Harding College, Searcy, Arkansas, two-year military service in New Jersey, then various jobs, college at West Texas A & M, marriage, home-ownership and parenthood in Amarillo, Texas. He never returned to live in Oregon, but our families exchanged visits, each visit memorable.

Verlin met Carol while he worked for Wm. Volker Company, a furniture freighting firm. An office co-worker invited him to a party at her home. "I'm having a bunch of nice young ladies as my guests tonight. Wouldn't you like to come?"

At the party he was attracted to a beautiful brunette wearing red velveteen pants. She looked into Verlin's blue eyes and lost her heart. "We were always so comfortable together," she said in later years.

Verlin and Carol's Wedding

Verlin and Carol married October 6, 1961 and parented two little boys of whom they were very proud. As their boys grew into teens the couple experienced two of the hardest situations parents can encounter; Vic, the oldest, was addicted to alcohol and drugs, Everett was diagnosed with schizophrenia. Doctors finally prescribed a drug for Everett that could greatly minimize his symptoms and return a degree of normalcy to their lives, but Vic's addiction controlled him for years and brought its own kind of chaos. Verlin and Carol held on to their faith, endured the problems, and supported their sons.

Of all the memories I collected while visiting in Verlin and Carol's home, my favorite ones involve sitting in their living room watching Verlin and Carol laugh at their cats and hearing them tell long-winded stories about what this cat and that cat had done. The cats accommodated our attentions at times and surprised us by giving live demonstrations of their unique abilities! Those memories still bring happy smiles.

We exchanged phone calls, each one a treasure. One memory that never fails to make me smile is about five years old. As we talked on the phone, Verlin told me, "I wanta get me a new cycle; one of those Goldwings. But Carol said if I get a Goldwing I can just keep on riding off into the sunset!"

The next call came about a month later. "I got my Goldwing; I got a really great deal."

"But Verlin, Carol didn't want you to get it. Did you have to 'ride off into the sunset?"

Verlin chuckled, "No, because I bought Carol a new Lexus at the same time!"

By this time, Verlin could afford the cycles and the Lexus. The Amarillo Deep Steam Company he founded after the Town Crier Steak House burned down had finally become profitable. He bought the very finest steam-cleaning machines, did his very best work, and spent extra time with each customer making sure he met all of their expectations. Referrals came, and his business continued to grow.

During the summer of 2005 Verlin was diagnosed with a skin melanoma which had spread to his lymph nodes. Surgery and recovery followed, Verlin maintained his optimism through it all. By this time, Mother lived with us in Washington State. When I noticed increasing confusion and decreasing energy in Mother, I called Verlin, knowing how much he loved and cared. "Wouldn't you like to come and see Mom while you can enjoy one another?"

Verlin left his business in Everett's hands and flew to Washington State to see Mom. Mom and Verlin were a joy to behold. Verlin slept on the couch in the living room. While he was here, Mom got up every morning, shuffled to the living room, bent over him, and kissed him on the cheek. Verlin bragged about those kisses to anyone who would listen. Little did we know these would be 'last memories' of both of our dear ones.

I called the other siblings and invited them to join us for a visit, thinking we could all see Verlin at once and save him a long trip. However, Al did not think he should leave his work or his horses. The only solution to that was a more than five-hundred-mile round trip. I loaned Verlin my car.

As Verlin was leaving for Oregon, he noticed a box in my back seat. "What's in the box, Margie?"

"Oh, it's just a crock pot. I bought it and decided I should take it back."

"What if I said you should keep it? I want to give you the money for it."

"No, Verlin. I don't want you to do that. I'm taking it back."

The crock-pot accompanied Verlin to Oregon and back. I took Verlin to SeaTac airport and we said goodbye.

After Verlin arrived home he called me. "I'm home safely. Have you returned your crock pot yet?"

"No. I just haven't gotten around to it."

A silence followed. "Well, I think you should go look under the box."

When I looked under the box in the back seat I found two bills totaling sixty dollars. I could have sent the money back to him, but that wouldn't have made him happy. So I kept the money and the crock pot. Using it always brings back the wonderful memory.

During the summer of 2006 melanoma was found again in Verlin's lymph nodes. Surgery was repeated. A brain scan revealed that he had a tumor in his brain. The family in Amarillo noticed increasing confusion. Verlin went into the hospital for tests. He called us, but told us that nothing was going to get him down, and not to worry. He bragged on the hospital staff and how well they were treating him. He had so many visitors that the staff dubbed him "The Visitor King."

On a Monday night he had a massive heart attack. The hospital staff treated it successfully, and Verlin kept telling us he was going home and planning more motorcycle trips. He fully intended to get well. But the hospital allowed him to go home for the weekend; he collapsed in the bathroom the first morning he was there; Friday, October 13, 2006. He was seventy-three years old.

I wrote the following message to him following his death.

Goodbye, Dear brother and friend. I miss your smile, your hugs, and your wonderful sense of humor. I loved your ability to listen and understand what was being communicated. I loved your generosity wherever and whenever you saw a need, and your kindness. I loved your willingness to share your life with those less fortunate. I loved your unfailing optimism, and your unwillingness to say you were sick.

I appreciated and loved your care for us, your long-distance family, and the lengths to which you would go to keep us from worrying. I loved your love of life, and the fact that you never stopped believing you could overcome obstacles, no matter how great they might be.

I love you for loving our wonderful, forgiving, Father in Heaven. I rejoice that you are now in glory, a member of that "great cloud of witnesses" which is watching us from above, encouraging us to never give up our faith in God. I rejoice that you are now a recipient of that wonderful promise, "And the tabernacle of God shall be with men, and He shall dwell with them, and they shall be His people. God Himself will be with them and be their God. And God will wipe away every tear from their eyes, there shall be no more death, nor sorrow, nor crying. There shall be no more pain, for the former things have passed away." Revelation 21:3-4

Epilogue
Seizing the Treasure

Y life, as is yours, is full of huge disappointments. Disappointments in love and marriage, abusive or unfaithful spouses, lost children, illness, accidents, and loss of loved ones make all our lives less than idyllic. In order to deal with these disappointments, pains, and uncertainties we need resources outside ourselves. Only faith in God and reaching up to Him can heal the hurts inside us and give us happy productive lives in spite of the realities of our existence.

His comforts are real. My grandparents walked daily with Him through the difficult days of the Dust Bowl and the Depression. My mother, Marion, reached up to Him through twenty-five years of poverty and difficult abusive marriage, keeping her smile and her spirit to pass on to her children.

I reached up to Him when my baby's life hung in the balance. He was there. I needed Him in the uncertainty of my third pregnancy. He came to me. Through the last tumultuous years of my first marriage he comforted me daily. When the marriage ended, He saved me from the poisons of resentment and anger and helped me choose the paths of forgiveness. The loss of my mother and my brother in the same year struck like a ton of bricks. Faith in God gave me faith in the future.

God is always near us, loving us. Remembering His promise, "I will not forsake thee or leave thee," helps us to count our blessings instead of our sorrows. It helps us to praise Him rather than complain. And if we do that, we find our spirits lifting and the blessings in our lives more than we can count.

PART NINE

More about the Vaughns and Kilpatricks

Prologue to Vaughn Ancestor's Stories

THIS writing is not to be regarded as pure history, for the history that is contained in it is clouded by time and many tellings. I learned what I know from a tape recording made several years ago by one of my cousins, Jeane Coon. She had encouraged her dad, Maynard Vaughn—youngest son of Charles Clarence and Laura Felter Vaughn—to tell his story, and recorded while he told it. Since the story was far from chronological, assembling it in sequence has been a job.

My sister, Mona, and I listened together to the tapes during a visit this past summer. Each of us scribbled frantically hurried notes. I have tried to assemble the information gained into sections according to where the events took place. Mona and I have collaborated, trying to sort out confusing information or misunderstandings, but strictures of time and distance have limited the effectiveness of this "editing." Please read this story with forgiveness, and enjoy the characters I am trying to bring to life.

A second source of information was a history put together by our Aunt Pearl, one daughter in Great Grandpa Thomas Vaughn's 'second' family with Annie Arneson. From this history Mona was able to construct a 'family tree' back to Samuel Vaughan. I have put Aunt Pearl's information in its historical setting. I hope you enjoy your reading of this trip through Vaughn family history.

One: More about the Vaughn Ancestors Famous Friends

MY GGG grandfather, Admiral Samuel Vaughan lived in England during the years when Napoleon ravaged Europe, 1803-1815.

This notorious general respected no human right or country boundary. Excusing his treatment of people, Napoleon said, "Among those who dislike oppression are many who like to oppress," and he continued his oppression.

Bent on his own dreams of glory and of conquering England, he reached as far as Egypt and then India in his search for conquest and allies. For twenty three years the people of England lived in fear of occupation by the French army. First the French Revolutionary Wars, then the Napoleonic Wars threatened their peace and well-being.

Eventually Napoleon was captured. He surrendered and was banished to the Island of Elba in 1814. He escaped within a year's time and made his way back to France, challenged his army and regained their support. Temporarily, for One Hundred Days, he ruled France again.

But he did not rule without opposition. The countries of Britain, Germany, Belgium, and Holland formed the Seventh Coalition and allied against him. Napoleon confronted them at Waterloo in Belgium. Confident of his military strategies, he expected victory.

The Duke of Wellington said of Napoleon, "I used to say of him that his presence on the field made the difference of forty-thousand men." Due to the capriciousness of History, the skills of The Duke of Wellington and Blucher's Prussian army, Napoleon met his "Waterloo."

ONE: MORE ABOUT THE VAUGHN ANCESTORS FAMOUS FRIENDS

The Duke had many military victories to his credit. His defeat of Napoleon won him a permanent position at the head of the British army and a permanent place in history. It ended Napoleon's rule in France, and the despot was banished to St. Helena where he died in 1821.

My GGG grandfather, Samuel Vaughn, reportedly sat, honored to be present, at the Duke's victory celebration. I am assuming he was an old man by this time. How many battles he had shared with the Duke or how many ships he had commanded remains a mystery.

As he sat at that banquet he would have witnessed the Duke's jubilance over his victory at Waterloo. He would have heard the Duke's comment after the battle:

"Nothing except a battle lost can be half so melancholy as a battle won."

He would have shared the meal, a meat pie made from fowl and lamb. He would have observed the unusual cutlery which divided the pie among the guests. And he would have met the veteran of the battlefield who tradition claims cut the pie with a sword.

But my GGG grandfather did not return home to his family. He died that night at the victory celebration.

Perhaps the celebration and his part in the victory crowned his life's achievement. Perhaps he would have agreed with Napoleon's words,

"Death is nothing, but to live defeated and inglorious is to die daily."

I am proud to think my GGG grandfather participated in such a memorable historical event.

Discontent

TIMES were ripe for political unrest, protest, and radicalism in England following the Napoleonic wars in 1815. Famine and chronic unemployment coupled with recognition of unfair representation in parliament spurred city-dwellers into political activism. Higher food prices and lower wages propelled the people into desperate circumstances and dramatically increased demands for parliamentary reform.

Two of Samuel Vaughan's sons played active rolls in the protests that resulted. John William and Thomas entertained views that went so far as to encourage revolt against England's rule. Thomas's activities resulted in his capture and banishment to Australia. John William avoided capture by making repeated trips to America, leaving his family in a state of almost perpetual loneliness. Charles—a Methodist minister— may also have been involved.

John William, my GG grandfather, married Elizabeth Lovett at an unknown date, probably close to 1822 or 1823. Their first child, Mary Ann, was born in 1824; James in 1832, John in 1836—John died at a young age— and Thomas in 1840. That same year William moved his family to America, to Norristown, Pennsylvania—about six miles northwest of Philadelphia— leaving the temperate maritime climate of England/Wales for a climate with slightly more extreme temperatures.

In 1845 when Thomas was five years old his father took him to get his naturalization papers. The family name on those papers was changed to Vaughn; leaving out the last a. 'Vaughn' became the legal spelling after that date.

The family lived in Norristown for nine years. The children had access to good schooling in Pennsylvania, and William plied his shoe cobbler trade. The family had a good life; but apparently the lust for land drew William on.

In 1849 William took his oldest son, James, then 17 years old, and traveled to Iowa to establish a new family home. Later that same year Elizabeth followed with Thomas, 9. Mother and son traveled by boat on the St. Lawrence River Waterway to Chicago where they were met by William driving a "one horse open wagon" —in Aunt Pearl's words—which provided their transportation on to Jackson County, Iowa, where they were to live for many years.

I can't help noticing the differences in climate between England/Wales and that of Jackson County, Iowa. Iowa is a state of extreme high and low temperatures, prone to high winds, and even tornado. The adjustments needed must have been difficult for people accustomed to the much more temperate climate of England.

Though schools were not available in Iowa, Thomas enjoyed riches of another kind. The family lived along the Mississippi River where he could hunt, fish, and swim. He became an excellent swimmer. His brother James ran a wood boat on the Mississippi, from Galena, Illinois, to St. Louis, Missouri. He must have gone along many times.

In 1861 Thomas Vaughn, then a grown man, answered Lincoln's call for ninety day volunteers after the attack of the Confederate Army on Fort Sumter and the beginning of the Civil War. He was sent to St. Louis where he became a part of Company H of the Iowa Cavalry. His cousin—Mary Ann's son—became part of the same company. They served in that company through much of the war, doing reconnaissance.

Another of the company's assignments was to accompany Sherman on his destructive March to the Sea as far as Atlanta. Sherman continued on his course of destruction through the state of Georgia, ending at Savannah, but Company H was re-assigned and involved in only one battle formation after that, named the Battle above the Clouds because of the foggy conditions on that day. Confederate troops occupied the table-flat top of the mountain. They were driven from it by Union troops who celebrated their victory by planting the Red, White, and Blue on the mountaintop.

At some time during these years Thomas' cousin, William Jones–five years his junior–was taken prisoner and sent to Andersonville prison, a prison notorious for its inhumane treatment of prisoners. Fifteen foot high stockade walls surrounded the compound which was much too small for the increasing number of prisoners. The prison was built to surround a swamp and, because of its lack of toileting or washing facilities, the swamp became the only choice. As more and more prisoners-of-war packed into the area they were forced into this uninhabitable swampy area. Nearly thirteen thousand of the forty-five thousand soldiers incarcerated at Andersonville died there, victims of starvation, malnutrition, diarrhea, disease, or gunfire— immediately inside the walls was a three-foot wide no man's land known as the "dead line." Any prisoner going inside that area was summarily disposed of and buried in a mass grave, a standard practice at Andersonville.

Union soldiers lived in horror of being taken prisoner, and after the war ended, many empathetic servicemen went to Andersonville to rescue those soldiers imprisoned there. William Jones survived his stay at Andersonville, possibly because my G grandfather, Thomas Vaughn, went there after the war in search of his cousin.

Greener and Greener Grass

MY paternal grandfather, Charles Clarence Vaughn, was born in Yankton, South Dakota to Thomas Vaughn and his wife, Donna Emerancia Hazen in 1869. A brother, John, two years older and his parents welcomed him.

A year after his birth his parents set out for Webster County, Nebraska in a covered wagon and driving a herd of cattle. Donna was burdened with the care of a one-year old and a three-year old over this difficult journey. In 1871 a little girl, Irene, joined their family—by August of 1872 Donna, then the mother of three small children, died on her 32nd birthday. Charles Clarence, my grandfather, lost his mother at only three years of age. His distraught father, perhaps as a matter of necessity, married Annie Mathia Arneson only one month later.

Thomas and Annie eventually had a family of nine, and by the time Charles was fourteen and his brother John sixteen, they had been sent out of the home to earn their own way. They rented a farm and milked cows, raised hogs and grew corn and alfalfa. Apparently they sold milk and hogs for income. Corn and alfalfa provided feed for the animals.

The Thomas Vaughn family stayed in Nebraska through 1899. Charles was 20 years old.

***

Charles moved to Winfield, Sumner County, Kansas, apparently following his parents, and there, at age 23, married Laura Alice Felter. They became the parents of nine children, six boys and three girls: Clarence, Ray, Vesta, Alice, and Bland—my father—Chester, Hazel, Merle, and Maynard.

The year after their marriage the government opened land in northeastern Oklahoma for settlement. Charles and his new bride, Laura, set out for Oklahoma with his brother John. When the Cherokee Land Rush began they witnessed at least one death as a rider rushed out ahead of the signal. Officials shot him.

Charles rode his horse, Laura and his brother followed in a covered wagon. They brought a plow horse and tools that would be needed to 'prove up' the land.

Charles' ride proved a little too eventful. As he crossed a creek he somehow broke the horse's bridle, leaving him no way to guide the horse. The horse covered lots of land, and when he "came to" some bottom land bordered by a creek, Charles, somehow, stopped the horse and planted his stake near the present Ponca City, Oklahoma. The settlers around him and the Vaughn family spent much energy putting up a sod house using the plentiful grassland of the prairie. They also began plowing.

Here lack of information raises questions. Uncle Maynard's story seemed to indicate that Charles left the claim. My summary of Maynard's story is below.

However, doubts arose when another rider rode in and planted his stake. After much mulling the situation and fearing that the other man had already filed his claim, Charles surrendered the land. Later, he learned that the man never filed a claim on the land he had given up, and that the improvements he had made saved the land for six months in his name. Charles later filed on two city lots in Blackwell, Oklahoma where he built and operated a meat market for an unknown number of years.

Aunt Pearl's account indicates that Grandpa Charles 'had' a claim which he acquired in the Cherokee Strip Run.

"Charles C. and Laura Felter were married at Winfield, Kansas, March, 1892, living in Geuda Springs. Clarence E. was born November 30,

1892. (Charles Clarence) made the run into the Cherokee Strip, had a claim about 3½ miles south of the state line and west of the Sumner and Cowley County lines, where Ray Thomas was born August 21, 1896, also Vesta born on February 5, 1899. He sold the homestead and moved to Sheridan Township, Cowley County, Kansas, in 1903, where Alice was born August 25, 1903, also Leslie Bland, July 2, 1907, Chester C. born July 8, 1909. The house Charles built still stands the north side of Highway 160 just east of Silver Creek." (*Wallace Howard, son of Vesta and Ray Howard, replaced the house with one he built. Wallace still owns a portion of the acreage purchased by Grandpa Vaughn.*)

Hazel, Merle, and Maynard were born in Harper County, Oklahoma. Ray and Clarence, Charles' oldest sons, helped Charles with the farm he had purchased thirteen miles northwest of the present Selman, Oklahoma. When Maynard was three years old in 1920 and the new town of Selman was being incorporated, Charles rented the Harper County wheat farm to Ray and Vesta Howard, and moved his family to town.

In 1921 the city built a new school building. The beginning of the new town excited Grandpa Charles and made him think of how he could earn a living without working so hard. He applied for the janitorial position at the new school, and was hired.

He started building a big house in Selman. His family lived in a wash house while he built it. After he finished the house the family moved in, and Grandpa Charles offered boarding for teachers. Word is that he loved to tease and play tricks on them—Bland would have been thirteen years old at this time.

The janitorial work proved much more demanding than Grandpa Charles had expected. Not only was he responsible for all the floors in the three story building, he had all the gas lamps used for lighting to clean, light each morning and put out at night. He also supervised the playground. His work hours stretched from 4:00 in the morning till 10:30 in the evening—he definitely did *not* have easier work!

Clarence and Ray decided to open a garage business in the new town of Selman. They called it Vaughn Brother's Garage. The family's stay in town lasted about five years. Maynard said he was eight—1925—when the family moved back to the farm.

Bland would have been 18. I am guessing this would be the time he went to Normal school at Stillman, Oklahoma and trained for teaching.

Since the farm was so far from school, the Vaughns purchased a Model T Touring car to get the kids back and forth. That solution to the transportation problem proved too expensive and time consuming with the price of gasoline and distance. The roads were dirt, and had to be driven in low gear. So Grandma Laura took the kids and moved back to town to batch in a rental house during the school year, leaving Grandpa Charles to run the farm alone.

The Vaughns owned the wheat farm until October of 1929 when Charles sold a portion of it. With money from the farm in his pocket, he decided to take the family to visit some of his half-brothers and some of Laura's sisters. Some of them lived near the present Jay, Oklahoma in the northeast part of the state; the trip also included locations in Arkansas and Texas.

They didn't return until the winter had passed into the spring of 1930. They spent a short while in Oklahoma visiting Vesta and Ray, and then went to Southeastern Colorado where they bought 160 acres from John Kilpatrick— Bland was teaching school by this time and driving back and forth to his assignments. His salary was $60.00 per month. He paid $10.00 monthly to his parents and lived at home while they were in Colorado. Maynard remembers that Grandma Laura did his washing and ironing. During 1930-1932 Bland courted young Marion Kilpatrick. In August of 1932 they married and moved to Lone Star where Bland continued to teach.

The property in Colorado was near Two Buttes in Baca County located in the extreme southeastern part of the state. The pioneers there had built a dam on Two Buttes Creek for the purpose of storing water for irrigation.

Nevertheless, the farming venture in Colorado proved difficult. At first they had milk cows but moved to herding cattle on the range.

Wind, being a major factor in the weather on the plains, began to bring with it soil made fine and light by drought. The drought lasted through the five years they owned this property and into the next decade.

At first the broomcorn, alfalfa and maize they planted grew, but soon the irrigation water in the dam reservoir played out. The dust storms and the drought continued. The water in the reservoir disappeared, drunk up by thirsty skies. Maynard said he saw cracks in the reservoir bottom that were so large he could see twenty feet into the ground.

Growing a crop became impossible. They harvested their last crop of broomcorn after the Depression started. They received eight dollars for the whole crop; not very good pay since "Harvesting broomcorn was a dirty, hot—thankless—job."

What alfalfa continued to grow was invaded by goat heads and Texas burrs, but they continued to stack it, and the desperate cows picked their way through it. The plant that continued to thrive was Russian thistle, also known as tumbleweed. The family harvested it; it kept the cows alive through winter, but just barely. The dry air pulled the moisture from the cows' hides, causing them to crack with the slightest bit of rain.

The dust invaded their homes. They tried vainly to keep it out, putting sheets and blankets over cracks around windows and doors, but dust made it dark inside. Light produced by two kerosene lamps proved insufficient. Light from a match that had been struck could barely be seen. The family went to bed at night with clean faces; by morning their faces were black.

By 1935 Grandpa Charles grew restless and discouraged. He gathered his family and started for Washington State in a 1928 Chevrolet, pulling a four-wheel trailer with a tent over it. In Washington the family camped in someone's yard until they learned of a farm west of Amboy for sale. Grandpa traded his 160 acres in Two Buttes for the 200 acre farm **30** miles north of Vancouver and 25 miles south of Mt. St. Helens. He borrowed money from Production Credit to furnish the farm with milk cows and sold milk for income. The payment to Production Credit was $13.00 per month. "When we went back to Colorado for a visit, they thought we were doing pretty good."

The family at home now consisted only of the parents, Merle, and Maynard. The boys loved the farm In Washington because it had lots of fruit trees. In fact it had trees everywhere. Washington seemed a huge improvement over Colorado and the dusty drought.

Vaughn Grandparents

Grandma Laura was ill. At 59 years old her stomach had swollen, but she ignored the pain and canned the abundant fruit. When she finally saw a doctor he diagnosed cancer and gave her a year to live. She started a grapefruit diet, and at first thought it was helping, but Uncle Maynard said, "every time she ate solid food she went downhill." She died in May of 1937, the same month and year the author was born.

After Grandma Laura's death Grandpa Charles found it difficult to stay in Amboy, and when he visited Bland in Vale and learned about a neighboring farm just north of Bland's forty acres he traded the farm in Amboy for it. Maynard, now almost twenty, and Merle felt happy at the Amboy farm and wanted to stay, however the move was made to Vale. It was not accomplished without difficulty.

The family could not bear to leave all Grandma's work, the 800 quarts of fruit she had canned. They loaded their four-wheel trailer with their household goods and the fruit and started the trip. "We hadn't gone ten miles before the axle on the trailer broke." They left the trailer on the road and drove the additional twenty miles to Vancouver where they replaced the trailer. Much work reloading followed, and they proceeded on their way; but their problems were not over. One flat tire followed another until they finally learned to over-fill the tires. The four hundred mile trip took the tired crew four days.

Bland had a forty acre farm with milk cows and grew alfalfa and corn as feed crops. The farm Grandpa traded for was north about one half mile through a small canyon, and was similar in nature; part of the land remained in sage brush.

While Grandpa lived in Vale, Verlin and Margie, Bland and Marion's children, enjoyed their only years with their Grandpa, as did Mona when she came along in 1939. He made frequent visits to their home, and probably shared many of those lemon drops he always carried and stories he loved to tell with his Oregon grandchildren.

Merle, no longer interested in farming, went off to Chicago to study electronics. Maynard and Grandpa stayed on in Vale until "Dad and Bland got to having trouble."

Grandpa traded his farm for a place in Ontario, Oregon in 1942. Merle had returned from Chicago by this time and met Betty in Ontario. After they were married they lived at the Ontario place.

Grandpa went back to Oklahoma. Ray and Vesta Howard had a large house with a basement near Selman or Woodward, and Grandpa lived with them until he became "lonesome." One of his nieces, Rosa—always a good friend to Grandpa—had been asking him to live with her for years. She had a farm and could use his help, and she didn't drive, so the partnership would be mutually beneficial.

Grandpa moved in with Rosa. He earned a bit of money herding cattle for her, and Maynard, having been drafted into the military service, sent back an allotment to help Grandpa with his living expenses. Grandpa put away for Maynard what money he didn't need; Maynard was saving all his military pay, too. When he got out of the service **in** 1946 he used this money to buy his farm near Jay, Oklahoma.

When Maynard found the farm near Jay he also found Eunice, the widowed daughter of the man he bought the farm from. She lived in a larger house up on the hill with her two little girls, Jeane and Patsy. She also had a mean cow to take care of and milk.

Maynard lived below in the "Rock House." At mail time every day they encountered one another while gathering their mail.

Within a month Maynard said, "Marry me."

Eunice said, "When?"

Maynard said, "Tomorrow." They went off across the Kansas state line to get married, finding the Kansas laws more accommodating to their needs, and hurried home in time to milk the cows.

Later, jokingly, Maynard said, "She had two kids and a mean cow, and she was looking pretty hard."

Eunice turned off the tape recorder.

Grandpa, back in Oklahoma, began to miss Maynard's presence, so eventually he went to northeastern Oklahoma. Rosa turned her farm over to friends or family and went along. Maynard had fixed up a little rock chicken house behind the Rock House he and Eunice lived in; Grandpa and Rosa lived there.

Maynard and Eunice had a little boy, Ronnie. Ronnie, at thirteen years old loved to eat breakfast with mom and dad, then "sneak over to Grandpa's and have pancakes with him." Grandpa loved his lemon drops. "He had a lemon drop every night before he went to bed, and when I stayed all night he gave me a lemon drop too."

Grandpa decided he was going to walk a mile every day, and even after he was blind walked back and forth along a rope until he had completed his mile. Maynard tied the rope to the back door and to the gate for him. "Grandpa was blind and he painted one lens of his glasses black. That was the way people did then."

Grandpa Vaughn

Eventually Grandpa became both blind and deaf. He became despondent, and mixed nights and days. He told stories on and on during the night. He began making threats; he would go out on the freeway and try to be hit by a car, or electrocute himself with his electric blanket. His care became so difficult that Maynard and Eunice decided to take him to Vesta and Ray thinking the more affluent family could afford to pay for a caretaker. No such caretaker was found, and Grandpa spent his last days in a nursing home. He died in Buffalo, Oklahoma, October 1, 1961 at age 92.

Two: More about the Kilpatrick Ancestors
Obituary, Samuel Allen Kilpatrick, June 10, 1952

O N Monday afternoon, April 21, 1952, the earthly life of Brother Samuel A. Kilpatrick came to a close after eighty-five years, ten months, and six days. Born in Lawrence County, Tennessee on June 18, 1866, he was destined to father one hundred descendents up to the time of his earthly departure.

Samuel and MaryLee Kilpatrick

In the fall of the year 1890, six months prior to his marriage to Merica MaryLee Kelley on April 2, 1891, he heard that a Brother Goodson was conducting a gospel meeting in Lawrenceburg, Tennessee, some twenty-five miles away, and rode horseback the entire distance for the specific purpose of obeying the gospel. After their marriage, his wife obeyed the gospel in 1891, and from that time on the two of them raised ten children, forty grandchildren and fifty great grandchildren, always nurturing "them in the chastening and admonition of the Lord."

In addition to his wife, surviving him are his ten children: Mrs. W.S. Maynard of Beaver, Oklahoma; Mrs. Elbertha Murray of Fresno, California; Mrs. A.C. Williams, Parsons, Kansas; Mrs. Ross Indermill, Visalia, California; Mrs. Bland Vaughn, Vale, Oregon' Mrs. L.D. McKinzie, Chowchilla, California; John, Colorado Springs, Colorado; Barney, Bolivar, Missouri; W.A. and Bonnie E. Chowchilla, California. Of the remaining ninety descendants, all but one survive him.

From the time he became a Christian sixty-two years ago, he was active in the work of the church in so far as he was physically able. Around the turn of the century, while still living in the hills of Tennessee, the Kilpatrick's placed their children in a one-horse hack and rode seven miles through the timbers every Sunday to "worship in Spirit and in Truth" and to hear Brother T.B. Larimore preach the gospel.

In 1904 the family moved west and homesteaded in "No Man's Land" which is now Beaver County, Oklahoma. It was there in the community of South Flat that Brother and Sister Kilpatrick, along with the Wesley Smith and Henry Mitchell families, established the church of the New Testament, the first organization of any kind in that area. Here Brother Kilpatrick served as an elder for twenty years, praying that the truth would triumph over the very-much-present error. Today that congregation, meeting in a beautiful new edifice, is the only active religious group in the community. His grandson by marriage and his family are still active in the leadership and work of the church there.

In 1928 the Kilpatricks moved to Colorado. Brother Aubrey J. Bradshaw...

Two: More about the Kilpatrick Ancestors: Obituary, Samuel Allen Kilpatrick

now an elder in Weatherford, Oklahoma, also one of the first preachers active in the South Flat work…came to hold a meeting in the school-house auditorium in Two Buttes, and another congregation of the Lord's church was established. Brother Kilpatrick served this group as an elder for some seven years.

Moving to Chowchilla, California, in 1935, the Kilpatrick family joined forces with the small group of saints then meeting, and for some five years Brother Kilpatrick served as elder to this good congregation, but became fairly inactive over the last years due to ill health.

His main interest in life was centered around spiritual things, even so much so that the greatest consolation he received during his last hours were the words of the Scriptures read to him by his family. All through his married life he taught and studied the Bible with his family day by day. He "so let his light shine" throughout the years that he was instrumental in encouraging Brother A.C. Williams of Parsons, Kansas, a son-in-law, to preach the word, and also aided another son-in-law to find the truth. Brother W.S. Maynard now serves the church in Beaver, Oklahoma, as an elder.

In addition to these, his son-in-law, Ross Indermill, serves as an elder, as does his son, Barney of Bolivar, Missouri. Several of his grandsons are excellent gospel preachers. In fact, although perhaps some are not as faithful as they should be, with very few exceptions, each of his descendents from the age of accountability upwards are members of the body of Christ. This is a wonderful tribute to his consecrated Christian life.

He was laid to rest on Friday afternoon, April 25, 1952, in the Chowchilla Cemetery. Brother Porter Norris of Tranquility, California and Brother Robert A. Bolton of Chowchilla officiated. Brothers Vernon Norris of Visalia, California, Elbert Garretson of Caruthers, California, and T. Craig of Fresno, California, assisted.

Surely his life should cause those he leaves behind and all who knew and loved him to strive to make certain that the "circle will be unbroken," for indeed, "he being dead, yet speaketh." Robert A. Bolton

Copied from an article in Firm Foundation, circa 1952

Mother's Parents and Grandparents

MY great grandparents, members of the Kilpatrick, Kelley, Durham and Grinnell families intertwined families in Lawrence County, Tennessee in the mid 1800's forming the families which brought my grandparents, Samuel Allen Kilpatrick and Merica MaryLee Kelley into the world.

Some stories indicate that the great grandparents enjoyed a bit of prosperity, both families reportedly having slaves. John Franklin Kilpatrick owned a bond-slave who had the right to leave the farm if he chose, but he chose to stay. My grandmother (Kelley) Kilpatrick was reportedly raised by a Negro nanny and a stepmother. Samuel Kilpatrick, my Grandfather, had a fifth grade education, which is remarkable because before the first compulsory school attendance law was passed in Massachusetts in 1852, only sons of the wealthy had the opportunity to be educated. During the half century of his birth (1866) many more states followed the lead of Massachusetts and made school attendance compulsory. Was Tennessee one of those states? Most likely.

Samuel Allen Kilpatrick, aged twenty four—a serious and studious young man—upon hearing of a gospel meeting being held twenty five miles away, mounted his white horse and rode there for the specific purpose of obeying the gospel. Six months later he married Merica MaryLee Kelley (April, 1891), and several months after their marriage, MaryLee was baptized into Christ.

Their first five children were born in Lawrence County, Tennessee by November of 1899. That year, taking their five small children, they moved by rail to Washita County, Oklahoma Territory where another child was born about 1903. Their intended destination was Beaver County, Oklahoma, but

MOTHER'S PARENTS AND GRANDPARENTS

upon hearing that his mother, Melvina, was grieving their absence, they again uprooted their family of six young children and returned to Tennessee where they remained until her death in September 1904.

The dream of sharing in the bounty of the land give-away by the government was still calling them west, so shortly after Melvina's death, Samuel again took his family to Washita County, Oklahoma, which he apparently used as a base for his land acquisition efforts. That same year of 1904 he staked out two parcels in No Man's Land one half mile west of Old Sophia Post Office in Beaver County, Oklahoma, then apparently returned to Washita County. Another child was born to them there in January 1905, and when the child was six weeks old, Samuel Allen moved his wife and seven children by covered wagon to Beaver County where he had built a half-dugout for their home.

Apparently there were numerous returns to Washita County. He used many of his talents for supporting the needs of the claim and the family. Samuel farmed, picked cotton, ran a sorghum mill, and plied his carpentry trade.

The new land in Beaver County, Oklahoma, at first received abundant rainfall and enabled bountiful gardens and crops. Broomcorn and wheat, both dry land crops, could be grown and harvested regularly. The children attended school, but had to travel some distance, many times in inclement weather.

Samuel and Mary Lee's last three children were born in Beaver County. My mother, Marion, numbered eight in a family of ten. She arrived in 1912 with her twin, Mildred. Neva followed two years later. The family lived in Beaver County until 1928 when the twins were ready for high school.

At that time Samuel moved his family to Two Buttes. This book highlights Marion Kilpatrick, my mother, and my father, Bland Vaughn, whom she met and married in Two Buttes, Baca County, Colorado. I began with the facts and stories my mother told me and created an account of their early experiences, their subsequent marriage, and their experiences in that marriage. I hope you have enjoyed reading it.

About Two Buttes and the Kilpatricks

THE Samuel Kilpatrick's home was small and the living room contained a bed. A kitchen and a bedroom completed the layout. Ira thought the house stood on about thirty acres neighboring the section John farmed, and that Grandpa may have leased the property. They owned several milk cows—maybe three or four.

Ira hesitated to name the crops Grandpa grew, but identified broom corn as a possibility. People did not eat broom corn but sold it for the production of straw brooms, thus obtaining a bit of cash.

One of the Kilpatrick men later told a story about Grandpa growing a watermelon patch. The patch attracted neighborhood boys and results of their thievery in his field was obvious to Grandpa.

Samuel rigged the patch with wires, and then hid himself in a ditch with his gun. When the young miscreants appeared, the lurking grandpa fired his gun into the air frightening the guilty consciousness of the boys. They ran and tripped over the wires. Their bruised knees and elbows later revealed their identities. Their thievery stopped. Grandpa usually shared the watermelons he grew for seed with neighbors, requesting that they return the seeds, but he drew the line at thievery.

The family possessed a telephone, probably a wall phone, per Ira. Several families shared a party line and people were directed not to listen in. Each family had a particular ring. Operators at "Telephone Central" in town manually connected the caller to the receiver of the call.

Ira said the Kilpatrick parents owned a "Model T" car in Two Buttes but that Grandpa didn't do much of the driving. "He just didn't drive much." A story near the conclusion of this book shares his experience of *learning* to drive with the instruction of his sons.

The Kilpatrick kids walked back and forth to school in Two Buttes, probably about a mile, Ira thought. He said the frame school building consisted of four rooms and sat on property behind Dr. Verity's home and office. First through third graders, fourth through sixth graders, seventh through ninth, and tenth through twelfth graders—children of the approximately one-hundred people who populated Two Buttes while the Kilpatrick and Vaughn families lived there—shared the classrooms.

Poor Chicken

GRANDPA Kilpatrick's quick "trigger" temper is legendary. Another of Marion's stories about this quality follows.

Grandpa habitually came into the kitchen from his work in the field, sat on a stool by the door, and read his Bible. One day Grandma interrupted his repose by a request. Since her lunch preparations required an egg which she did not have in the kitchen, she sent Grandpa Samuel out to gather eggs.

Grandpa complied readily enough; he went to the coop and reached under a hen to gather the egg. The hen, taking large exception to his methods, reached out and pecked Grandpa smartly on the hand. Grandpa, taking larger exception to the treatment he had received, grabbed that hen around her neck and put an end to her petulant life! He brought provisions for an unplanned dinner of fried chicken into the kitchen along with the requested egg.

A Switch Story

THIS story is likely the inspiration my mom needed when she applied discipline. Mom told this about her father, Samuel, and Bill, and Barney her brothers—her memory was a bit hazy on whether it was Bill or Bonnie, but Barney took part for sure.)

Beaver County, Oklahoma—a dry-land-farm area where farmers used windmills for watering gardens and providing water for the home—sets the scene for this story. One day Grandpa, working at the top of the windmill—having secured the fans so they wouldn't hit him, and himself so he couldn't fall—observed his boys on the ground.

The boys fought angrily over some imagined grievance. Though they knew that Grandpa did not like them to fight when they were mad, they fought anyway. Grandpa would never stop what he was doing and come down to punish them, they thought.

As Marion told the story, "They thought wrong!" Grandpa did come down. He cut three tamarack switches, gave one to each of the boys and kept one for himself.

"If you boys want to fight, we'll just have some fun."

With that statement Grandpa started switching and strongly encouraged the boys to do the same. Round and round they went, having a wonderful time and learning another valuable lesson.

Marion's Memories of her Siblings
Stella Rachael Leona Kilpatrick

"STELLA had two kids when we were born, and she kind of took over since Mama wasn't feeling very well. Instead of her four kids she had to boss, she eventually had seven, and she did a good job of it." Her children were Carson, Estelline, Ruth, and Veva—There were two late-term miscarriages following Veva. The three Kilpatrick children included in 'Stella's Bunch' were Marion, Mildred, and Neva."

According to Mom, Stella's Bunch often heard Stella say: "Oh! I could just *stomp* every last one of you!"

"A lippy bunch we were: 'You can't boss me. You're not my mama!'"

"Stella was a good story teller. She told life experiences. They were better stories than you could make up. I can just hear her telling the story about Miss Tanie Pollen, an 'old maid' school teacher."

"When Neva was born Miss Pollen said to Mama, 'Mrs. Kilpatrick, I just don't know how you can love em, you've got so *many!'*

"Miss Tanie Pollen!" Mama burst out. "You're a school teacher, and you do a good job at that. But you've never had children, and you don't know *how* to love 'em till you've *had* a few!"

"We didn't have very much then, and Stella was always making sure we had a suitable dress to wear for school occasions. Sometimes she even *made* them for us."

"Stella was married to Will Maynard, whom she called 'Mr. Bill. Will was quite a lot older than Stella, and sometimes he treated her a lot like a kid.

For instance—on one occasion—Will went off and left her when she wasn't ready to go to church on time!"

"Sometimes our family would ride along to church in Will and Stella's great big Studebaker car."

Marion's Memories of her older brother, John Franklin Kilpatrick

"I don't remember very much about John since he was so much older than I. He married Bertha Adams in Sophia, Beaver County, Oklahoma—The Kilpatricks, Adams and Davis families all lived in this community—John and Bertha's children were Earnest (1916) Ira, (1919), Juanita, (1927), John Jr., (1929), and Sheila, (1937)".

"When Ira was born we wanted to go see him, but Stella said it was 'too soon.' Ira was about seven years younger than Mildred and me."

Mom remembered John telling her this story while they were driving past the place where he went to school. "One day I was sitting on the schoolhouse steps holding Bertha in my lap. Bertha must have seen the teacher coming and disappeared. I never did know what happened to Bertha!!"

"John was a sweetheart. He was tender-hearted. He understood kids pretty well, and he was not afraid to cry."

In answer to my question, "What else can you remember about John?" Marion replied, "I just know he was a good big brother."

"Papa gave John part of his two sections in Beaver County (Sophia) when John and Bertha were married. There are a lot of oil wells there now."

More on Uncle John Kilpatrick,
per Ira Kilpatrick, October 1, 2009

JOHN'S family lived across the field from Grandpa and Grandma on 160 acres bought by John. This property near Two Buttes was split and divided; sold to Ira's Uncle, Roy Adams, and part traded to the Vaughns for a car and a combine. The walk between the two homes was about ¾ mile across a field.

Uncle John was a creative mechanic, building various machines to do whatever needed to be done. Ira said that after John's place was split, half of the property didn't have a well. Uncle John had previously observed how wells were dug, created his own drilling device, and completed a well on the property that needed it. As a consequence other neighbors ask him to help solve their water problems. Ira was John's "right hand man" during these jobs. They did "several" according to Ira. A man "down by the creek on the south" had artesian wells, but they were covered with slate so he didn't have access to the water. Ira said his dad "cleaned them out so the man could put in windmills." Ira and his Dad had a "well drilling business" there for awhile.

Another machine John created was to facilitate removing seeds from cantaloupe and watermelon. Ira said John started with a Ford engine and made a machine with gears, rods, shafts, rollers, two by fours, and piped water.

John grew seeds for a local seed company; Ira wasn't sure which company, but it may have been the D.V. Borough Seed Company. Apparently there was some agreement between Grandpa and John, because Grandpa also had a field of watermelons, and Ira said he would bring his melons over to be cut and seeded.

They also grew squash for the seeds. Ira said they stacked left-over un-needed squash and rinds at the end of John's machine in a pile four to five feet high and fifteen to twenty feet in diameter. The cows enjoyed these left-overs.

While we were talking about watermelons, Ira told me about how the farmers would take large quantities to the "Labor Day Parade"—Music Day— every September and sell them from produce stands. Grandpa and Uncle John both did this. Dr. Verity's band was always performing on Labor Day; marching down Main Street and playing from the band stand in a park that was "one block square." Seating was provided in the park so people could sit and listen. People came from neighboring towns—Ira mentioned Vilas— to take part in the celebration.

Two Buttes Creek ran north and south. It was dry much of the year but in flood stage was a good sized river. There was a dam and reservoir on Two Buttes Creek. The Arkansas River was fifty miles north of Two Buttes, coming from the Northwest into Kansas and Eastern Oklahoma. The Cimarron River was more than an hour away from Two Buttes.

Sue Kilpatrick—wife of Frank Kilpatrick, son of Ernst Kilpatrick, son of John Kilpatrick—confessed to being Grandpa John's side-kick as he continually visited city dumps and salvaged parts which he then used for all his creations. They shared this activity so many times that Sue began to call John by a new name: John Kil-pack-*rat.*

Marion's Memories of
Tenney Elbertha Kilpatrick

"I don't remember too much about Tenney. She was the second oldest sister, and of course, was married with children by the time we came along."

"Tenney was married to Cole Murray. She had attended Normal School—a teacher-training program—about the same time John attended, and they both taught school before they were married. I don't know whether she taught afterwards or not."

"Tenney was pregnant with her third or fourth child when Papa went over to check on Tenney and Cole during a bad snow storm. Though Tenney's baby was nearly due, he found Tenney alone. Papa wanted to stay there until Cole returned home and teach him not to leave his wife alone like that anymore, but—to Tenney's relief— he changed his mind and went home."

"Tenney didn't talk much about her relationship with Cole." She eventually took the children and went to California when Samuel and MaryLee followed Bonnie and Bill west. There she raised her children, apparently alone, and in thankfulness that her parents were there to help.

Marion's Memories of Mayme Melvina Kilpatrick

"MY earliest memories of Mayme are of the time while Clyde was serving in the army during World War 1. Mayme had met Clyde Williams in Beaver County, and they had been married. They had only three months together before Clyde was drafted. Mayme moved back home to live with the family while Clyde was gone. I was about six years old, and my strongest memories are of Mayme's crying. We all felt like we needed to comfort her, but she seemed to take more comfort from four-year old Neva, the baby. It was a long time, but the war did end, and Clyde came back home. Mayme had a nervous breakdown waiting for him."

"After Clyde came home he taught school at Greenough in Beaver County, Oklahoma. When he was a young man he used to go out on the farm and get up on a tree stump and preach to the tree stumps."

"Clyde and Mayme eventually had five children. I remember that Clyde insisted that his kids sit on the front row at church. And while he preached, they had better be listening. If he saw any misbehavior, he would stop his preaching and call their names in public."

"I remember staying with Clyde and Mayme for a while when she wasn't very well. The children were little, and Clyde (A.C.) was away a lot, so I was there to help out. Mayme was still quite emotional. I remember her giving the children their baths. I thought she was going to scrub their skins off. I told her that I thought she was too rough on them. She just laughed at me like she laughed at everything."

"Mayme was very home-centered as far as I know. She had her hands full with five little children running around, and then growing up. Being a preacher's wife I suppose she did her share of typical preacher's wifely tasks, but I don't remember much of that."

Marion's Memories of
William Allen Kilpatrick

MOM'S first reaction when I said, "Tell me about Bill," was "He was a prankster!" But when I tried to learn what pranks earned him such a reputation, I was not able to stir up even one. If other's tales of woe had been spoken in her hearing, she could not remember them. There was nothing Bill did to her or any of the siblings. Perhaps Bill just gave that impression with his happy face and smiling eyes.

Mom finally remembered when the boys, Bill and Bonnie, tried to teach Grandpa to drive. The boys had the car in the driveway in front of the house. They put Grandpa in it and showed him all of the buttons and gadgets and pedals. Then he drove off to great 'hurrahs.' He drove down to the neighbor's house, circled around, and drove home again. He drove up to the house and just kept going, back out into the street, down the street to the Terry's' house, circled around again, and drove home into the driveway, back out into the street, and there he went again.

Back at the house folks wondered when Grandpa would have enough of the new-fangled car. They watched him arrive and go for several more trips before it occurred to them why Grandpa didn't stop. He couldn't remember how!!

On his next trip in, Bill and Bonnie began shouting directions to the frantic driver as he drove into the driveway. Finally, the mystery solved, Grandpa stopped the car and got out.

No one dared laugh in the driveway. Marion and the others disappeared into the house and were fighting uncontrollable giggles. When Grandpa went into the house, they went out the back door to prevent his seeing them laugh. He didn't think any of it was at all funny.

Remember, cars were for the adventurous in those days. Grandpa did gain a measure of confidence on that embarrassing day. He wasn't afraid to get in that car and drive any more, and the traumatic way he learned to stop the car stayed with him forever. He eventually used the car regularly to take the cans of milk to Two Buttes.

Marion's Memories of
Barney McCoy Kilpatrick

"BARNEY and Nona lived fairly close to us after they were married. I remember one Christmas time while we still lived in the half-dugout. You know, we were probably considered poor, but we didn't know it. We had everything we needed."

"Barney evidently thought we needed some candy for Christmas so he came over to our house bringing a big bag of hard candy. He thought it would make our holiday a little merrier. We were still kids, so I remember him putting the candy up high above the steps where it would be hard for us to reach. We could have gotten to it, but we knew it was for Christmas, so we didn't try."

"Barney was always very sweet and gentle. When we were on the farm in Vale and Bland got so hard on Verlin, I always knew I could call Barney. He would understand."

"So I called Barney and he said, 'Send him down here to me. I need a son.' I sent him. Verlin was a junior or senior then. He lived there until he graduated. Uncle Barney bought him the suit he needed for graduation and paid the expenses that seniors have."

Barney enjoyed having Verlin in his home and having the 'son' he never had. But he may not have been prepared for all the mischief and inconvenience teenagers can bring into life. One thing that happened was that Verlin used the car Barney had loaned him to drive to take the girls—Shirley, Carolyn, and Norma Lou—fishing. They were successful in catching some fish and decided to store their bounty in the car while they attended to other matters. They forgot to reckon with the Missouri summers and the temperatures inside a closed car. Verlin said Aunt Nona never did figure out how 'that smell' got inside the car, and none of the participants ever volunteered any information.

Marion didn't remember what Barney did for a living. "Farmed, I think." But she remembers that he "was always building something. "He must have gotten his building talents from Papa." The last thing Marion remembers that he built was church furniture for the Church of Christ in Bolivar, Missouri. She remembers that after he got sick with leukemia, he built a communion table and a podium, and that he worked "until he couldn't work any more."

Memories of Bonnie Edwin Kilpatrick

"BONNIE was always getting in trouble," Marion said. "When he was in about the eighth grade and was with some neighbor kids playing ball, a ball got away and went through another neighbor's window. The kids, hoping to escape taking responsibility, ran for home and went to bed. Unfortunately the neighbor followed Bonnie home."

When the neighbor asked Mama about Bonnie, she said, "No, my kids are in bed." When the neighbor said that he had followed Bonnie home, Mama had to believe him. "She told Bonnie that *she* was going to have to pay for the window because *he* had broken it, and that now *he* would have to *work* for her until he earned the money to pay her back. He worked a long time for that window."

Marion didn't remember more of the "trouble" Bonnie was "always" in. But she remembers his reputation!!

Bonnie and Myrtle left Colorado during the "Dust Bowl" days—their daughter, Luetta, remembers the family sleeping under the truck after they got to California.

Bonnie and Myrtle had four children: Edwin, Erlene, Luetta, and Bonna. Bonna died suddenly on a Sunday afternoon of spinal meningitis at age fifteen. She was one year younger than Luetta. Edwin Dale died of cancer in his late forties.

***

Ira Kilpatrick's memories were that Bonnie really liked to laugh, and that Bonnie and Myrtle (Miller) had a good marriage. Ira remembered also that before he enlisted in the Navy in 1940 he worked for Uncle Bonnie in

California driving trucks and tending the station—Ira eventually worked in the NASA machine shop for the Aeronautic and Space Administration.

Bonnie and Myrtle followed Bill Kilpatrick and his wife Myra (Davis) to California during the Depression. They survived by helping with harvesting and doing miscellaneous jobs that became available. Work they did also included running a service station, working for a building contractor, and opening a machine shop.

Eventually, Bonnie owned a fleet of trucks and operated a business hauling crops in season such as cantaloupe, grapes, melons, cotton or hay. Bonnie had his trucking business for most of the years he lived in Chowchilla.

Bonnie and Bill finally convinced "Mama and Papa" to leave Colorado and join them in California. The senior Kilpatricks settled in Chowchilla in 1935 and lived there until their deaths.

Marion's Memories of her Twin Sister, Mildred Raye Kilpatrick

"I was born twenty minutes ahead of Mildred. My birth weight was nine pounds, Mildred weighed eight and three-quarter pounds. She was born shorter and stayed shorter all her life than I was."

"Mildred was always a busy child. Mama said that when we were little and Mildred fell down, I would stop and try to help her up even when I was too small to do so. Mildred, according to Mama, never even stopped when I fell down."

"I used to feel kind of neglected because Mildred and Neva were always hanging around together, and leaving me out. I was always a little older than their interests. Mildred, however, was kind of the leader while we were in school."

"I needed a lot of help in algebra when I was a sophomore. Algebra was very easy for Mildred, so she worked hard to keep me from failing. I have always been very grateful to her for that."

"When we were in the ninth grade, Mrs. Carter found out that I could sing harmony and that Mildred and I sounded good together, so she started casting us in plays together where we had singing parts. The biggest production we were in was *Windmills of Holland*. We also starred in *Daddy Long-Legs*, our senior class play."

"Mildred and I were also in the high school band together. Mildred played clarinet and I played trumpet. Neva played a baritone. Dr. Verity enabled our participation by providing instruments for all of us who could not buy them ourselves. For this reason the band came to be known as Dr. Verity's Band.

We played at basketball and baseball games, and marched in several parades every year. Mr. Backus was our director, and he really demanded performance. He wouldn't dismiss class until we got the music right! Bland Vaughn, my eventual suitor, was a part of this band, playing sousaphone."

"Two Buttes was a small high school, so we got to participate in lots of activities. There were so few students that we all had to take part to enable the school to do anything. Seventeen—approximately the number in her graduating class—keeps coming to my mind"

"Mildred met Ross Indermill, a Two Buttes resident. They were married in a double wedding with Estelline Maynard and J.P. Underwood, and eventually moved to California where Ross started his coffee-vending machine business."

"On the way to California during their honeymoon Ross and Mildred stopped when they heard a train approaching. They climbed up on top of the railroad bridge, thinking they would watch the train go by. Little did they know what the train held in store for them!"

"As the train crossed the bridge, the engineer decided it was time to blow the whistle, and Ross and Mildred got a thorough blacking by the smoke from the whistle. Lesson learned!"

Ross did very well in his business, enabling him and Mildred to travel around the country to visit family members. We lived up in Oregon, and could not spare the money or the time from our farm to travel, so Ross and Mildred visited us there.

We, being lonely for family members, really appreciated and welcomed those visits. We children enjoyed our farm and each other while we shared one experience after another. Wise in the ways of the farm, we initiated Richard and Rosilee into all the familiar activities. Many a story could be told here.

"Mildred and I are ninety one this year."(2003).

Marjorie's Note: One of my vivid memories of Aunt Mildred is from a visit when I was, perhaps, in eighth grade. Mona and I didn't get many new clothes, and Aunt Mildred apparently noticed. She went to town, bought new fabric, and made dresses for both of us. We felt very beautiful in those dresses. Aunt Mildred was a great seamstress.

Marion's Memories of Neva Kilpatrick

NEVA was the youngest of the ten Kilpatrick children. She was born two years later than Mildred and Marion, thus earning a lasting name: The Baby. Neva came to hate that name!! Neither did she like to be bossed by Stella. This the three youngest Kilpatricks had in common.

"Stella knew how to tease Neva and always get a reaction. She would say, 'Mama was my Mama before she was your Mama!' And Neva would cry."

"Neva was in the band with Mildred and I, and she also took part in the musicals we were in. We enjoyed singing together."

"Neva was still living at home when Mama and Papa moved to Chowchilla, California. She met and married L.D. McKenzie in Chowchilla, and they lived their entire married life there." Neva and L.D's children were Daryl and Jack.

"Neva died younger than any of us siblings. She had ovarian cancer and died at age 65. I was with her near the end of her life. I asked her if she'd like a prayer before I left, and she said 'yes.' But when I couldn't find any words, Neva said, 'It's okay Marion. The Holy Spirit knows what you want, and He will carry your prayer through.' That was the last time I saw Neva."

Kilpatrick family picture circa 1946
Left to Right, Back Row: Stella, John, Bill, Barney, Bonnie, Mildred
Front Row: Mayme, Grandpa Samuel, Grandma MaryLee, Neva, Tenney
Marion sits on arm of sofa.

Thank you for following me through my journey. I hope my stories and the characters in them have brought you pleasure. There is much more to tell, but I will leave it to my children. God bless you, every one.

Marjorie

About the Author, Marjorie Vaughn-Eldred

How can one trace the roots of passion?

Only in looking back at one's life can one begin to see threads woven through its tapestry

Margie experienced life's beginnings on a small dairy farm in Eastern Oregon.

Her father, an outstanding teacher, taught over forty students in a one room country school while also clearing his forty acres of sagebrush. Her mother-an amateur poet-found only bits of time to express her poetic talent as she worked alongside her husband to develop their land. Both instilled love of land and learning in their children.

An older brother and three younger siblings comprised the family. Each member shared tasks and responsibilities. Hard work was expected and valued.

Margie learned the values of persistence and of seeing a job to completion. Her love of the land later expressed itself in her beautiful gardens.

Though being a loyal supporter and encourager of her siblings she felt deeply the isolation from grandparents, aunts, uncles and cousins. She longed for extended family connections.

As the years passed, the desire grew strong to preserve for future generations what was so precious to her. When her aged mother moved into her home she used the opportunity to record her mother's stories and memories.

She rediscovered her passion for writing which had lain dormant during the years she was raising her four children and fulfilling her family responsibilities.

After her mother's passing, the momentum grew as she gathered and researched family roots. Her writing and preserving became a passion undergirded by her commitment to see her vision through to completion. You are holding a part of her dream in your hands.

—*Mona Armas*